SUSAN'S QUEST

SUSAN left Boston with mixed feelings. She had never known any other home. But she knew if she stayed, she would always be the daughter of Irish immigrants. Even if Donald were dead, or if she could not find him, she could at least start a new life in California.

She watched, with no regrets, as the Boston shoreline receded in the distance. The breeze caught the sails, billowing them into great white globes. The rigging creaked in protest, the water sparkled in the rising sun.

Susan drew a deep breath of the fresh salt air, and watched the sun climb above the far horizon, where the water stretched as far as she could see. As the sun rose higher, she felt her spirits rise with it.

She was on her way to California.

SUSAN'S QUEST

by Jacquelyn Hanson

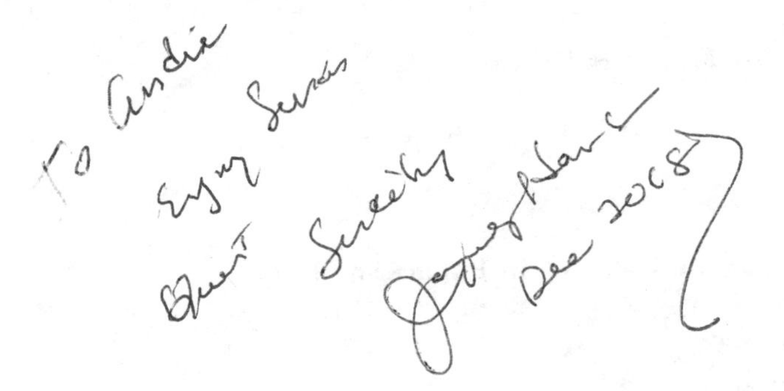

Glenhaven Press Modesto — 1998

SUSAN'S QUEST
by Jacquelyn Hanson

Published by:

GLENHAVEN PRESS
2401 E. Orangeburg Ave.
Suite 675 - 109
Modesto, CA 95355

This book is a work of fiction, and, except for actual historic figures, places, and events, is a product of the author's imagination.

First Printing — October, 1998

1 2 3 4 5

Publisher's Cataloging in Publication Data
Hanson, Jacquelyn,
Susan's Quest

Bibliography: p.

1. A Historical Romance based on the life of Irish Immigrants. 2. Boston, 1848—Boston society. 3. California Gold rush, Sailing ships—Passage around the Horn. 4. Romance, Intrigue 5. Valparaiso, Old San Francisco—1851, Early Sacramento.

Library of Congress Catalog Card Number: 98-72508
Hardcover ISBN 0-9637265-7-9
Paperback ISBN 0-9637265-2-8

Typeset with PTI LaTeX
Font: ITC Souvenir Light
Cover Art by Studio II

DEDICATION

This book is dedicated to the memory of the passengers and crew of the Bark Hersilia, whose careful records allowed me to describe Susan's voyage in detail.

BOSTON

1848 to 1851

Chapter One

SUSAN ROSE from the desk and walked to the window. She gripped the curtain so tightly her knuckles turned white. She stared across the street into the Boston Common as tears filled her green eyes. The sprinkling of freckles that covered her short Irish nose stood out against her pale skin. How, she wondered, could the scene be so peaceful? Children played in the warm April sunshine. Old men sat on park benches gossiping, enjoying the first warm day of the year. Shadows from newly budded leaves speckled their faces. The children jostled each other, laughing at the freedom to be out of doors after the cold winter.

Her head pounded. She felt as though the floor had dropped from beneath her feet. Taking a deep breath, she ran her fingers through her red curls and tried to get her heart rate back under control. The world looked the same. How could her small part of it be so changed?

I'm only seventeen, she thought. How can I manage? What can I do? Surely there must be some mistake!

But the papers she had pored over for hours left no room for doubt. Her father's death had left her penniless. His debtors would soon be demanding payment. The house and its furnishings were the only assets she possessed.

He did it all for me, she thought. The house here on Commonwealth Avenue. The sacrifices for the French lessons, for the piano, for the books. She grimaced. Perhaps had he not made the attempt, had he left her with a smaller house and no debts, she and Bridgit might have been able to take in sewing or washing, and Susan could have given reading or English lessons . . . . Stop it, she told herself. It's behind you now. Thinking of what your poor father should have done will not help you. He did what he thought best. But, she thought, panic again threatening to overcome her, what can I do?

Susan took another deep breath, forcing herself to relax, to slow the heart pounding against her ribs. She stared at the playing children, thinking perhaps she could be a governess. Stricken by the knowledge of her inexperience she thought, a little frantic at the idea, how does one get to be a governess, anyway?

She remembered her French lessons, and the hours she spent practicing on the piano. Did she know either one of those well enough to teach? Her love of literature might save her, but she knew only too well that even in the modern year of 1848 the types of jobs available to women, especially young women, were very limited.

It had happened so fast! The fever that took her mother in two days took her father only three weeks later. The tears in her eyes overflowed and rolled down her cheeks as she remembered holding her father's hand, begging him not to leave her. She had not realized he was dead until she felt Bridgit's arm around her shoulders pulling her away from the bed.

"Come, love," the old woman had said. "Poor baby, to be left all alone, and you jest a lass." Her Irish brogue full of sympathy, she led the stunned Susan from the room.

The faithful Bridgit stayed with her, even though Susan had no money to pay her. In fact, Bridgit's money fed them now.

"Don't worry your little head," she burred. "For the nonce we will be foine. I've a wee bit stowed away."

But Bridgit's 'wee bit' would not last long. The merchants demanded cash as soon as they heard of Seamus McGuire's death. She had already received several polite letters from his debtors. How could there be so many debts? She knew only too well that the letters would soon become less polite when they realized she had absolutely no source of income.

She looked around the room. Her emerald eyes filled with tears again. The comfortable bed with the quilt she and her mother had tied that reminded her of the companionship they had shared as they worked. The dressing table with the tortoise shell toilet set, a Christmas gift from her next door neighbor and best friend, Abigail Chase. The lamp she and her mother had selected together, with the spray of roses on the round glass shade. Her father had protested the lamp was too gaudy when they had proudly presented it.

The memories made the tears overflow. She sank into the little chair in front of her reading desk, her favorite piece in the whole room. The cherrywood top shone like a mirror. Bridgit polished it with beeswax every week. With loving fingers, Susan caressed the desk's smooth finish, thinking of the many happy hours she had spent there reading her beloved books.

The books themselves stood on the shelves of her bookstand against the far wall, the dark wood outlined on the bright floral wallpaper. The roses on the paper matched the lamp. She smiled as she recalled selecting the lamp because of the roses on the wall.

To give it all up! She inhaled deeply, taking in the familiar aroma of the books, the furniture polish, the slight odor that clung to the lamp's wick. The day to day smells that said this was home, and all of the memories they brought back to her.

She returned to the window to look again at the governess and the children in the park. She tugged at the long, red curls she could never control. Can I be a governess? She wavered, then made up her mind. Of course I can, she told herself firmly, taking a deep breath. I will find a job as a governess. I will even persuade my employer to hire Bridgit so we can stay together. After all, she thought, Bridgit has been with the family since Father was a child in Ireland. I can't leave her. It would break the old woman's heart.

She would sell the house and the furnishings. That money would enable her to pay the debts and have enough for a small room for herself and Bridgit. It should last them until Susan could find work.

Tears stung her eyes again, but she pushed them back. For the first time since her father's death she felt energy surge through her body.

"Bridgit," she called, her voice filled with determination. "Come up here, please. We have something to discuss."

Three weeks later, Susan and Bridgit stood arm-in-arm under a huge elm tree across the street from the house and watched as item after item fell to the auctioneer's gavel. Perspiration beaded Susan's forehead, and she felt it running in little trickles down her back, although the weather that May morning was pleasant. She set her jaw, determined not to let any of those grim men see a sign of weakness in her.

She wavered when her reading desk reached the block, then felt a hand grip her arm. She turned to find her friend Abigail Chase standing beside her. The girl's bright blue eyes sparkled with mischief.

"Susan," Abby whispered. "I've told Charlie to buy your desk. Mother and Father forbade me to come, but we snuck out. I told him how much that desk meant to you, and that we had to save it."

Susan, touched by her friend's thoughtfulness, held Abby close, the tears again threatening to overflow. Dear, loyal Abby, who had defied her mother's admonitions against playing with 'that little Irish girl' since they were children, spending every possible moment with Susan.

"Oh, Abby, you are the only real friend I've ever had, other than Bridgit. How in the world did you persuade Charlie?" Susan knew Charles Chase was as big a snob as his parents. He frequently complained because Abby refused to give up her friendship with Susan, no matter how concerned her brother was about what his friends would say.

"Easy. I found out he's been seeing a girl Mother and Father would never approve of, and that he doesn't want any of his upper crust friends to know about either. You just have to know how to handle brothers is all."

Susan laughed in spite of her leaden heart. "You blackmailed him! Abigail Chase, you are devious. And I love you."

"There it is," Abby murmured as the cherrywood desk came to the auctioneer's block, dutifully purchased by the obedient Charles. "Now I had better get back before Mother learns I am gone. As soon as you are settled, give me your direction and I'll have one of the servants bring the desk over to you."

Susan had refused to subject Bridgit to the ordeal of walking the streets of Boston to find a room they could afford. She blushed at the memory of her interview with the landlady when she finally discovered a suitable one they could pay for with their meager funds, in one of Boston's poorer areas, close to the waterfront.

"And what would a fine lady like you be a-wantin' with a place here?" she had queried suspiciously, looking Susan up and down. "Ye're not some man's fancy piece, are ye? I'll hev ye know I run a proper house, no goin's on, if you get my meanin'." She scowled. "Place might look a mite shabby, but I'm a good Christian woman, I am."

Susan hastened to assure her she sought just such a place, that her only companion would be Bridgit, and had finally managed to convince the good lady of the house that hard times, not a desire for a clandestine relationship, had driven them to this part of town.

Abby accompanied the servant that delivered the reading desk to the cramped quarters, and stood aghast at the dinginess of the tiny room. Susan's decision to become a governess also horrified her.

"Oh, Susan," she gasped. "I hear governesses are dreadfully mistreated. You'll be stuck in a stuffy little attic room, and fed only bread and water!" She dropped her voice. "And I hear the master will make improper advances to you." Abby's knowledge of the outside world came only from some of the cheap novels they used to smuggle in and hide, reading them when they could be sure of no interruptions.

"What other choice do I have, Abby?" Susan shook her head. "Work at one of the dance halls? Be a maid? Serve meals at a restaurant?" Or worse, she thought.

Abby sighed. "I suppose you're right. Just promise me you'll be careful. I'll ask around. Some of my mother's friends are always looking for a governess." She frowned. "But some of them are so disagreeable no governess ever stays for long."

Abby proved to be an even greater friend than Susan had anticipated. In the end it was Abby who discovered the Andrew family sought a governess, and it was she who persuaded Mrs. Andrew that she also needed a cook so Susan and Bridgit could stay together. On Abby's recommendation, Susan and Bridgit were hired and moved into the Andrew house on Commonwealth Avenue, not far from the home Susan had been forced to sell.

Their new life was not as bad as she had feared, in part, Susan felt, because Mrs. Andrew wanted to please Abby, but also because she was a kindly soul. Susan took over the education of Mary and Elizabeth, ages nine and eleven. She and Bridgit had a small, but comfortable room on the second floor. Abby remained loyal. They kept in touch, meeting in the park on sunny days when Susan's duties allowed her to get away. Abby seemed much relieved that Susan's lot was not as bad as Abby had predicted. Susan laughed to herself, remembering the hours she spent trudging the streets of Boston until Abby sent her to the Andrew residence, thinking how much worse it easily could have been.

Mary and Elizabeth were bright and eager to learn. Susan found teaching a real pleasure, and quickly grew to love both girls. Bridgit was happy. She loved to cook, and had been so fearful of a separation from Susan. Two maids did the other household work, to Susan's relief, for she had some concerns about Bridgit's health. Her feet swelled, often so badly she could not stand, and she had to take the steps very slowly. To sleep at night she had to prop herself up on three pillows, almost into a sitting position. If she lay flat, she could not get her breath.

Mrs. Andrew, when Susan voiced her concerns, called the family physician to see Bridgit.

"Dropsy," he announced. He took some blood from her arm and gave her some pills. "And I recommend a room on the first floor if it can be arranged."

Bridgit did seem to feel better after the doctor's visit, even though she continued to climb the stairs each night to the little second story room. Susan, annoyed when Mr. Andrew refused to 'coddle' Bridgit by giving her a room on the first floor, relaxed a little when Bridgit assured her she could handle the stairs "long as I kin take me time," as she put it.

They settled into a routine. When Susan turned eighteen the following August, Mrs. Andrew gave her a small party. It did not, Susan noticed with a wry smile, include any of the Andrew's social set, but Abby attended, as did Bridgit and the two housemaids, and Mrs. Andrew and the two girls.

The weeks passed, pleasant weeks in which nothing out of the ordinary happened. Susan felt her life drifting by. Sometimes she thought about what would become of her, a vague, uncomfortable feeling that she immediately dismissed.

Then, on the following Christmas, her life again changed forever.

Chapter 2

THE CHRISTMAS TREE sparkled as Susan lighted the last candle. The Andrew household smelled of holly and ginger. The aroma of Bridgit's freshly baked gingerbread brought back memories of the happiness of the previous Christmas, but Susan shoved the memories back in her mind. She had learned not to dwell on the past. Except for her weekly trip to the little cemetery where she visited the graves of her parents, she put her former life behind her.

"Oh, Miss Susan, it's so lovely!" Mary's blue eyes widened at the sight of the tree. The candlelight reflected in her eyes. The girls' red-gold hair revealed their Scottish heritage. Not the red of Susan's hair, or Bridgit's before the gray became dominant. More a gold with hints of red. The short noses and freckles they shared suggested some border crossings among their ancestry.

"Nothing but the best for your brother's homecoming," Susan laughed. The whole household could talk of nothing else but the return of young Donald for the Christmas holidays. Mr. Andrew had decided his only son should be educated at the University of Edinburgh, so he had spent the previous three years in Scotland. Just why he was returning in what should be the middle of a school term remained a little vague. To Susan, it seemed a strange time of year for a sea voyage, while storms raged across the northern Atlantic.

"He is transferring to Harvard," his step-mother explained. "Now we will be able to see him more often."

Susan had studied the painting of Donald that hung over the fireplace. His coloring, according to Mrs. Andrew, reflected the dark hair and hazel eyes of his deceased mother.

Susan had learned Donald's mother died at his birth, but other than that, no one ever mentioned the first Mrs. Andrew. The painting depicted him as a charming young man, full of fun, but somehow Susan detected a weakness in his face. She dismissed the feeling. Maybe the painter didn't portray him accurately. How could she judge? She hadn't even met him.

Mrs. Andrew hurried in. She added her admiration of the tree to Mary's. "But come and help Bridgit in the kitchen now, please, Susan. Dinner must be perfect. After all, Donald's not been home in over two years." She glanced in the mirror and patted a stray strand of the golden hair into place. "Everything must be perfect," she repeated, a little breathlessly. She scurried from the room, continuing to mumble. Susan smiled to herself. To the flighty Mrs. Andrew, everything became a major production. Obediently, Susan followed her from the room.

Since dinner would be for just the family, they invited Susan to join them. She took pains with her dressing, selecting a favorite dress she had rescued from the auction. The white wool dress bore sprigs of tiny red flowers. The bodice fitted like it was pasted on, and showed her figure to perfection. The skirt, just full enough to emphasize her slender waistline, flared around her.

Carriage wheels crunched on the gravel and she hurried to the window in time to see a tall young man jump lightly down. His voice floated up to her. "Thanks, Jasper. Sorry you had to wait so long. Blasted longboat took forever to get us ashore."

Jasper touched his hat in reply. "My pleasure, Master Donald. Welcome home."

"Donny, Donny," came the squeals from the girls as they threw themselves on him. "You're home at last!" The party passed into the house and out of Susan's sight.

So that was Donald, she thought. She returned to her

dressing table and brushed her hair until it shone, the flame of the lamp catching the highlights. Her green eyes danced in anticipation. What if he falls in love with me, she thought, enraptured with the idea of marrying into one of Boston's most aristocratic families. Visions of inviting Mr. and Mrs. Chase to a soiree ran through her mind. She stroked the smooth finish on her reading desk and chuckled at the thought of the high and mighty Charles Chase kissing her hand and reminding her it was he who had saved the cherrywood desk from the auctioneer's block.

Then she laughed at her fantasies. Forget it, she told herself. You've been reading too many of Abby's cheap novels. He'll never even notice you.

As she descended the stairs, Donald and his father stood beside the marble fireplace talking, each holding a glass of brandy. He stood several inches taller than his father, slender yet well-muscled. He looked even more handsome in person than in his portrait, the dark hair with the widow's peak on his high forehead contrasting with his father's fairness. At the rustle of her skirts, the two men looked up.

"Here she is now, Donald. May I present Miss Susan McGuire? She has proven a most admirable governess for your sisters."

Susan's heart gave a little leap. Forcing down her irritation at Mr. Andrew's reminder to his son that she served him as a mere employee, she managed to smile.

As she placed her hand in Donald's, she met the hazel eyes. Looking deep into those eyes roused feelings in her she had never felt before.

"Miss McGuire." He acknowledged the introduction with a nod. His smile emphasized the dimple in his chin. "Please, allow me to escort you in to dinner." He drew her hand through his arm and led her through the double doors to the dining room where he seated her, then took the chair beside her.

Susan tried later to remember what she had eaten, but all she could think of was the hazel eyes smiling into hers. Donald refilled her wine glass so often she felt giddy. It took all her concentration not to show the effects. She knew what Mr. and Mrs. Andrew would think if they thought she allowed herself to get drunk.

After dinner, Mary and Elizabeth begged Susan to play the piano. "You have to show Donald how pretty you play."

Mrs. Andrew added her entreaties. "Play some of that new music you have been teaching the girls. Perhaps the etude of Mr. Mozart that Mrs. Griffin presented at her last musical afternoon."

In her relief at the prospect of getting away from Donald's constant refilling of her wine glass, Susan agreed. They adjourned to the music room, Susan taking deep breaths, trying to clear her head. He sat beside her on the bench and turned the pages while she played. She tried to concentrate on the music. She did not know if the dizziness came from the wine or from his proximity to her. Whenever his hand brushed against hers, a shock shot up her arm and through her whole body.

After she played several selections, Susan glanced at Donald's father to find him scowling. Oh, dear, she thought. He's not happy that Donald finds me attractive. When she finished the next piece, Mr. Andrew rose to his feet. "I think it is time for you ladies to retire," he said sternly. "Donald and I need to talk."

Susan lay awake for some time after she crawled under the covers. As she listened to Bridgit's uneven, rattling breathing, for once her own feelings drove away her concern for Bridgit. Could this be love? she wondered. Does love happen this fast? Can it really be happening just like I imagined?

Give it up, she told herself. Mr. Andrew may like you just fine as a governess, but the daughter of Irish immigrants as a wife for his son? He would never hear of it. Even though her father had earned enough to buy the house on Commonwealth Avenue, it had never gained them admission into Boston society.

Tears stung her eyes as she thought again of her father's sacrifices for the French lessons, for the piano, for the books, all in his attempt to get them accepted into Boston society. All was gone except the desk Abby had saved for her and some of her favorite books. Tom Jones, of which her father would never have approved, her beloved Dickens, and Mr. Dana's recently published *Two Years Before the Mast.* This she kept because the magical country he described fascinated her. California. She often thought about it. She sighed. Highly unlikely she would ever get to go there.

She heard some exciting rumors about a gold strike in California. She read about it in an article that had been copied from one of the Baltimore papers, but most people discounted the story. With a little chuckle, she remembered Bridgit's reaction when she mentioned the tales to her. "Some folks now, they'll believe anythin' they read in the papers," Bridgit had snorted with derision. "They be the same folks as believe in the little people."

Susan had nodded and sighed. "You're probably right." But, she thought, remembering the conversation as she snuggled deeper into the warm quilts, if it is true, it sounds so exciting.

Donald came home frequently after he enrolled at Harvard. During the long winter evenings, he often asked Susan to be his partner for a game of whist. He turned the pages while she played the piano to entertain the family. He even escorted her and the girls to one of Mrs. Griffin's musical afternoons, although Susan knew the whole affair bored him to the point of almost yawning the whole time.

* * *

The first warm April afternoon of the following spring, Donald invited Susan to take a stroll through the Common with him.

"It's such a lovely day, Miss McGuire, and you have been cooped up in the house all winter. The fresh air will do you good."

Susan's eyes sparkled. "I'd be delighted. Let me run up and get my shawl. It may be sunny, but there's still a chill in the air."

Bridgit lay back against her pillows, her shoes off, but her eyes as bright as ever. "And where be ye a-goin', Missy?" she inquired as Susan dug her shawl out of the small chest at the foot of her bed.

"Donald has asked me to take a walk in the Common with him," Susan replied, trying to keep the excitement out of her voice.

As usual, Bridgit saw right through her. Her eyes narrowed. "Not becomin' too fond o' the young man, are ye?"

Susan blushed at Bridgit's perspicacity and hurried to murmur a disclaimer. She gave a little laugh. "It'll just be a nice change. The weather has been so miserable lately, and it's such a lovely day."

Bridgit sighed. "I jest fear he'll hurt ye, Lass, is all. These rich young men, they think nothin' o' toyin' with the affections of lasses like yerself."

Susan nodded. "I know, Bridgit. I'll remember."

But as Donald's eyes lighted up at the sight of her descending the stairs, she could not keep her heart from giving a little leap. Maybe, just maybe, she thought, she dared to dream.

They strolled among the newly budding trees in silence for a while, Susan's thoughts on the previous April when she stared out at these same trees after her father's death. The same old men sat on the park benches. Children ran past, shouting in glee at the freedom to run after the long winter.

One boy rolled a large metal hoop down the path directly towards Donald and Susan.

"Careful! Watch out." Donald's arm circled her, pulling her close to him to evade the boy and the hoop. The lad raced past, but Donald continued to hold her securely. She felt his heart pounding against her. She looked up and met the hazel eyes. They stared into hers with an intensity she found disconcerting. Her heart beat so loudly she feared he would hear it.

"Susan, Susan," he murmured against her hair. "You are so lovely, so charming, so . . . , so everything!" He held her away from him, his hands on her shoulders. "I think I have fallen in love with you. Can a person fall in love so fast?"

"Donald, no." She shook her head. "We can't. You know your father would never give his consent. I don't belong to the right society. My parents, as I am sure your father has told you many, many times, were Irish immigrants. You know what people from England and Scotland think of the Irish."

"This is America," he grumbled. "I thought we came here to get away from the rigid class structure they have in the Old Country."

Susan gave a shaky little laugh and pulled away from his embrace. "They haven't been away from the Old Country long enough yet. Before we take on all of Boston Society, let's wait until we get to know each other a little better."

"Ah, Susan," he sighed. "Your wisdom is exceeded only by your beauty. You're probably right. At least, give the Pater a bit of time to adjust to the idea."

They tried very hard to be discreet, but the glances that passed between them, the slight lingering when their hands touched could not, as Susan had feared, long be missed. As she passed the door to the library one morning in May, she heard Donald and his father talking.

"Donald," Mr. Andrew's voice said in his emphatic, no argument tone, "I have noticed you taking an unseemly interest in our lovely Susan."

"She is a charming young lady, Father," Donald began, his voice revealing the slight slur she had heard before when he had imbibed a little too much of his father's brandy. "She's . . . ."

His father interrupted him. "She's no one. Her parents were Irish immigrants, for God's sake." Susan heard these words with a pain in her heart. Poor Father, who tried so hard. What snobs these upper crust Bostonians were! She wished she could tell them all the members of her father's family were landed gentry in Ireland. Too many brothers and too little land made him decide to come to America. For me, she thought, tears springing into her eyes. For me.

"If you wish an innocent flirtation, Son, so be it," Mr. Andrews continued. "Just be sure the subject of matrimony never comes up between you."

Susan fled, not wanting to hear more. Reaching her room, blinded by tears, she threw herself on the bed and wept, thankful for Bridgit's absence. Good enough to teach his daughters to be proper young ladies, but not good enough to marry his precious son.

Her first impulse, to march out of the house, raged through her. But where would she go? If she tried to get another job as governess, she would need a reference from Mr. Andrew. If she stomped out in a fury, she would never get it. And what about Bridgit? She was happy here. Would they throw her out too? She had to take care of Bridgit. She could never get another position with her poor health. No one would hire a cook who could barely catch her breath and had to rest every hour. They were just fortunate Mrs. Andrew was kind-hearted enough to overlook Bridgit's infirmities, and the two housemaids had grown fond enough of the old woman to take over some of her duties.

Susan pulled herself together. She had known all along it could never be. Getting up, she dipped a handful of water from the basin that stood on top of the commode and bathed her face, trying to erase any sign of the storm. She would just forget she had fallen in love with Donald. Maybe he did not love her after all. He had never said anything about marriage. Had she built all those dreams on nothing? Was Abby right when she said he just played with her affections?

"These rich boys do that," Abby had declared to Susan on one of her visits when Susan had confessed her feelings for Donald. "I've heard Charlie laughing with his friends about some poor housemaid or governess who thought the master's son loved her." She scowled. "It's just a game to them."

But her resolution faltered whenever their eyes met. After his classes at Harvard ended for the summer, he came home even more frequently, and he often contrived to arrange for a few moments when they could be alone.

"Father has forbidden me to marry you," he told her at last, tenderly kissing the hand he held. "But I've only one more year of college. Then I'll be of age and can get a job. Please wait for me."

Joy rushed through her. He does love me, she thought. He does want to marry me. The future looked rosy after all. "Oh, Donald! Of course I'll wait." Her eyes shone with love for him as he swept her into his arms.

By the summer of 1849, everyone talked about the gold strike in California. The papers filled column after column with reports of riches being found by men who had only to look for the gold lying about on the ground. Susan read the reports with fascination.

"Just imagine," she said to Bridgit. Her eyes sparkled as she looked up from the morning's copy of the *Boston*

Globe. "Imagine being able to pick up your fortune as easily as gathering chestnuts from beneath the trees."

Bridgit snorted. "Believe it when I sees it, I will. Sich stories as that have a way o' gettin' better wi' the tellin'. Sounds ta me like chasin' after the pot of leprechaun gold at the end o' the rainbow, it do." She shook her head. "They be them as spend their whole lives a-chasin' jest such a will-o'-the-wisp."

Susan laughed. "My beloved but ever practical Bridgit." She folded up the paper. "You're probably right. But it does sound like a fascinating country."

One evening in July, Donald burst into the house and swept Susan into the library. He told her, with great excitement, that he had decided exactly what to do.

"I'll go to the gold fields in California." His eyes sparkled. His breath had that hint of brandy she tried to ignore. "Men are getting rich there every day. Really rich! And when I've made my fortune, I'll come back for you. Then we can be married and my father and all his snob friends can go straight to the Devil!"

"But, Donald. It's so far! And what about Harvard? You still have another year to finish."

"We'll be so rich with the gold I won't need any college. I'll write to you. You'll see. This is the way." He tugged her hand. "Come on. Where's my father? Let's go tell him right now." He dragged the reluctant Susan along behind him.

They located Mr. Andrew in his study. He looked up with a scowl when he saw Donald holding Susan's hand, but he heard Donald out in icy silence. Susan could see the fury mounting in Mr. Andrew's face. He turned so blue with suppressed rage Susan feared he might have an attack of apoplexy.

"Have you lost your mind?" he shouted when Donald

finished outlining his plans. "I've already made arrangements for you to join the business as soon as you graduate. Is this what your puppy love for the lovely Miss Susan has led you to?"

Susan stood speechless. A furious blush washed over her face. How dare he discuss her as though she did not even exist! She controlled her rage with an effort. After all, his attitude should not surprise her. He always treated the hired help as if they were part of the furnishings.

"It's not puppy love, Father," Donald replied quietly. "I have had some experience with puppy love. Susan is the only woman for me. I'm sorry you can't accept her as my wife."

"Then you are no longer my son." He turned on his heel and stalked from the room.

"Oh, Donald," Susan gasped as they watched his retreating back. "He'll blame me. He'll dismiss me without a reference. What will I do?" Her heart quaked as the thought of Bridgit flooded into her mind. "And Bridgit, with her poor health . . . ."

Donald gathered the shaking girl into his arms and kissed her gently on the forehead. "Don't worry. He'll get over it. The girls love you too much to let him dismiss you." He grinned. "I'll tell them not to let him. Everything will work out. You'll see."

Susan, although not completely convinced, allowed him to persuade her. After all, she thought, what options did she really have?

The arguments raged. Mr. Andrew stormed and threatened to dismiss both Susan and Bridgit. The girls wept and pleaded with him not to blame Susan. Even the timid Mrs. Andrew added her pleas to those of the two girls. Bridgit said nothing, but Susan knew she worried about the future. She also knew most of Bridgit's concerns were not for herself, but for Susan.

After one particularly loud quarrel, one that ended with Donald stomping out of the house and slamming the door, leaving the girls in tears, Susan fled to her room. She stood at the window looking out over the Common, her mind in a turmoil.

Guilt tore at her as she realized the conflict her presence had caused. Donald had been the obedient son, his father's pride and joy. She tried to understand Mr. Andrew's point of view. After all, he had hoped his only son would follow him in his business. The Andrew Import/Export House was a thriving one, dealing in large numbers of expensive textiles, and Mr. Andrew had been grooming Donald to become his partner . . . .

She shook her head with a heavy sigh. Behind her, Bridgit spoke.

"Ye canna blame yerself, Lass," she soothed. "T'were destined, it were. Those two would never a' got along." She smiled at Susan and opened her arms. Susan threw herself into Bridgit's embrace and wept.

Donald stood firm in his decision, and on the 14th of August, 1849, Susan stood on the pier with Mrs. Andrew and the two girls and watched his ship sail out of Boston Harbor. Her cheek tingled from his farewell kiss. She would savor that kiss. It had to last her for a long time.

Mr. Andrew had angrily refused to join them. Susan was proud of Donald, for he continued to declare his love for her in spite of his father's opposition, but her heart ached as she watched him leave. He stood on the taffrail, waving. The girls jumped up and down, shouting "Good-bye! Take care of yourself! Write to us!" until long after he passed beyond hearing range.

Susan stood silent and unmoving. She hoped she could pretend to be patient until he returned for her.

Chapter 3

THREE DAYS AFTER CHRISTMAS of 1850, Susan stood on the pier looking out over Boston Harbor. As the chill wind wafted over her, she thought of the many times she found herself on that very spot since the sultry August day in 1849 when she watched Donald sail away from her. Drastic changes in her life had followed that fateful day. Mr. Andrew continued to blame her for Donald's departure.

"If he hadn't been so besotted with you, he'd have stayed here like a proper son, finished Harvard, and never taken this fool trip to California," he accused. "Never should have let the Chase girl talk the wife into hiring you. Told her we didn't want any Irish. Nothing but trouble ever comes out of Ireland."

Susan made no reply. She had heard comments like that so many times before she had built a shell around her feelings to make herself immune to the insults. The girls, true to Donald's prediction, had begged and pleaded until their father agreed not to dismiss her, but the whole atmosphere changed. She continued to do her best for Mary and Elizabeth, and spent any free time either in her room, in the kitchen with Bridgit, or, weather permitting, walking in the park with Abby. She frequently thanked her lucky stars for Abby's loyal friendship.

She also often visited the pier, where she anxiously scanned the faces of arriving passengers, looking for Donald. Sometimes, if a man looked like a returning miner, she would approach him, asking timidly if he had known a

Donald Andrew. She showed each of them the miniature portrait of Donald he had given her before his departure.

"Sorry, Miss." The reply never varied. "Never seen no one like him. So many men. Never even knew the name of most."

But no word in a year and a half! He had promised to write. She knew mail came in on each boat. She wondered if his father received the letters and never gave them to her, but she dismissed that idea. If a letter had been received, Mary and Elizabeth would have chattered about it for days.

Abby begged her to forget him. "He's gone and got himself another sweetheart, mark my words!" Abby had recently had a bad experience with a young man and had declared herself off men for good. "You're young and pretty and shouldn't be wasting your time waiting for him to come back."

Susan smiled at Abby's loyalty, but she had promised Donald she would wait. She had to know. Of course, she thought wryly, it wasn't like she had half the eligible young men in Boston knocking at her door.

She turned her steps back to the Andrew house. Bridgit had stayed in bed that morning, saying she 'felt poorly', and Susan did not wish to stay away from her for long. She knew the old woman's heart grew weaker each day. The thought of losing Bridgit frightened her, for then she would be all alone.

One of the housemaids met her at the door. "Oh, Miss Susan," she whispered. "Bridgit were askin' fer you." Fear showed in the girl's eyes. "She were breathin' kinda hard, she were."

Susan gathered her skirts and ran up the stairs. Bridgit smiled at her as she entered the little room they had shared for so long.

"Are you worse?" Susan gasped, out of breath herself from the run up the stairs. "Do you want me to send for the doctor?"

Bridgit smiled and held out her hand. "No, child." She shook her grizzled head slowly from side to side. "I jest wanted ye wi' me. It's time."

"Time?"

"Time fer me to go to me reward. I want ye to know how much ye've meant to me across the years. Me own little datter would'a been like you, had she lived, God rest her soul." The old woman paused to catch her breath. "She an' her da died o' the fever . . . jest afore I went into service with yer grandfolks, while yer pa was jest a bairn. Never wanted to marry again, so ye became me family."

Bridgit paused, out of breath, her lips blue with the effort of speaking. Susan placed her hand against the bony chest and felt Bridgit's heart, appalled to find it racing rapidly.

"Don't try to talk. It's exhausting you. Are you sure you don't want me to get the doctor?" She clung to the work-worn hand. "Please, Bridgit. I don't want to lose you. You're all I have left!"

Bridgit patted Susan's hand and shook her head. "Time's are changin'," she panted. "The girls . . . are 'most growed up. When I'm gone . . . ye'll be free. Won't allus . . . be a-worryin, how . . . ye're to take care o' me." Her eyes closed.

Susan did not reply, but sat watching Bridgit's rapid, shallow breathing. She matched her own respirations to Bridgit's until she began to feel dizzy and had to take a deep breath. Tears slowly trickled down her cheeks as she watched a bluish hue creep across Bridgit's face.

Susan lost all track of time as she sat by the bedside holding Bridgit's hand. The old woman had lapsed into unconsciousness and Susan knew the end approached rapidly. When the breathing stopped, she gently pulled the sheet over the face of the faithful servant, her childhood nurse, and life-long friend.

"Goodbye, Bridgit," she whispered. "I love you, and I'll never, ever forget you."

Susan buried Bridgit next to Seamus and Mary McGuire, so they could be together in death as they had been in life. After the handful of mourners left, she stood by the graves for a long time in the light sprinkling of snow that covered the ground. The cold crept up her feet until it reached her heart. She had never felt so lonely in her life. Her parents gone, Bridgit gone, Donald so many thousands of miles away . . . . What would she do now?

She shook her head. She would think about it later.

Susan stood looking across the harbor on a clear, cold, January day two weeks after Bridgit's funeral, wondering what she should do with the rest of her life. The girls would not need her much longer. Elizabeth had begun finishing school in January, and Mary would join her in another year. Mr. Andrew had already dropped several hints in the past month that her services would soon no longer be required.

A magnificent bark, the *Even Tide,* stood at anchor in the harbor. Susan had seen the ship before. She knew Captain Griffin often took his wife with him on his voyages, for the Griffins and the Andrews were friends, and Susan frequently attended the afternoon musical recitals at the Griffin home. Mrs. Griffin had regaled Susan and the girls with some of her adventures with her husband. Mrs. Andrew had been horrified, but the tales fascinated Susan. They made her realize what a circumscribed life she led.

On impulse, ice crunching beneath her booted feet, she strode to the dockmaster's office and asked when and where the *Even Tide's* next voyage would be.

"She's loaded and ready. Planned to leave on January 6, but she's waitin' 'til the ice clears the harbor. She'll round the Horn by the end of April, before the winter sets in hard.

Dock in San Francisco probably late July, early August." He chuckled. "She's carryin' a bunch of minin' equipment for all them men gettin' rich in the gold fields."

"Thank you." Susan made her decision and headed for the Griffin residence.

Persuading Mrs. Griffin had not been hard. She greeted Susan with enthusiasm, for they shared a love for Mozart, and even though she knew Susan worked for the Andrew family, the gracious woman always treated Susan as an equal. If Mrs. Griffin had any negative opinions about Irish immigrants, she kept them to herself. Susan had grown to love and admire her.

Susan explained her circumstances, omitting any reference to Donald. If Mrs. Griffin had heard gossip, she was polite enough not to mention it.

"With Bridgit gone, and Elizabeth already in finishing school, well, the girls don't really need me any more. I can't picture Mr. Andrew wanting to keep me after the girls are grown. And I admit I've a great curiosity to see California. I've heard you speak of it so often in your stories of your travels . . . ."

Mrs. Griffin nodded in understanding. "It is a fascinating place, and I do admit I miss having a feminine companion on the long voyages. The men, for the most part, are a rough lot, although the officers, of course, are gentlemen. But Howard is often busy, so I am alone much of the time." She paused long enough to refill Susan's teacup before she continued. "We sail with the morning tide one week from tomorrow. The ice should be clear of the harbor by then." She smiled as delight lighted Susan's face. "I will arrange for a cabin. Please plan to be on board the day before we sail. The cabins are small. I trust you will not have much luggage?"

Susan laughed grimly. "Very little, I fear. And I can pay my passage. I have some money saved up."

Mrs. Griffin shook her head. "Don't even think of it. I should pay you, to be my companion. We will be delighted to have you with us." She smiled. "Besides, if you stay in California, you will need your funds until you can get situated there. Hotels are quite expensive, from what I understand."

Mr. Andrew sneered when he heard of her plans. "Chasing off after him like the slut you are. Good riddance to you. You've sent him to his death is what you've done. We'd have heard from him by now if he were still alive."

In her heart, Susan feared he could be right. The other alternative, that Donald simply chose not to write, she refused to accept. No, she reassured herself. He's just been where he can't write.

Mrs. Andrew, timid soul that she was, could not believe Susan would actually go.

"But my dear, it's so far! And what about Indians, and cholera, and shipwreck?" She shuddered. "And seasickness?"

Susan smothered a smile, knowing Mrs. Andrew was remembering one ill-fated sailing trip on the bay. "Mrs. Griffin has survived many trips, so I'm sure I can manage one," Susan assured her. Dear Mrs. Andrew. Susan knew she tried to compensate for Mr. Andrew's vindictiveness, holding Susan blameless for what she openly called 'Donald's foolishness', not realizing that her attitude was as much of an insult as her husband's.

The girls, delighted, begged her to take them with her. They had read many romanticized stories about the fabled land of gold and were innocently eager to see it.

"Sorry, I'm afraid your father would never permit it." Laughing, she hugged them. "I love you both. I'll never forget you, and will write every chance I get."

"And find Donald for us," they both cried.

"I promise."

Susan left Boston with mixed feelings. She had never known any other home. But she knew her life would go nowhere if she stayed. She would always be the daughter of Irish immigrants. Even if Donald were dead, or if she could not find him, she could at least start a new life in California. Surely the society there would not be as rigid as Boston.

So, on Tuesday, January 18, 1851, her cherrywood desk and all but a few of her cherished books entrusted to Abby, her few remaining belongings stowed in the tiny cabin, she watched, with no regrets, as the Boston shoreline receded in the distance. The breeze caught the sails, billowing them into great white globes. The rigging creaked with protest at the strain the strong northwesterly breeze put upon them. The water sparkled in the rising sun. Little froths of white foam ran across the tops of the waves. Gulls swooped and screamed as they squabbled with each other over tidbits.

She drew a deep breath of the fresh salt air, savoring the smell of the sea mingled with the odor of pitch from the caulking. She watched the sun climb above the far horizon, where the water stretched as far as she could see.

As the sun rose higher, she felt her spirits rise with it. Her old life was behind her, and her new one began at that moment.

She was on her way to California.

THE PASSAGE

January to August

1851

Chapter 4

THE WIND out of the northwest drove the ship steadily on its southeasterly course. By mid-day, Susan could no longer see land. As the afternoon progressed into evening, the wind blew with greater and greater force. That night, she fell asleep to the sound of water slapping the side of the ship and rushing past the hull. At first she found the noises frightening, but reassured herself that the *Even Tide*, a sturdy ship, had made the trip many times. Still, the howl of the wind intimidated her, and she covered her ears with the blanket.

The next morning she discovered the motion of the ship made her queasy, so she climbed the ladder to the deck. There she saw a boy of about fourteen dragged forward by one of the crew, the back of his ragged shirt clenched tightly in the fist of the scowling crewman.

"Stowaway, Sir," the seaman reported to the First Officer. "Found him hidin' aft, behind some of the cargo. What'll I do with 'im?"

"Should throw him overboard," said the officer, a young man Mrs. Griffin had introduced to Susan as Peter Thomas. "Would be a good lesson to those as think to do likewise." He glanced at Susan, who watched the scene with horror. "Up to the Captain, of course," he hastened to add.

Summoned from the chart house, Captain Griffin smiled at the frightened boy. "Relax, Son. No one will be thrown from this ship while I am the Captain. We'll let you work off your passage. Have you any sea-faring experience?"

"No, Sir, thankee, Sir," the boy stammered, his relief so patent Susan felt it. "Apprenticed to a blacksmith, I were." He dropped his eyes. "Couldn't take it no more, Sir. Rather be thrown overboard than go back." Susan noticed the burn scars on the boy's hands, and a crooked arm. He gave the captain a shy smile. "Name's Barney, Sir. Don't know my other name. My parents died when I was too young to remember, and Master took me to work for him."

Susan noted the red hair and the green eyes. Freckles stood out on the boy's pale face. Irish, she thought with a smile. We could be kin. What would have happened to her, had the fever that took her parents taken them when she was only two or three? Would she have wound up apprenticed to some cruel dressmaker, or worse? She shuddered. The world could be a harsh place for those with no one to care for them.

The seaman's face relaxed into a smile. "Come, lad. I'll find ye a place to bunk and lay out yer duties fer ye."

The next day they entered the Gulf Stream. An obliging young officer explained the unique ocean feature to Susan. "It's a current that begins down off the Florida Keys," he said. "Brings warm water up the coast and across over to England. Keeps the ice out of the North Atlantic and warms the whole north coast. Moves fast, too. Can carry a ship up to five or six knots. Have to take our bearings more often, to be sure we're not carried off course. Seen it happen."

Frequent rain squalls kept Susan confined below decks for several days. She learned as long as she lay quietly on her bunk, the motion could be tolerated. At least the wind held steady, and the ship plowed through the waves at an encouraging rate of speed.

On Sunday, January 30, the crash of a wave over the bow woke Susan to the fury of a storm. Frightened, she tried to go on deck, only to be driven back by the torrential rain. The frigid wind, blowing at gale force from the north, took her breath away and stung her face. The fury of the wind lashed the waves in front of it into a white froth. The ship scudded along with close-reefed main and top sails. She watched the wind pull at the sails and wondered how the fabric could keep from tearing, with so much pressure from the wind upon it. The masts creaked and groaned until Susan, who stood fixed in horror at the scene before her, expected any moment to see one splinter and crash to the deck.

Mrs. Griffin heard the girl's frightened gasp and hastened to reassure her that Captain Griffin knew exactly how much strain he could put on each mast. "That's why he ordered the sails reefed last night when the barometer began to fall," she explained. "Some captains wait until the storm is upon them to shorten sail, to make all the speed they can, but Howard prefers to be cautious." She chuckled softly. "At least, he does when I am with him!"

By mid-afternoon, the clouds broke away, though the wind continued and the seas remained turbulent. Susan, feeling queasy after being confined below all morning, mounted the ladder to the deck to get some fresh air. She emerged from the companionway in time to see Barney fall from the rigging.

With a little cry, she hurried forward as fast as the pitching deck would allow. Pushing aside the sailors crowded around, she reached his side. His right leg, twisted beneath his body at an odd angle, was obviously broken, even to Susan. Tears of pain streaked the boy's face, though he remained silent.

"You poor lad," Susan murmured, stroking the tumbled red hair back from his freckled face. The tear stains made him look even younger. She wondered how old he was, or if he even knew. She pulled her handkerchief from her sleeve and wiped away his tears.

First Officer Thomas pushed his way through the crowd of seamen, a tall, clean-shaven man at his side.

"This is Dr. Alexander, Miss McGuire," the man said. "He can tend to the boy."

Susan looked up and into the bluest eyes she had ever seen. Her heart lurched. She noticed the blond curls just touching the collar of his topcoat, the quality cut to his clothes, the width of his shoulders, and took a deep breath. She forced her mind from him and returned to the business at hand.

"I fear his leg is broken, Doctor," she reported, trying to get her unexpected emotional response under control, annoyed with herself for her reaction. After all, she was on her way to search for her Donald. She should not have any interest in strange doctors, not even one with the most striking eyes she had ever encountered.

Dr. Alexander immediately took charge. He gently probed the injured leg, then carefully untangled it from the coil of rope the boy had landed on. "You," he ordered a nearby seaman, "bring me two slats of wood. We need to splint this leg to prevent further injury before we can move him."

Susan cradled Barney's head to her breast and stroked his face as he grimaced in pain. Tears of sympathy ran down her cheeks. The poor boy had endured so much suffering in his short life.

The seaman reappeared with the two ordered supports, and Dr. Alexander finished splinting the leg. "Take him to my cabin. I will set the bone there. You," he beckoned to Susan who had stepped back to allow the seamen to carry Barney below deck. "Come with me. You can assist me. I will need a nurse."

With trepidation and a lot of care, for the slippery deck still rocked and heaved, Susan followed the small procession down the companionway and into the cabin amidships.

The doctor's quarters, twice the size of Susan's, boasted two bunks. She also noted it rode much more smoothly than her cabin in the aft. When the three of them were alone, Susan asked the doctor, "Why have I never seen you before?"

"I have remained in my cabin," he replied curtly. "I prefer to be alone. My books are my companions."

Having no reply to that comment, she fell silent and watched him prepare a dose of laudanum for Barney.

He handed her the medicine. "Have him drink this," he ordered.

Susan took the small cup, suppressing the sharp retort that sprang to her lips as anger surged through her at his imperious attitude. Not even a 'please', she thought as she urged Barney to sip the concoction. "This will stop the pain," she soothed the frightened boy.

"Thankee, Miss," he whispered. His eyes darted from her face to the doctor's. "Will I . . . will I . . . lose my leg, Sir?"

"No, lad," the doctor assured him, "it's not likely you'll lose the leg. 'Tis not a bad break. Go to sleep now. Let the medicine take effect so I can set the bone." With a large pair of scissors, he cut away the ragged trousers to expose the point of the break, which swelled rapidly.

When Barney's eyes at last drifted shut under the influence of the opium, the doctor prepared his splints and bandages. Susan tried to keep the leg steady in the pitching cabin. Between the smell from the smoky oil lamp and the motion of the ship, nausea again threatened to overcome her. She took a deep breath and forced the feeling away, although she almost lost the battle when the doctor fished two leeches out of a bottle and applied them to the swelling. She saw him watching her face and erased the feeling of revulsion. She refused to show any weakness in front of this grim man.

She marveled at how he seemed unaffected by the lurching of the ship. The small lamp swayed back and forth, casting eerie shadows across his face. As he worked, the sullen look vanished, replaced by concentration and interest. She hoped he was a competent doctor. He seemed, to her untrained eye, to know his profession.

"Hold him still," he ordered curtly, "while I get the bone in place. When I tell you, tie the bandages to secure it." He seized the boy's foot with both hands and tugged gently. Susan felt, rather than heard, the ends of the bone grate together as they slipped into place. Barney cried out in his drugged sleep.

"Now," Dr. Alexander snapped. "Hurry, before the next blasted wave knocks the bone out of line again."

Susan hastened to obey, tying the bandages securely around the leg, binding the strips of wood in place.

Dr. Alexander poured a packet of powder into a small basin of water. He stirred it, then dipped a piece of cloth in the solution. Wringing the water out of the rag, he folded it into a square about the size of Susan's hand.

"Watch closely," he ordered. "You will replace this every fifteen minutes until the swelling is gone." He placed his big watch on the table where she could see the time.

She must have looked startled, for he smiled faintly. "Do not fear. I will take over when you return to your cabin to retire for the night. Meanwhile, since I will be up all night, you will excuse me while I rest now." Taking off his shoes, he lay down on the other bunk, pulled up a blanket, and fell asleep almost at once.

Susan sighed and returned her attention to the injured boy. She smoothed the red hair back from his sweaty forehead and stroked his smooth cheeks, feeling just the bare beginnings of a beard. He must be about fourteen. Her heart went out to him. He had been alone all of his life, and could not remember having anyone to love and care for him. Well, young Barney, she thought, although surprised herself at the depth of feeling for the boy that ran through her, I care. As long as you and I live in the same world, you will never be alone again.

Two days later, another storm struck. Susan, still exhausted by the first one, and from caring for Barney, greeted the newest storm with exasperation. The ship continued to battle the seas in a southeasterly direction. As Susan clung to her rocking bunk, she almost regretted her decision to come. She wondered why anyone would follow the sea for a living if it meant putting up with feeling as bad as this half the time. She sighed. The sailors probably got so accustomed to the motion they no longer noticed it. She hoped she would get her sea legs soon.

"Why are we going so far east?" Susan asked the captain's wife two days after the second storm while they shared a quiet cup of tea in the small parlor that adjoined the cabin Captain and Mrs. Griffin shared. "I thought we had to go south." The seas were finally calm. When the ship had finally settled down to a steady pace, Susan could only marvel at how much better she felt with the bark again riding on an even keel. Maybe she could say she had her sea legs at last. Barney no longer required constant care, leaving her freer to move about.

"We have to go where the trade winds blow, my dear," said Mrs. Griffin with a gentle smile. "And we have to clear the bulge of South America." Susan conjured up her geography lessons in her mind and saw the eastern edge of the South American continent jutting out into the Atlantic. She smiled as she remembered her childish comment to her tutor that it looked like South America had been pulled away from Africa. The tutor had treated her comment with scorn.

"How in the world could that possibly happen? Everyone knows the continents are fixed and unmoving."

But as she gazed at the small globe on its stand by the tea table, she could only think her first impressions had to be correct, no matter how illogical.

"We will be passing by the Cape Verde Islands, just off the coast of Africa," Mrs. Griffin continued. "We come to within a hundred miles of Africa itself."

"Have you been to Africa?" Susan asked in awe. The Dark Continent held a fascination for her.

"Only the Cape, coming back from the Far East. Africa itself is still mostly uncivilized," she replied. "There is a thriving European settlement at the Cape. All ships rounding the Cape of Good Hope stop there to re-supply."

Susan sipped her tea in silence, feeling young and inexperienced in the presence of such a woman of the world. She thought suddenly of Dr. Alexander. Mrs. Griffin would surely know something about him. She hesitated, then posed the question to her companion.

"He is a well qualified physician," Mrs. Griffin replied with a smile. "We are fortunate to have him with us, especially in view of the serious injury to the boy. He hails from Scotland, and is a graduate of the University of Edinburgh, one of the finest medical schools in the world." She chuckled. "He was appalled to learn so few Americans are vaccinated against the Pox. He says the Pox is almost unknown in England and Scotland now."

Susan had never heard of such a thing. "If the disease can be prevented, why isn't it done in America?"

Mrs. Griffin shrugged. "Many American doctors disagree with the practice of vaccination, even with cow pox, let alone using the exudate from the Pox itself." She laughed and added, "Probably because of Dr. Boylston's experience in Boston's smallpox epidemic of 1721. I understand he was the first to try the method."

Susan had never heard of Dr. Boylston. In fact, she had never heard of the epidemic of 1721. Obviously her tutor had not felt information on the history of Boston critical to her education. He had placed more emphasis on teaching her the names and reigns of the English monarchs. Her curiosity immediately aroused, she asked. "What happened?"

"He vaccinated his son and two slaves. When they survived, he did the same for another two hundred or so colonists. Unfortunately, six of those died."

"But more than two hundred lived!" Susan knew the numbers of people that died when they took the Pox exceeded six out of two hundred. "Surely they could see the advantage of the procedure."

"Apparently not. They rioted and tried to hang him." With a chuckle, she added, "So you can see why other doctors were loathe to experiment."

Susan nodded. She could see very well, wondering vaguely how many lives such stupidity had cost. She shrugged it off and returned her mind to her original subject. "Why did Dr. Alexander leave Scotland?"

"That I cannot tell you, for he is silent on the subject. He came to Boston several years ago, and had a thriving practice there. All he will say now is he has heard so much about California that he is anxious to see it." She laughed. "I fear I contributed to his curiosity, for when he came by to treat one of my maids for a whitlow on her finger, I told him about the lovely climate in California." She took another sip of tea and refilled Susan's cup. "It was a particularly vile day, with sleet dashing against the window pane. One of those times when one could not get warm anyplace except within a few feet of the fire."

She frowned. "He did make one comment though. He said he found society as rigid in Boston as in Edinburgh. A strange comment to make, since he is obviously an educated man, and speaks as one who has had genteel breeding."

Susan made no reply. She could certainly understand his point, having had her own experiences with Boston society.

Mrs. Griffin continued. "But I know nothing more. He has never mentioned his family, and never says anything about himself. He seems to prefer his own company. Howard and I have invited him to dine with us, but he refuses. He says he prefers to take his meals alone in his cabin."

With a soft laugh, she glanced at Susan. Her eyes twinkled. "And he does have the most remarkable blue eyes!"

Chapter 5

BY SUNDAY, FEBRUARY 6, the weather had turned pleasant and warm and the seas moderated. Susan found it hard to believe they were on the same ocean that had tossed her about so violently such a short time before. Feeling the fresh air and sunshine would be good for Barney, Susan asked two crewmen to carry the boy up on deck. She found herself growing more and more fond of the plucky lad.

As soon as she overcame his reticence at talking to her, finally convincing him she really did care what became of him, he told her all he knew of himself. He thought he was about fourteen, although he could not be sure. He said his parents came from Ireland, but he did not know their names or when they migrated.

"Master, he was a mean 'un, I'll tell you, Miss Susan. Used to whup me all the time." Susan knew he had been beaten, for she had seen the scars on his back when she bathed him. "His wife, she was real nice. Used to sneak me food when he wa'n't lookin'. He'd whup her, too, especially when he got drunk. That bothered me more than him a-hittin' on me." He scowled. "Man hadn't oughta hit a woman."

"And your arm?" Susan hesitated to ask, but had to know how the arm had been injured.

"I stepped between him and her one time and he twisted my arm 'til it broke. Wouldn't call me no doctor. They's laws against mis-treating apprentices, an' he knew it, so's he wouldn't have me a doctor."

"And how did you get away from him?"

The boy's eyes fell, but not before she saw the flash of fear. He did not reply, nor did he need to. She knew. "You were protecting her, weren't you?"

He said nothing, but when he looked up, she read the answer in his eyes.

She squeezed his hand. "Don't worry. It will be our secret."

When Susan got her young patient settled, a nondescript mutt belonging to one of the passengers ambled up and laid his chin on Barney's chest, gazing at him with soulful brown eyes. Barney's hand came up to ruffle the dog's ears. The dog licked the boy's chin, eliciting the first laugh Susan had ever heard from him. She feared he had not had much reason to laugh in his harsh life.

The dog's owner watched as well, as the love between the boy and the dog became apparent. "Knows the boy needs company, Jake does," the man said. "Boy should have a dog. Ever had a dog before, lad?"

"No, Sir." Barney's face glowed as the dog continued to gaze at him with adoration. The boy's eyes shone as he stroked the silken head.

Jake became Barney's constant companion, whenever he and Susan were on deck. Susan would read to Barney while Jake snuggled beside him or rested his chin on the boy's chest. The two became inseparable.

Dr. Alexander assured her Barney's leg was healing well. "You're a good nurse. Very few of you high society ladies have any practical skills," he said, his scorn for such women clear.

"Is that what you think I am? A high society lady?" She almost laughed at the irony. He thought she, who had been shunned by all of Boston's society except for dear, loyal Abby, was a high society lady.

Their eyes met and her heart lurched again. Angry with

herself for her reaction to his presence, she lashed out at him. "And what if I am? What do you care?"

"I don't, my dear. I don't care a whit."

He turned on his heel and left her staring after him, open-mouthed.

She saw little of Dr. Alexander after that. Barney had recovered sufficiently to move back into the crew quarters. Susan still read to him when he lay up on deck, with the faithful Jake by his side.

The days passed, lazy days of warmer and warmer weather. One evening, a shower of rain left them with a brilliant rainbow. The colors seemed so much more radiant than on land.

On Saturday, February 12, they crossed the Tropic of Cancer. They would soon be far enough east to get the Northeast trade winds, a few hundred miles off the coast of Africa. The weather felt like May instead of February. Susan spent more and more time on deck, preferring that to the stuffy cabin with the suffocating smoke from the oil lamp. Many of the passengers slept on deck in the fresh air. Some took salt water showers behind a make-shift screen in the bow. Susan declined the offer of a grinning crewman to pour water for her, and continued to bathe in her cabin from the tiny basin of fresh water allowed her each day.

Six days after they crossed the Tropic of Cancer, they encountered the Trades and the wind shifted to the northeast. The helmsman changed their heading to southwest. Susan's excitement rose as Captain Griffin set the ship's course for Brazil. She found herself longing to see land again.

The following morning, she woke to the sound of sails flapping idly against the mast, and arrived on deck to find herself surrounded by calm seas, with virtually no wind at all. A slight breeze helped cool her face a little, but the mighty ship lay dead in the water.

Shouts of excitement drew her to the rail. A school of porpoise frolicked about the ship. Fascinated, she watched the graceful creatures circle around and around. Several men tried to harpoon one, but, to Susan's relief, their efforts proved futile.

She returned to Barney's side and confessed, a little sheepishly, that she was glad the men had been unsuccessful.

His hand on the head of the faithful Jake, the boy said, "I'm glad they couldn't cotch one, too, Miss Susan. I used to watch the porpoises play in the harbor. Master, now, him bein' a real strict church man, never worked on Sunday. Said it were sinful to work on the Sabbath. So I sometimes got a few hours to myself. Onct in a while, when the master be a-sleepin' off a drunk, the missus could get away and come with me. She loved to watch the porpoises, too."

Susan wondered how a 'real strict church man' could beat both his wife and his apprentice and spend the Sabbath sleeping off a drunk. She shrugged, doubting she would ever understand such a person. A pang of pity surged through her for the man's wife, a gentle soul, judging from her treatment of Barney, trapped in a marriage to such a man. With a smile, she stroked Jake's floppy ears and opened the book. She had chosen her well-read copy of *Two Years Before the Mast,* for they both wanted to learn as much as possible about the land to which they journeyed. "Where were we?"

"We just got to where he was a-rollin' the hides down offen the cliffs onto the beach. I can't imagine cliffs like that. Sure don't have nothin' like that in Boston!" Barney's eyes shone. "I sure wish I could'a learned to read like you, Miss Susan."

Susan laughed at his enthusiasm. "I guess I will just have to teach you, Barney." She located the page and began.

Susan quickly tired of the gentle side-to-side motion of the becalmed vessel. Two days later, to her relief, the wind picked up again and the ship once more moved forward at a steady pace. In the middle of the afternoon, one of the seamen caught a large shark. As the men brought the shark on board, Jake got so excited he began to run around in circles, barking. Barney and Susan laughed at his antics until one of the men shouted "Look out! He's rabid!"

Others took up the cry. "Mad dog! Mad dog! Throw him overboard or we'll all die!" Panicky hands grabbed the unfortunate dog and, before saner heads could prevail, they hurled poor Jake far over the taffrail.

"No!" Susan cried. She ran after the men, but she arrived too late. "Jake, Jake," she cried as she watched the doomed dog paddling valiantly behind the ship, growing ever smaller as the distance between them widened. "You fools!" she shouted. "He wasn't mad. He just got excited at seeing the shark is all. Poor Jake. And he meant so much to Barney."

"Seen a mad dog take a whole ship onct, leave a ghost ship," one man muttered. The others looked a little abashed.

Dr. Alexander joined the group. Some of the men tried to defend their actions. He merely looked at them with scorn. "Ignorant fools." He took the weeping Susan's arm and led her away.

She glanced at his grim face. "Thank you," she said softly, surprised to find him so sympathetic. She took a deep breath and wiped her eyes. "I dread telling Barney."

But when she returned to the boy's side, she saw in his face that he knew what had happened. With a sigh that broke Susan's heart, he said, "Guess I wa'n't never meant to love nuthin', Miss Susan."

On Saturday, February 26, they crossed the Equator. Susan's sex spared her the indignities usually heaped upon those making the fabled crossing for the first time. She saw several men sloshed with grease and tar, and one man's beard shaved off with a rusty iron hoop. Some paid their tormentors a bottle of wine or brandy and thus escaped further abuse.

Susan retreated to the haven of her cabin, leaving Barney on deck to watch the tomfoolery. The boy never mentioned Jake again, and he put on a brave front, but she knew he still deeply felt the loss of the companionship the dog had given him.

Dr. Alexander pronounced Barney's leg healing well, although he still could not bear any weight on it. He instructed Susan how to move the leg several times a day.

"Exercise is good," he said. "Rebuilds the strength in the leg and keeps the joints from stiffening."

The days continued hot. Below decks became unbearable, so even Mrs. Griffin spent most of her days on deck. A crewman arranged a special area on the poop deck for her, with a small sail rigged to provide protection from the blistering tropical sun. Susan avoided the sun whenever possible, for her fair skin burned so easily. Barney's nose peeled constantly, for he, too, paid the price of a skin which refused to turn brown.

Susan often joined Mrs. Griffin on the poop deck, and the two watched the action on the deck from their elevated post. Several times they saw other ships, but only once did one come close enough to hail. Since the ship drifted slowly in a calm, glassy sea, the captain allowed some passengers to row over for a visit. Once a passing ship flew a flag Susan did not recognize, and she asked about it.

"Why, that's a Russian flag," Mrs. Griffin told her. "They roam the northern Pacific coast looking for furs, especially the sea otter. Otter furs are greatly prized in Russia."

Susan stared, excited to see a ship from a country on the other side of the world. "I've never seen a Russian flag before," she said. "Not even in Boston Harbor."

"They seldom come by the eastern seaboard. After they spend a season hunting, the ships return around the Horn, cross the Atlantic, and go through the English Channel into the North Sea and on to the Baltic. Most of the ships we pass are on their return trip to St. Petersburg, which is a port Peter the Great built for Russia on the gulf of Finland off the Baltic Sea." She chuckled softly. "I understand that is a whole story in itself."

On Sunday, March 13, Susan and the captain's wife again sat at their small table on the poop deck after church services were over. About two in the afternoon, the cry of "Land ho!" rang from the lookout high up in the mast.

Susan jumped to her feet. "Where? Where? Have we reached Brazil?"

Mrs. Griffin laughed. "Relax, my dear. Yes, it is Brazil, but we won't see it for another couple of hours. Unless, of course," she glanced upward, "you wish to climb the mast."

Susan looked up at the top of the mast, swaying from side to side, and shuddered. "I can wait," she decided.

By four o'clock, everyone could see the line of peaks along the horizon. By dark, they were within ten or fifteen miles. Susan retired to her cabin, thrilled to think she could be on land again as soon as the following day.

The next morning, Mrs. Griffin joined Susan at the rail. "The city yonder is Saint Catherine," she told the excited girl, who stood in awe at the sight of the first foreign port she had ever seen. "The natives call it Santa Catarina. A string of islands guards the mainland, making a perfect natural harbor. The channel ranges from two to five miles wide. Two of the islands have the ruins of old forts on them, from when the Spanish threatened to take the land from the Portuguese." She motioned to the smaller of the two islands bearing a fort. Susan could just make out the ruins. "We usually stay there."

As the *Even Tide* eased towards her anchorage, a small boat with a Brazilian officer rowed out and the nattily dressed gentleman climbed aboard. About five in the afternoon, Susan heard the chain rattle in the hawse pipe as the *Even Tide* dropped anchor.

When the ship rode securely at anchor, Captain Griffin approached Susan and his wife at the rail. "Fifty-four days out of Boston, my dear." He smiled at Mrs. Griffin and squeezed her hand, his face lighting up as he reported, "Logged 7,587 miles. Not a bad passage."

"Can we go ashore?" Susan asked eagerly, fascinated by the strange houses and magnificent foliage. She also thought it would be a relief to stand on land again.

"We are in quarantine for six days. If no one shows any sign of any sort of disease by then, we will be free to go ashore. You are not to go unaccompanied. In these countries, ladies are never allowed to go anywhere alone. I'm afraid I must ask you to conform to that restriction. I must also advise caution. There have been reports of Americans being killed here, although we are more popular than the British. I suspect, however, that the incidents resulted from some kind of confrontation between sailors and natives, so I doubt you will be in any danger."

Mrs. Griffin's eyes twinkled. "Perhaps the good doctor will accompany you."

Susan doubted that. She had seen him only briefly since Barney no longer required their mutual care, and on those few occasions he had been so gruff it bordered on rudeness. Not wanting to dash Mrs. Griffin's romantic hopes, she just murmured, "We'll see."

Six days. Well, she had waited fifty-four. She could wait another six. She looked back at the beautiful city so close, yet so far beyond her reach.

Chapter 6

THE FOLLOWING MORNING, shouts roused Susan from a sound sleep. She shook her head to clear it. Remembering they had anchored the previous day, she scrambled into her clothes and hurried up on deck to see the cause of the excitement. She arrived in time to watch several crewmen pay a line over the starboard rail.

"What's happening?" she asked the nearest man.

He grinned, a wide smile showing gaps from a number of missing teeth. "Natives, Miss McGuire," he said. "Come to swap stuff. They bring chickens an' eggs an' fresh fruit. Mighty tasty, after two months of ship fare."

"How can they do that? I thought we weren't allowed to have any contact with the natives until the six days of our quarantine have passed."

"We can't let a little thing like a law to protect the health of the citizens interfere with business, can we?" Dr. Alexander spoke from behind her.

The seaman, wiser in the ways of the world than Susan, chuckled. "He's right. Natives pay off the port officer, and trade away to their heart's content."

Susan shook her head. "Then what's the point of keeping us here for six days?" she muttered, to no one in particular. Her mouth watered at the sight of baskets with lemons, limes, and bananas coming over the side. The chickens, hauled up by a cord around their legs, squawked in protest. Another basket carried a number of small, brown eggs.

"Fresh eggs for breakfast!" she marveled. Her concerns about violating quarantine vanished. "I'd almost forgotten how good they taste."

The six days passed slowly, lazy days spent reading to Barney or chatting with Mrs. Griffin on the poop deck.

In spite of her eagerness to reach California, Susan enjoyed the respite. It felt good to be able to relax, not constantly battling the motion of the ship. She watched the colors of the sky change from purple to light blue to bronze as the heat of the day progressed, then revert slowly again to purple as the sun disappeared behind the lofty mountains. She had never seen mountains so majestic, with peaks that rose so high the tops frequently disappeared behind the clouds. Quaint one-story homes marched up the sides of the hills, clinging to sides so steep Susan wondered why they did not slide down.

She posed that question to Mrs. Griffin. With a little laugh, her companion replied, "Sometimes they do, my dear, in a very heavy rain. But the owners are undeterred. They just dig out and build again."

When finally released from quarantine, the ship moved to the mainland, and anchored in front of a small, shabby town several miles down the coast, so far from St. Catherine's Susan could barely make out the buildings.

Disappointed, Susan turned to First Officer Thomas, who, she had noticed, she frequently found beside her. "Why are we staying so far from the city? Why don't we go closer?"

"Have to anchor here, in front of Santa Cruz," responded Mr. Thomas. "Only place the water is deep enough. Way too shallow in front of St. Catherine's. If you want to see the city, one of the locals will be happy to drive you. Many of them make their living transporting passengers and personnel back and forth." He chuckled. "I suspect they are not anxious to make any improvements in the anchorage that would cut into their income."

"The homes in St. Catherine's look so beautiful. The ones here, well . . ."

He nodded in assent. "Yes. That's because many retired merchants have built their homes around the suburbs of the city. Only natives live this far down the coast."

Mrs. Griffin approached, accompanied by Dr. Alexander. His lugubrious expression made his slender face seem even longer. Susan, with some effort, repressed a wild, almost irresistible urge to giggle. Mrs. Griffin's eyes sparkled.

Uh-oh, Susan thought. She's match-making again. She's determined to develop a romance between us. Mrs. Griffin's first words proved Susan's instincts had not misled her.

"My dear," she began, "I told Dr. Alexander how eager you were to see the countryside while we are here and he has agreed to accompany you on a visit to St. Catherine's."

Susan looked into the cold blue eyes, wishing she could read the man behind them. "Really?" she managed to choke out.

"I will be pleased to escort you, Miss McGuire," he said. "I, too, would like to see the city. We will go ashore in the morning. Please arrange for a basket of food to take with us, for we shall be gone all day." He turned on his heel and walked away.

Rage swelled within her. Just like that, she thought. We go when he wants to go, and I make sure he will be fed. She suppressed her first impulse, to refuse to accompany him, but knew if she did, she would be stuck here on the ship and never get ashore. She bit back the sharp retort on her lips and forced them into a bright smile. "Thank you, Mrs. Griffin. I shall enjoy a little shore excursion. Now, if you'll excuse me, I think I had better consult with the cook!"

Susan rose the next morning to the sound of the slight creaking in the rigging and the screams of seagulls. She blinked away a fading dream and hurried to dress. If I'm not there when he's ready to go, she grumbled under her breath, he'll probably leave without me. She wished she could take Barney, for she knew he would enjoy the excursion, but knew he could not come with his injured leg. Dr. Alexander still kept the leg splinted, but allowed the boy to hobble about with the aid of a cane. The First Mate had put him to doing a lot of little minor chores, like unraveling small pieces of rope to make oakum, which they used for caulking.

She chuckled as she fastened her second shoe. She had helped Barney one day, working with the fragments of rope until it took the skin off of her fingers. When she commented on how the crew seemed to be working all the time, Mrs. Griffin had laughed and quoted what she called the 'Philadelphia Catachism' to her.

> "Six days shalt thou labor
> And do all thou art able,
> And on the seventh
> holystone the decks and scrape the cable."

Susan thanked her lucky stars she did not have to be a sailor. The quote seemed appropriate, for they were always busy, scrubbing, repairing sails, replacing caulking that always managed to work its way out, braiding bits of rope around grommets to form cringles . . . .

Heavens, she thought, listen to me! I'm starting to speak their language. How was any land-lubber to know, for example, that a scuttled-butt was a cask for drinking water? Or that earings were small ropes used to attach those cringles to a yard? Maybe they wanted a separate language so it sounded mysterious, and no one would know what they were talking about.

Susan pulled the brush quickly through her long red tresses and bound them into a snood to keep the recalcitrant curls under control. A quick glance in the mirror revealed the sparkle in her eyes. He doesn't want to take me, she thought, so let's be as demure and polite as possible. Make him feel guilty for being so boorish about agreeing to be my escort. Picking up her parasol and reticule, she left the cabin.

When she reached the deck, the sun had just cleared the row of islands on the seaward side of the channel. She cast an uneasy glance at the clouds massing on the tops of the mountains to the west.

"Is it going to rain?" she asked the first seaman she saw.

He squinted at the clouds. "Mebbe. Mebbe not," he said with a characteristic shrug.

"Well, it's nice to know for sure," she responded, her sarcasm lost on the sailor. She looked around. Dr. Alexander had not yet put in an appearance. Good. She had time for some breakfast. She also hoped the cook had prepared the basket as she asked.

The cook, as it turned out, had not only prepared a basket, he planned to accompany them. "Got to see Mr. Cathcart," he explained. "Got to order some supplies from him for the next leg of the voyage. Usually get eggs 'n' oranges 'n' bananas. Last time, even got a hog to butcher. Got a fine plantation, does Mr. Cathcart."

Susan, her curiosity easily aroused, asked, "Who is he?"

"American as come down here twenty-odd years ago. Seems when he got home from a voyage, found his wife had up and run off with another man. So he come down here and fell in love with the Governor's daughter and married her." The cook grinned. "Sold the ship and cargo and set himself up in a right fine plantation. Even got him some Negro slaves. There are some as say the ship and cargo wa'n't his to sell, but he done it anyway. Guess as long as he stays down here, ain't no way the owners can get back at him."

* * *

The sailors assigned to take them ashore brought the longboat to the port side and secured the lines. Susan watched with horror as the cook scrambled down the rope ladder slung over the side. Her heart quailed as she watched the swaying grid. Would she be expected to climb down that rickety contraption as well?

Dr. Alexander took her reticule and parasol and handed them, along with the basket the cook had prepared, to a seaman who lowered the articles into the boat. Then the doctor turned to Susan. "I will descend first. Follow me closely, so if you fall I can catch you."

She glanced around to notice all of the men watching her. Determined not to show fear to any of them, she set her jaw and swung herself over the side. She clung to the rope with all her strength, and eased one foot at a time down to the next rung. So intently did she concentrate on keeping her footing she did not realize she had reached the boat until she felt Dr. Alexander's hands on her waist.

"You can let go now," he said, impatience in his voice. "Let me bring you aboard."

Susan opened her eyes and realized she had reached the safety of the boat. She clung to him for a moment, then met his eyes. Her heart gave that familiar unwelcome lurch as she found herself wanting to kiss those lips that were so close to hers. Angry with herself for her reaction, she flushed and pushed away from him. "Thank you," she murmured. "I'm sure I can manage now." Afraid to move in the rocking boat, she sat in the first seat she reached.

"You have to come aft, Miss," the seaman said. "Rower's got to sit there."

"Of course." She carefully edged her way towards the stern of the rocking boat, accepting a helping hand from the cook. There was more to this boating business than she realized.

* * *

They disembarked at the little pier and Susan watched with interest as the cook haggled with a young man standing by a small cart. She had never seen the animal in the traces before. He looked like a small mule. This must be one of the burros they talk about, she thought.

"What an adorable creature," she exclaimed, reaching out a hand to pet the patient animal.

"Careful!" Dr. Alexander grabbed her hand and snatched it back. "They are famous biters." He looked at her, Susan thought, as he would a precocious child for whom he had been given reluctant guardianship. She glared at him and climbed onto the seat. The driver and Dr. Alexander squeezed Susan tightly between them on the narrow bench. Susan hated herself for how conscious she was of the doctor's thigh pressed against her. The cook climbed into the back, and the little burro started down the narrow, rutted track, pulling the cart with apparent ease.

Susan tried to get her mind off of the proximity of the doctor by looking at the scenery. What a change from Boston, she thought. The lush countryside grew fruit trees in abundance, and she saw fields of what the cook said were cotton, coffee, and corn. She even saw vineyards. Some of the one-story houses were made of stone, but most had been constructed with the sun-dried adobe bricks. All had been plastered and white-washed on the outside, giving the whole countryside a clean, sparkling look. Roofs of the smaller dwellings were straw. As they approached the city, she began to see larger houses, and some of these boasted tile roofs.

Two things struck her as strange, and she asked the cook, "Why is there no glass in the windows? And why don't any of the houses have chimneys?"

"Don't need glass," he replied. "Open windows let the breeze through, and it never gets cold enough to want to shut the house up. Same for fires. Never have fires except for cooking, and do most of that outside. Only cook inside when it's raining. They just let the smoke find its way up through the roof. Them straw roofs got plenty of spaces for smoke."

"Fascinating." Intrigued by the passing sights, when they reached the city, Susan was astonished to find two hours had passed. She did not even notice the jolting of the little cart as the wooden wheels bounced over the ruts.

At the order of the cook, the driver pulled the cart to a halt in front of the store of Mr. Cathcart. A rapid-fire conversation in Portuguese ensued, then the cook returned to Susan and Dr. Alexander.

"Told the driver to take you around, show you the sights, then bring you back here in an hour. Should have my business taken care of by then, and we'll be ready to go back to the ship."

"So soon?" Susan, unable to hide the disappointment in her voice, suppressed a sigh. I shouldn't complain, she thought. At least I've been able to see this much. If I'd stayed on the ship, like Mrs. Griffin says she always does in these foreign ports, I'd never have seen any of this.

An hour later, when their escort returned them to the square, they found the cook in earnest conversation with a tall, portly gentleman who sported a full beard just beginning to show touches of gray.

The cook hastened to meet them. "Dr. Alexander," he began, a little hesitantly, "I wanta introduce Mr. Cathcart. I told him you was a doc, and seems he's got one of his slaves as is in a bad way. Wants to know if you could come out to his plantation and have a look." The cook glanced over at Susan. "I told him you was escortin' Miss McGuire, and I didn't know if you'd be willin' to go . . . "

"I am a doctor." He turned to Susan. "Miss McGuire, it seems you are going to get to stay ashore a little longer after all."

Chapter 7

"WE'LL TAKE MY BROUGHAM," Cathcart said. "My plantation is only about an hour out of town. Wife and I'll be happy to have you as our guests tonight. Don't get many visitors from the States. Tomorrow morning I'll return you to your ship."

"I'll tell the Cap'n," the cook promised as he climbed onto his seat. Mr. Cathcart's helpers finished loading the little vehicle with crates of oranges, limes, lemons, bananas, and some items Susan could not identify. They stacked the crates so high Susan feared the cart would overturn. She felt a pang of sympathy for the burro, wondering how he could pull such a heavy burden, but the little animal did not seem to notice.

The cook waved to Susan as he started his return voyage. "See you tomorra, Miss McGuire, Doc." The two pigs he had attached to the ends of lines behind the cart grunted as they trudged along.

Dr. Alexander assisted Susan into Mr. Cathcart's brougham. She sank back against the cushion. What a change from the board planks of the cart! The good gentleman has indeed done well for himself, she thought, with a little chuckle, remembering how the cook said he got his start.

Mr. Cathcart pointed out all the sights along the way, and extolled the benefits of living in such a salubrious climate. "Not much sickness, long as we can keep the ships from bringin' in the Pox or the Cholera. Alluz a problem here convincin' folks they should wait to trade until the quarantine's up. Might just as well shout at a hurricane. Keep tryin' to tell 'em it's for their own good, but all they can see is the money they get off the folks on the ships." He sighed. "I know that ain't yer problem, Doc. Nuthin' you can do about that. But this Nigra woman o' mine, she's been ailin' for several months. Don't seem to get better, no matter what we try. Sure appreciate you comin' to see her. She and her husband been with me for years."

They left the buildings of the city behind, and passed by fields which Mr. Cathcart said were cotton, and part of his plantation. Thick bushes that sagged under a heavy load of coffee beans marched up the side of the slope.

"Grow mighty fine coffee," he bragged. "Sell it all over, especially to the States. Our coffee's famous all over the world. Got ships comin' in here just to buy my coffee." He waved his arm to the right. "The trees there, now, them's guava apples. Bet you've never ate one, Miss. They're right tasty. Got fig trees, too. Other side of the house I grow sugar cane. These folk around here, they're real neighborly, but awful lazy. Never try to grow any more than they need for themselves. Grow a little extra to sell in town to buy a few things, is all." He chuckled. "You see what can be done with a little Yankee enterprise. Well, here we are!"

He pulled the horse to a halt in front of a large, one-story building with a tile roof. A chimney rose from the east side.

"A chimney!" Susan exclaimed. "It's the first one I've seen."

Cathcart nodded. "I think it's the only one. I'm from Boston. House just didn't seem complete without a fireplace. But I have to admit there's seldom a fire in it."

A young native boy ran to greet them and led the horse and brougham away as soon as Dr. Alexander had helped Susan to alight. She looked about eagerly as they entered the house. The coolness of the interior amazed her, and she commented on it.

"Walls're real thick," their host pointed out. "Keeps the cool in."

"And why is there so little furniture?"

"Hardwoods don't grow here. Wood comes from the States by boat." He chuckled. "And termites eat it almost as fast as we can bring it in." He ushered them into a small side room where an old Negro woman sat, her eyes closed, her head lolling back against a stack of pillows. She had an ageless, leathery skin, and grizzled hair. Her labored breathing sounded loud in the tiny room.

"Shouldn't she be in bed?" Susan asked.

"Cain't lie down. Cain't ketch her breath if she does." The old Negro man beside her patted her shoulder. "Momma, kin you hear me? Mr. Cathcart, he done fetched a doc offen one o' the ships fer ye."

The old woman opened lusterless eyes and attempted a smile. "I . . . thank ye . . . fer comin'," she managed to gasp out.

"Don't try to talk," the doctor ordered. He pulled out his big watch and counted her pulse. With a frown, he knelt by her swollen feet and pressed his thumb into the flesh just above her ankle. The indentation formed a white pit which remained after he removed the thumb. He put his ear to her chest and listened to her heart.

"Dropsy," he announced. "Her heart rate is too fast. She is not cleansing her blood as she should."

"Does she need to be bled again, Doc?" Mr. Cathcart asked. An anxious frown creased his brow. He really does care about her, Susan thought. "A doctor on another ship bled her once, three, four months back," he continued, "but she didn't seem to get no better."

"Bleeding is a barbaric practice still far too common, I'm afraid," Dr. Alexander scowled. "No, what she needs is medication to slow her heart rate. Are you familiar with foxglove?"

"There's an old woman in town as sells all kinda herbs. She might have some."

"I must go and see. May I have the use of your brougham, with a driver to show me the way?"

"I'll take you myself. My dear," he said to the attractive young woman who entered the room, "allow me to present the good Doctor Alexander and his companion, Miss Susan McGuire." He smiled. "My wife," he said. "Her English is very limited, but she does understand a little." He spoke rapidly in Portuguese for a few moments, then turned to Susan. "She will be delighted to entertain you until the doctor and I return."

Susan refused to let Dr. Alexander see her disappointment at being left behind. She just nodded in agreement.

When they returned, the sun hung near the tops of the mountains to the west. Dr. Alexander held up a small bag in triumph. "She had it. I can't remember what name they use for it here, but it's foxglove, all right." He extracted a small leaf. "Now, the trick is to find the right dosage. You," he spoke to the old man, "fetch me a teacup of boiling water."

The old Negro hastened to obey. When he returned, a steaming cup in his hand, the doctor crumbled the small leaf into the water and stirred.

"Ain't that poison, Doc?" The man's eyes watched the procedure with anxiety.

"It can be. The secret is not to give too much. This will slow her heart and allow it to work more efficiently." He handed the cup to the woman, but she could not hold it in her shaking hand, so he passed it to the old man. "Have her sip this until it is gone." He smiled faintly as the old man continued to hesitate. "Don't worry. The effect is cumulative. You can't poison her with the first dose."

"Now," he turned to Susan, "I believe our host mentioned something about supper. Although the picnic lunch the cook prepared was quite tasty, I, for one, am ready for a hot meal. We can check on our patient again after we have dined."

Susan could not recall dining so elegantly in some time. She had to laugh at the irony. Here they sat, in the middle of a wilderness, but they ate a delicious, well-cooked meal served on fine china, with crystal goblets for an excellent wine, a wine which their host bragged came from his own vineyards.

Sated with ham, honeyed yams, fried plantains, light biscuits, and fresh fruit, some of it unfamiliar, she sighed with pleasure at the coffee served in fine china cups.

"I can't tell you enough how delightful this meal was," she exclaimed. "Please," she told Mr. Cathcart. "Tell your wife how much I have enjoyed it. And this coffee is wonderful as well."

He grinned. "We do like our little pleasures. Not a lot of social life, so we take advantage of our opportunities."

Dr. Alexander rose. "Now," he said, "I think it is time to check on our patient. Mr. Cathcart, Miss McGuire, if you please."

Susan followed the two men obediently as they returned to the old woman's room. Susan could detect no change in the woman's appearance, but Dr. Alexander, counting the woman's pulse as he watched the second hand sweep around the face of his large pocket watch, nodded with satisfaction.

"Slower and stronger," he reported. "She should feel much better by morning." He motioned to the old man hovering close by. "Come. You must learn to check her heart rate." Susan admired the patience with which he taught the old man how to find the throbbing pulsation in the old woman's wrist.

The old man's eyes brightened. "I feels it, Doc, I feels it! Now what?"

"Now you must count the pulses. Follow the sweep of the second hand on this watch Mr. Cathcart has been so kind as to provide for your use."

The man's face fell. "But I cain't count. Never learnt numbers."

Dr. Alexander rubbed his chin for a moment, then smiled. "But you can move coffee beans." He rose and returned a few minutes later with a double handful of the beans. A young servant girl followed with a tray, a puzzled look on her face.

"Move coffee beans?" Susan almost laughed at the blank look that crossed the grizzled old man's face.

"Yes, for each beat you feel, move a coffee bean from one side of the tray to another. I have counted out sixty beans." He placed the sixty beans on the tray and demonstrated, moving a bean with each pulsation, then had the old man repeat the action. "Any time you don't move all of the beans across in the time it takes the second hand to make a complete sweep, we must reduce her dosage." He smiled as comprehension dawned in the wrinkled face.

"This is extremely important," he explained to both of them. "Since we have no way to measure the amount of the foxglove exactly, we must go by her heart rate. I will write out a formula for you to follow. Mr. Cathcart can help you with it. And someone must stay with her all night. Should her condition worsen, please waken me."

The remainder of the evening passed pleasantly. Mr. Cathcart's young wife played several selections on the harpsichord, and Susan, who loved to sing, sang along. To her great surprise, Dr. Alexander joined her, in a mellifluous baritone which contrasted nicely with her soprano. When she retired for the night, Susan slept soundly on the soft, goosedown bed. The strange sensation of motion puzzled her, for she knew the ground was firm beneath her, yet she felt herself rocking like she still slept in her small bunk on the ship. In the morning, she awoke to a delectable aroma and opened her eyes to see a young girl delivering a cup of coffee on a tray.

She sat up with a smile. Coffee in bed! What a treat! "Why, thank you," she exclaimed, unable to remember the girl's name, and any smattering of Portuguese she had learned vanished from her mind. The girl dropped a small curtsy and fled.

Susan sipped the delicious brew. She thought it the best she had ever tasted. No wonder ships came from all over the world to buy Mr. Cathcart's coffee beans. She drained the last drops from the cup, then hurried to dress. She knew that at any moment, Dr. Alexander would want to return to the ship, and, she thought with some irritation, he would expect her to be ready. Angry with herself for hurrying, she tied her petticoat so hard she pulled off the string. She forced herself to be calm as she struggled with makeshift repairs. He could just wait.

The girl returned with a plate of sliced fruits and saw Susan struggling with the recalcitrant string. Putting the plate down on the small table by the bed, she produced a needle and thread and, with a shy smile, swiftly repaired the damage. Helping Susan pull her dress over her head, she said, in her broken English, "The doctor, he asking after you."

"Well," Susan said, recovering her courage, "he can just wait." She seated herself on the wall bench and proceeded to devour the delicious fruit in a leisurely fashion. "Please tell him I will be there when I have finished my breakfast."

When she reached the dining room, she found the doctor and Mr. Cathcart in conversation over their coffee. They looked up as she entered the room.

"I trust you slept well, Miss McGuire," her host said politely. "Your patient is much improved."

She looked at Dr. Alexander for confirmation. "Yes," he said, "her heart is now beginning to clear her body of the dropsy. If they can maintain the correct dosage of the foxglove, she should soon feel much better. Come and see her."

The difference struck Susan as soon as she looked at the woman. The misshapen feet and ankles protruding below the ragged hem were still swollen, but she sat up straighter, and her eyes had lost much of the desolate look. Her breathing had improved markedly, and she greeted Susan with a bright smile.

"Mornin', Miss," she paused to take a deep breath. "Still . . . a bit short . . . but breathin' ever so much better." Her work-worn hands fluttered to her chest. "Pore ol' heart, now, she's not . . . a-poundin' near so bad."

"Hush," Dr. Alexander interrupted her gently. He placed his ear next to her chest again and concentrated on her heart sounds.

Susan laughed to herself. He treats his patients with such kind consideration, but won't give the time of day to well people. Especially me, she thought with some irritation. Not that she cared, of course, she told herself. She tried to ignore the pleasure she remembered feeling as they had sung together the previous evening, how well their voices had harmonized. After all, Donald was the man she wanted. She shook her head and returned her attention to the scene before her.

The old man rambled on, saying he could not believe the change. "Doctor Alexander, he's a miracle man, sent straight from God," he declared. "He's saved her life."

"It's up to you now," Dr. Alexander praised him. "Keep track of her heart rate and measure the foxglove like I taught you and she should do very well." He grinned. "And don't let anyone bleed her." He turned to Susan. "Now, Miss McGuire, unless you and I wish to remain here while our baggage continues on to California, I suggest we return to the *Even Tide*."

Chapter 8

AS SOON AS SUSAN and Doctor Alexander were safely on board and the longboat secured, the chain rattled in the hawse pipe as the crew weighed anchor in preparation for departure. Susan checked the date in the small diary she wrote in every day. Sunday, April 3. I have been gone from Boston for just over two months, she thought, and already I have trouble remembering what it looked like. It seems so far away. Another lifetime ago. And we still have another four months of voyage ahead of us. Some of the stories she had heard about rounding the end of the South American continent ran unbidden through her mind. She felt a small stab of fright, then shook her head and chased away the fears.

The next morning, the sound of thunder and lightning aroused her, and rain fell in torrents, great sheets of it sweeping across the deck. Much to her surprise, Susan discovered the rain was warm, not cold like the rains of the North Atlantic. Barney loaned her an oilskin coat and she stood out in it, letting the soft water run over her hands and splash on her face, soaking her hair. She had never dreamed standing in the rain could feel so good. It reminded her of an incident when she, as a child of four or five, had walked through a summer rain with her father. She smiled as she recalled how her mother had scolded them both when they returned home sopping wet.

Dr. Alexander's voice cut through the memory. "Really, Miss McGuire! You'll take a chill standing out here in the damp."

* * *

Three days later, as Susan read in her cabin, Barney hobbled up to her door.

"Miss Susan, Miss Susan, come quick! Come see the whale." He tugged her arm in his eagerness. "One of the crew spotted a finback whale. Biggest whale I ever seen, and he's headed this way. You gotta see 'im."

She hurried on deck in time to see the huge creature rise out of the water almost the full length of its magnificent body and splash down again, sending a plume of water high into the air. The animal dove beneath the water, then rose in a leisurely fashion, spraying a fountain of fine mist from the blowhole in the top of the huge head. She and Barney watched spellbound as the whale continued to rise out of the water and return with an easy grace. She thought of the whalers that hunted these animals, and felt a pang of pity that anyone could kill a creature of such grace and beauty.

"Ain't he sumthin', Miss Susan?" Barney marveled as they followed the whale's trail with their eyes until it passed out of sight. "Ain't he just sumthin'?"

First Officer Thomas stood behind them. As the whale disappeared beyond the horizon, the man clapped his hand on Barney's shoulder. "Lad," he said, with a smile, "you've a watch coming up. You'd best be getting some rest. Got to take care of that leg. Run along, now." His eyes met Susan's as the boy scurried forward towards the crew's quarters. "He's a fine young man," he said, with a sad shake of his head. "Pity his life's been so harsh. Wonder what will become of him when we get to California. That's a rough country for a boy."

Susan had thought a lot about Barney, and she had already determined her course of action. "He'll stay with me," she said. "I'll take care of him."

The officer looked at her with surprise. "But you're just a lass yourself. You'll be needin' a man to take care of you, not a boy."

Susan suppressed her irritation at his condescension. She resisted the impulse to tell him she had taken care of herself quite nicely for the past several years without any help from a man, knowing it useless, since most men thought as he did. She only smiled and said, "Thank you for your concern, Mr. Thomas, but I'm sure we'll manage."

On Saturday, she saw her first albatross, accompanied by what a seaman told her were stormy petrels and cape pigeons.

"Gettin' south, now, Miss McGuire," he advised her. "Won't be long now 'til we be passin' by the Falklands. Couple weeks at most. Lotsa sea birds close to them islands. Weather be gettin' rougher here pretty soon. Lot colder, too."

"What graceful birds they are!" Susan watched in fascination as the albatross soared over the waves, maintaining the same altitude above the water, just inches above the waves, following the contours. She wondered how they kept from being caught by a wave.

The seaman grinned. "In the air, yes, but you should see one of 'em tryin' to land. Fall all over themselves, they do."

Two days later, the first gale from the west struck, and they spent the next week under double-reefed fore and main sails as the winds battered the ship and the seas rose. On Thursday, April 21, they spotted the Falkland Islands in the distance, and Susan discovered the seaman was right about the number of birds. The whole area teemed with life. Literally thousands of feathered creatures surrounded them. When the cook's helper tossed the garbage over the side, the birds squabbled over the scraps with loud screeches. Susan, bundled against the cold under the care of the solicitous Barney, laughed at their antics.

The next day, a severe gale, directly ahead of them from the southwest, struck with a ferocity that forced the ship to lie to under only the close-reefed mainsail. Frequent squalls of rain, hail, and snow blasted the decks and kept them constantly wet. Seas as high as mountains surrounded them.

So this is what it is like to round the Cape, Susan wrote in her diary, huddled in her cabin under the blankets in a vain effort to keep warm. She glanced through her porthole from time to time at the huge swells. Sometimes the waves broke over the ship and she saw only water through the porthole. She prayed for Barney's safety, fearing he might fall on that treacherous deck, covered by a thick layer of ice and snow. If he slipped . . . she forced the thought from her mind.

By Sunday, the storm abated somewhat, and they made some headway towards the Cape. Susan remained huddled in her bunk, forcing herself to eat the food a worried Barney brought to her, although the food threatened to come back up. And she thought she had her sealegs!

"You got to keep up your strength, Miss Susan," the boy said. "We'll be roundin' the Cape in a few days, then it's gonna start gettin' warmer again. Reason it's so cold, it's startin' into the winter season down here. Days're real short. Only about eight hours from dawn to sunset."

"I'll be fine, Barney. Thank you for your concern. I just feel it's better if I stay out of everyone's way, with the weather so bad."

Without a word, he took her slop jar to empty. When he returned, he patted her hand awkwardly. "You just stay warm, Miss Susan. I'll be back after my watch with a cup of hot tea and some supper."

"Bless you, Barney." Susan watched him leave with a little smile. Yes, she thought. The decision to keep him with me was a good one. How anyone could have mistreated such a good-hearted gentle boy appalled her. The man must have been unimaginably cruel to drive Barney to violence. She sometimes wondered what had really happened, but Barney never brought the subject up again and neither did she. She stared at her water pitcher as it rocked back and forth on the little stand and thought, he'll tell me some day. In his own good time.

On Thursday, April 28, they passed the southernmost point of Cape Horn. Susan, bundled up in all the clothing she could wrap around herself, struggled to the deck to see it. To her disappointment, she saw only mounds of slate blue against the horizon.

Barney noted her reaction and grinned. "Don't wanta get too close, Miss Susan. The fellers tell me we can get caught right easy by a gale and get swept onto the rocks. Sure don't want that, we don't."

"We sure don't," Susan agreed, snuggling further into her muffler. The weather was clear and cold. Snow stood in little mounds around the corners of the deck where it had not yet been swept away. The sun lay low in the northern sky, a dim, red ball, even at midday. No wonder it's so cold, she thought. We never get any heat from that distant sun.

She saw Dr. Alexander had come on deck to view the Cape as well. He passed her on his way back to the companionway.

He spoke only briefly. "Try not to take a chill, Miss McGuire." He disappeared below decks.

"I'll try to stay well. I certainly don't want to do anything that would force you to have to see me," she muttered to his retreating back, careful to keep her voice low enough that he would not hear. He was the most arrogant man! Nothing like her Donald. Why did she keep thinking of him, when every time he saw her he brushed her off? Well, she thought, grumbling under her breath, two can play that game.

Three days later, a gale struck them from the west, forcing the ship to again lie to under close reefed fore and main sails. Susan spent May Day huddled under the blankets in her rocking cabin, attended by the faithful Barney. She thought of the daffodils that would be blooming along Commonwealth Avenue, comparing that with the cold, dismal scenes she had seen of the bare, rocky shores of the Cape. "This, too, will pass," she told the little mirror, appalled at her disheveled image. She took a deep breath and mumbled. "I will get through this." She thought of Mrs. Griffin, who, she knew, also huddled in her bunk. Mrs. Griffin had told Susan the only way to endure the cold of the Horn was under blankets.

By Wednesday, May 4, Barney reported improvement. "Wind's startin' to veer more southeast, so we're able to make some headway. Cap'n says by tomorrow we should be able to swing more northeast. We'll be around the Horn, and in only fifteen days." His eyes shone with excitement. "Sure never thought I'd see the Horn, Miss Susan. Funny how life works out sometimes, ain't it?"

Susan tried to catch his enthusiasm. She forced a laugh past the nausea that kept threatening to overcome her. "Barney, tomorrow, as soon as you're off watch, come and get me. I've had enough of this dinky cabin. We'll go up on deck together."

The next morning, true to his word, Barney appeared at her cabin with her breakfast and a set of oilskins. She forced down the food, trying to warm her hands by wrapping them around the tin coffee cup, absorbing the heat. Between the steam from the coffee and the steam from her breath, the tiny mirror fogged up.

"Got a southeasterly wind," he reported with glee.

"Course is nor'west, and got a spankin' good breeze on our quarter. Should be makin' good time."

"Heavens, Barney," she laughed, struggling into the heavy oilskins with his help. "You're beginning to talk just like them. Have you decided a sailor's life is what you want after all?"

His face sobered. "I ain't never goin' back to Boston, Miss Susan."

"That's right. I forgot. Well, neither am I, so we'll just have to figure out a way to make a living in California."

"I'll help you, Miss Susan. I'll do anything you want. I'm real strong, and I learn fast."

The fervor of his reply touched her. Resisting the impulse to hug him, not wanting to embarrass him, she only said, "I'll remember that! Come on, let's get up on deck. I am more than ready for a little fresh air." And I'd pay dearly for a bath, she thought. She had not even changed her clothes in so long she refused to think about it. The idea of undressing and bathing in that frigid cabin was more than she wished to contemplate.

When they reached the deck, the cold wind struck her an icy blow and she turned her face away to protect it from the stinging sleet. Barney led her to a nook where she stood in the lee of some barrels lashed to the mast. Ice and snow covered the decks, and heavy gusts of wind whipped snow squalls in front of them.

She had to breath slowly. The cold air hurt her lungs, but it smelled wonderful. Barney stood supporting her, for the rolling deck made it difficult to stand.

"Been seein' more porpoise," he shouted above the howl of the wind. "And yestiddy I seen another whale. Soon's this wind dies down, you'll be able to see all kinda sea critters."

By the following day, the gale had passed. A steady breeze kept the ship moving at a brisk rate, the sky cleared and the air, although still cold, did not make her lungs ache any more. She stood at the rail and watched the men attempting to catch albatross and cape pigeon with a hook and line. They enjoyed reasonable success, enough that the cook began talking about pigeon pie for supper. One sailor shouted in triumph as he caught an albatross with a wing span of over ten feet.

Mrs. Griffin joined Susan at the rail, admitting relief at being out in the fresh air again. "I believe that albatross has to be one of the largest I have ever seen," she told Susan. "Some of the sea creatures are truly amazing. Have you seen a sea tortoise yet?"

"Sea tortoise?"

"Yes. Some of them reach eight and nine feet in length." Her eyes twinkled. "And make delicious turtle soup. There are some islands we stop at en route to the Sandwich Islands that have huge ones that live on land. We often stop and get one or two for fresh meat. They are so big and so slow they are easy to catch."

After another week, the snow turned to rain. A gale from the southwest moved them along rapidly. "Makin' ten knots," Barney bragged to Susan. "Be in Valp'r'iso in a couple of weeks."

"I'm just glad it's not snowing any longer. I understand it never snows in California, at least not around where we will be, in the Valley of the Sacramento. Imagine a winter with no snow!"

Barney grinned. "I'm ready, Miss Susan."

Chapter 9

THURSDAY, MAY 19: We are passing Santa Maria Island. It's just off the coast of Chile. Some ships stop at a little port here, but we are continuing on. Our next stop will be Valparaiso. I can hardly wait. Thank Heavens the weather is finally getting warmer. I want to soak in the sun until the heat drives all of the cold out of my bones.

Monday, May 23: We still have a cool wind from the south, and Barney tells me we continue to make ten or eleven knots. After all that time hove to with a battering head wind, this is wonderful. We are now traveling within a few miles of the coast, for they tell me it is very deep here, all the way up to within just a few hundred yards of shore. The air is clear, and starting to get warmer at last. I am writing this on deck, as it is finally pleasant enough to do so. Before me rise the Andes mountains, thousands of feet above the sea. I thought the mountains at Saint Catherine's were high, but these are higher. They are covered with snow, and I understand they are so high the snow never melts. What a magnificent country this is. How I wish Mary and Elizabeth could share it with me.

Susan thought of Donald, and raised her eyes from writing in the diary to look toward the mountains, so clear she felt she could almost touch them. Donald must have seen this. Or did he go across the Isthmus at Panama? So many did, as it cut weeks off the journey, and all the miners were anxious to get to the gold fields. Well, she sighed, I will just have to remember what it looks like and describe it when I see him again. She pulled the little picture out and looked into the mischievous hazel eyes. She couldn't help comparing them with the striking blue eyes of Dr. Alexander. Stop that, she commanded herself. You are in love with Donald, and you are going to marry him. As soon as you find him, that is.

And if you can't find him? The little imp inside her mind took up the adversarial position. Be still, she retorted. I will.

But what if he doesn't want you, the imp persisted. What if that is why he never wrote? What if he doesn't really love you after all?

To force herself to stop thinking along those lines, she closed the diary, tucked it in her reticule, and walked to the rail where first officer Thomas stood. Mr. Thomas always greeted her with a bright smile, so she asked him when they would arrive in Valparaiso.

"Wind holds like this, should drop anchor by tomorrow."

"And can we go ashore?"

"Soon's we clear six days of quarantine. Ship last year brought the cholera in, so now all ships have to be quarantined. They are terrified of another cholera epidemic."

She sighed, although she could understand their fears. "Again? Can't Dr. Alexander convince them that we are all healthy?"

The officer grinned. "He could try, but I doubt it would do any good."

At noon on May 24, 1851, the *Even Tide* dropped anchor in front of the city of Valparaiso, sharing the anchorage with at least fifty other vessels.

Susan, watching the operation with Mrs. Griffin, marveled at the skill of the sailors. "How in the world do they keep all these ships from bumping into each other?"

Mrs. Griffin laughed. "They don't, always. Howard dislikes having so many ships this close together. But we need fresh water and fresh produce, so we are forced to stop. The next leg will be a long one, for we go far west, then north. From here, we will see no more land until we are off the coast of California. It will take at least two months or longer."

"Two more months?" Susan tried to hide her dismay. At least, she told herself, the weather should be better. She voiced her thoughts to Mrs. Griffin.

"Oh, yes, the weather will be good. Sometimes too good. There are parts of the Pacific where the wind is barely enough to move the ship."

The Captain joined them, the ship riding securely at anchor. "Another good passage, my dear," he said to his wife with a smile, nodding his greetings to Susan. "6,361 miles from St. Catherine's to Valparaiso in 53 days. We've averaged 120 miles a day, in spite of being hove to for weather a couple of times. Fifteen days to round the Horn! A very good passage indeed."

"Why did we go all the way around?" Susan asked. "I've heard there are a couple of channels that cut a lot of miles off the trip."

"They are also treacherous. Many a ship has foundered in those narrow, rock-infested short cuts. If the weather is clear and the wind stays favorable, it's true time can be saved." He shrugged. "I prefer to put the highest priority on the safety of my ship and her passengers."

Susan laughed merrily. "I'm inclined to agree with you, especially since I'm one of your passengers."

A small boat threw a line to a waiting crewman and Captain Griffin excused himself. "The officials approach. I will see you ladies at dinner."

"Can I go ashore when we have passed quarantine?" Susan asked as he rose to his feet. "I would love to see the town. How many people live here?"

"About 60,000. You can go ashore, but you must have an escort. I had two sailors beaten here on the last trip. It seems a group of Chileans went north to the gold fields and were treated rather badly by the Americans. Feeling against Americans runs high in some quarters, although I doubt they would blame a young lady. But the Spanish attitude towards young women traveling alone is very similar to the Portuguese. Now, if you will excuse me, I believe the gentlemen from the Port Authority are ready to meet with me."

He strode away. Susan sighed at the twinkle in Mrs. Griffin's eye. She's going to ask Dr. Alexander to escort me again, and I will go with him because there is no other way for me to see the city. Curses on men who think any woman alone is automatically a lady of the night. She sat back in her chair and sipped the cup of tea the young steward placed on the table in front of her. She might as well enjoy the respite and admire the magnificent mountains while she had the chance. Soon enough there would be nothing on the endless horizon but water.

On Sunday, the Port Captain lifted the quarantine and many passengers eagerly prepared to go ashore. Dr. Alexander appeared, glum as usual, and offered to escort Susan and Barney. Determined that the boy have the experience of at least one foreign city, Susan had persuaded the deck officer to allow Barney to accompany her.

"You might wish to take Joshua, Miss McGuire," the man added. "Since his home is here in Valparaiso, he speaks the language and knows the city well."

"What a wonderful idea!" Susan's eyes sparkled. She had noticed the brown-skinned, dark-eyed young man with the high cheek bones and wondered where he came from.

So the four of them climbed down into the longboat and were rowed ashore. The city climbed the side of the mountains. Buildings stood upon ridges separated by deep gullies. To reach from one ridge to the next, they walked down zigzagged pathways, crossed the bottom of the gully, then struggled up the pathway on the other side.

"Heavens," Susan panted as Barney gave her a pull up the third gully they crossed. "These women must have the strength of oxen." She marveled as she watched them walk up and down the paths with loads of laundry or wood or fresh fruit piled high on their heads. "Don't they have burros to carry the loads?"

Joshua laughed. "The men use the burros. They expect the women to carry their own loads. Only after a year in your country did I realize men treat women very differently there. Here, the wives of the important men have servants, but the wives of poor men work very hard."

Susan noticed with a start that several of the women were not only carrying heavy loads, but were very visibly pregnant. In Boston, any woman whose condition began to show stayed in her home until after the birth of the child. No proper Boston woman would ever let anyone outside of her immediate family see her in such an obvious state, especially men. Susan did not voice her thoughts to Joshua, but the difference in attitude towards pregnancy impressed her. Actually, when she thought about it, it made more sense. Certainly pregnancy was a perfectly normal part of life. Why it should be considered something to hide really didn't make too much sense. She shrugged and returned her attention to Joshua.

Joshua, or Josue, as he told them he preferred to be called, proved a very able guide. He showed them the church and the main square, which he called the *zocalo.* "Every town with more than a few houses has a *zocalo,* Miss McGuire," he explained. "It is where the men gather to gamble and talk the politics, and the women to gossip. The young men and young women come to stroll past each other and . . . how do you say it? To flirt, yes? To flirt with each other." He smiled. "On Saturday nights, while the strolling musicians play"

"You miss your country, Josue," Susan said. "Why do you not return?"

"My country is very poor. The Captain, he pays well. When we stop here, I visit my family and give them the money I have earned. After you return to the ship, I will go to them and stay until Tuesday morning, when Captain Griffin plans to set sail."

"We're keeping you from your family!" Susan exclaimed. "We could manage . . . "

He held up his hand. "It is my privilege to show you and the good doctor my city. Do not deny me the pleasure." His smile revealed a missing tooth, but lighted up his dark eyes. "And it is good also for the boy, is it not so, young Barney?"

Barney's green eyes sparkled. "Oh, yes, sir. Never seen nuthin' but Boston afore I come on this trip. Never knew there'd be so much to see!"

Even Dr. Alexander had to laugh at Barney's enthusiasm, and they continued their tour. They visited the market, where women sat on the ground on colorful blankets and hawked their wares. She saw mangos, papayas, bananas, and a number of fruits and vegetables she could not identify. One woman sold herbs of every description. Susan thought of Boston's strict laws against shops or any business operating on Sunday. She chuckled. Apparently they had no such laws here to hamper business.

In mid-afternoon, they stopped at a small sidewalk cafe for a cup of coffee. Susan sank into the chair with a sigh of relief. She felt they had been walking for hours. Barney had not complained, but she noticed he had begun to limp, so the leg obviously pained him. As they settled into their seats, Susan looked down the street and saw a sign advertising the Star Hotel. She laughed.

"That's not a very Spanish name," she commented to Josue. "Why do they call it the Star?"

Josue grinned. "The influence of the American and British ships. There is a Golden Lion Hotel as well. The restaurant where I will take you to eat is called the California Chop House. It is the best food in the city."

At the mention of food, Barney's eyes lighted up and his stomach growled. Susan felt some hunger pangs herself. Dr. Alexander smiled. "I do believe we are ready to dine, Josue." He put some coins on the table. "Come, I believe young Barney is not the only one who is hungry."

Susan drained the last of the thick, syrupy coffee, which, to her amazement, had tasted surprisingly good after Josue showed her how to dilute it with the hot milk served in a little pot with the coffee. Setting down her cup, she rose to her feet. "I'm ready."

The Chinese couple who ran the California Chop House greeted them cordially in both English and Spanish. They dined on a clear soup served in a small bowl with no spoon, followed by rice and a variety of vegetables Susan could not identify, and fish served with a delicious, tangy sauce. The tea they drank with the meal was the best Susan had ever tasted.

At first she hesitated, for some of the food looked strange to her, but when she noticed Dr. Alexander watching her, she attacked her plate with vigor, not about to let him think her fearful to try something different. The proprietor, with some amusement, tried unsuccessfully to teach Susan how to use the chop sticks he placed before her, then took pity on her and brought a fork made of bone.

"First time you have tried Chinese cuisine, Miss McGuire?" A smile twitched around Dr. Alexander's lips. "It's actually quite healthy, much more so than many of the foods Americans eat." He shuddered. "And especially better than we get on board a ship, even as well run a ship as the

Even Tide. So enjoy it."

The day passed all too quickly. The sun had passed its mid-point in the afternoon sky when Josue escorted them back to the dock where the longboat waited for them to return, rising and falling with the surge.

"Now," he said, with his charming smile, "I will go to visit my family."

To their surprise, one of the crewmen from the *Even Tide* awaited them with Dr. Alexander's medical bag in his hand, and a man ran up shouting, "Josue, Josue!"

Susan's eyes widened. What had happened?

Chapter 10

A RAPID CONVERSATION IN SPANISH followed. Susan caught the word *medico*, and assumed the word meant "doctor". She smiled in anticipation. Perhaps her adventure had not ended, remembering the stop at St. Catherine's. Perhaps someone here needed medical help also.

Josue did not keep his companions in the dark for long. He turned to face them, his eyes worried. "This man," he said, "is my brother-in-law, Armando. It seems my sister Consuela is having trouble with the *partida.* She cannot *dar la luz,* though she has toiled with the child for many hours. The *curandera* has said she and the *bebito* will die, and that it is God's will." His eyes flashed. "But neither Armando nor I wish to accept God's will so readily. He says he heard an American doctor is here in the *pueblo,* and that perhaps he can save the life of his beloved Consuela." He motioned to the crewman. "Armando requested one of my shipmates bring your bag to save time, Dr. Alexander, if you can be persuaded to come to her aid."

Susan looked at Dr. Alexander. Barney gaped, his eyes shifting rapidly from one to the other.

The doctor took the bag from the seaman. "Of course, we must try. I can promise nothing, for if she has labored for many hours, it is possible she will be too exhausted for me to help her."

"Armando has his cart, *Senor Medico.* Come, we have no time to lose."

"Is it far?" Susan asked.

"Just a short ways outside of the city, in a small village. How fortunate that Armando heard my ship was here in the harbor, and they were expecting me. Come, let us hasten." As he spoke, he hurried them back along the dock to where Armando's crude cart awaited. Barney ran along behind and assisted Susan onto the cart seat, then tumbled into the back. Susan smiled at Barney's determination to accompany them.

"Perhaps Barney and I should walk," Dr. Alexander said, eyeing the tiny burro. "We don't want to overburden the poor creature."

"No, no," Josue hastened to assure them. "He is used to carrying very heavy loads." They had barely gotten settled on the seat when Armando tugged on the beast's halter and the two of them started off at a trot. The little burro pulled the cart along behind him with no visible effort.

They reached a collection of small adobe shanties in a remarkably short period of time, breathless and bruised from the jolting ride, although the sun hung very low in the sky when they arrived. A large number of people of all ages immediately surrounded them. Never before had Susan seen so many children in one place.

"Who do all of these children belong to?" she asked Josue.

He grinned. "Not my sister. This is her first child. No, all of the children are here because they have never had a norteamericano come to their village before. Many have only seen them from a distance, or have never seen them at all. They are curious. We will leave young Barney to amuse them while we attend to my sister."

Susan entered the one room hut, appalled to find the expectant mother lying on a blanket on the dirt floor. In one corner stood a small table and two rickety chairs. A few dishes lined a shelf on the wall, and an open chest in another corner revealed some colorful clothing and a small pile of what appeared to be more blankets.

An argument raged between Armando and Josue and two old women. Another woman, of perhaps forty years of age, stood by, her jaw working with emotion, tears pouring unchecked down her cheeks. Probably Consuela's mother, thought Susan, confused by the squabble, wondering what in the world had caused the disagreement. We're here to help the poor young woman, she thought, although she had not the slightest notion what she could do, and they are quarreling?

Josue and Armando apparently won the argument, for the two women stormed out of the room, shouting what sounded to Susan like epithets as they left. Josue turned to Dr. Alexander and Susan and apologized for the disturbance. "Sorry, Doctor, Miss McGuire. The old women, they say a man cannot attend her, for it is shameful. Armando says he would rather have a living wife, even a shamed one, and wishes for you to try and save her. Also, I do not know your religion, Doctor, but here, the Church says you must save the child, even if you must sacrifice the mother. Armando does not agree. He prefers to have his beautiful Consuela if you must choose between mother and child."

Josue's dark eyes met Dr. Alexander's blue ones. "I agree. *Mi hermana* is very special to me. She is my baby sister. I used to carry her around when she was little. I would like very much for you to save her life, even if it means I must take her and Armando to California to spare Consuela the scorn of the old women and the wrath of the priest."

A low moan from the woman on the blanket spurred Dr. Alexander into action. "We can discuss religious philosophy later. We haven't saved either one of them yet. Right now I need clean water and a towel. I must wash my hands before I can examine her." He rummaged in his bag and dug out a small piece of soap.

The woman Susan took to be Consuela's mother hurried to obey, and returned in a few moments with a gourd full of reasonably clean water and a small, ragged towel. While the doctor washed his hands, he ordered Susan to do the same. She must have looked startled, for he smiled, a movement of his lips that did not reach his eyes. "Sorry, I know you society ladies are taught such things as childbirth do not exist, but you will have to help me."

Susan took a deep breath, ignored the insult, and pushed aside the panic at her lack of knowledge. "You'll have to tell me what to do."

"Hold her legs thusly." He demonstrated. While Susan tried to follow his instructions, she glanced at the girl. Even in her exhausted state she was still beautiful. Sweat poured from her, and fatigue lined her face. Susan smiled into the deep brown eyes and said, "We will help you."

The young woman could not understand the words, but the tone of Susan's voice seemed to reassure her. Hope replaced despair on the girl's face.

"This girl is only a child," Susan said to Dr. Alexander, appalled to realize just how young she appeared. "Can you help her?"

The doctor withdrew his hand from the woman's pelvis. "The infant is in breech position. That's why she is having so much difficulty. If we can turn it, I believe we can save her. She has not lost too much blood, and the mouth of her womb is dilating well."

"So how do we do that?"

"First, we turn her over and elevate her hips. I will try to push the child back into the womb and rotate him into the proper position, with the head presenting. If I can do this, she should be able to deliver without too much difficulty."

They enlisted the help of the puzzled but willing husband, and did as the doctor wished. Susan watched his eyes as he concentrated on his attempt to turn the child inside the woman's body. She was amazed. She had no idea childbirth could be so complicated, realizing how little she knew about the whole process.

"Good," he cried, his eyes lighting up. "The head is now in the neck of the womb. Return her to her back. You," he commanded Josue, "tell her husband to support her body against his knee. I want her head elevated." He shoved a pillow under the young mother's hips to maintain them above the floor. "Miss McGuire, keep your hand on her abdomen. When you feel the contraction start, tell me, for she must push the child out. Ready?"

"Ready." Susan, on her knees beside their patient, felt the wave start across the damp abdomen. "Now."

"Empuje!" the doctor ordered. Armando reinforced the instruction, and the exhausted girl tried to obey.

"Good," Dr. Alexander said. "Relax and wait for the next one." Josue translated. Susan kept her hand in place. "Now," she cried again, as she felt the next contraction start its rolling wave across the girl's abdomen.

Susan began to feel dark despair wash over her when contraction after contraction did not seem to be getting them anywhere, but finally their efforts were rewarded. With a grunt of satisfaction, Dr. Alexander helped the small head pop out. Consuela collapsed back into Armando's arms with a gasp of relief. In another moment, the whole tiny body squirmed in Dr. Alexander's hands. A shrill cry filled the dingy little room.

Susan laughed and cried at the same time. Tears of relief and joy poured unchecked down her cheeks. She had never felt such a surge of triumph before. Dr. Alexander grinned like a school boy as he held the baby aloft for the proud parents to admire. The candles on the table cast his shadow against the wall. "You've a fine son," he announced. "You," he said to Susan, "get that clean cloth from the weeping grandmother so I can wrap the child."

Susan looked about, realizing that, except for the candles, the whole room was dark. Had they been here that long? She looked at the tiny watch pinned to her blouse. It read 9:30. Startled, she realized the whole day had passed and night was upon them. How were they to return to the ship?

Susan left the newborn child nursing at the breast of the proud mother, with the solicitous new father hovering nearby, and emerged from the hut to tell Barney what had happened. Barney looked at her, the question on his lips answered by the joy in her face.

"Well, Miss Susan," he said, "looks like your little adventure is gonna continue a mite longer. Josue says we can't get back down the mountain in the dark, so we gotta spend the night here."

Susan could not suppress a feeling of dismay as she thought of the dirt floor and the blankets. She didn't recall seeing any beds. Oh, well, she told herself with a little chuckle, you probably aren't going to have too much luxury in the gold fields, so you might as well get used to roughing it a bit.

She laughed. "But we saved two lives, Barney." The feeling of elation that had suffused through her at the sound of that tiny cry washed over her again. "We saved two lives," she repeated half under her breath, as though unable to believe it herself.

Smoky candles lighted the crowded room as Consuela's mother served them a simple meal of rice and beans, with slices of fresh papaya. As they ate, seated on folded blankets on the floor, Armando began to string hammocks between posts along the walls. Susan must have looked puzzled, for Josue laughed.

"We sleep in the hammocks, Miss Susan," he explained. "Off of the ground, for the ground frequently has bugs and snakes, which are, unfortunately, deadly."

Susan looked around in apprehension. "They come into the houses?"

"Not often. They come in looking for rats and mice. In a way, they are good, for the rodents eat the people's food, so please, do not be alarmed. It is just a precaution."

"If you say so." Susan still felt some misgivings. She didn't know which she feared the most, the rats and mice or the snakes. The idea of sharing a hammock with either one had no appeal. Well, she told herself, you wanted adventures. Now you've got one. She knew the sailors used hammocks all the time, but found herself wondering how on earth one got in and out of those flimsy contraptions.

Barney must have read her thoughts, for he grinned at her in sympathy. "I'll help you, Miss Susan. Hammock's pretty good sleepin', onct you get the trick."

Susan only shook her head.

When Barney assisted her out of the hammock the next morning, she had to admit she had slept quite well. The fatigue and excitement of the previous day combined to overcome her fears. She had gotten into the hammock with Barney's assistance full of visions of either falling out or awakening to find a venomous snake coiled around her.

"Morning, Miss Susan," the boy grinned. "Everyone's havin' breakfast outside. Armando's ready to take us to the ship. I hev to git back or the first mate'll have my hide."

They made a more leisurely return to the harbor, and Susan thoroughly enjoyed her chance to see the countryside as the little burro pulled them down one side of the series of gullies and up the other. The vision of the happy parents cooing over the child nursing at his mother's breast, with no idea of all the fuss he had caused, kept popping into her mind. She had never known any feeling could give a person such joy. No wonder Dr. Alexander had chosen to go into medicine. To be able to save a life was an incredible sensation.

She found herself again wondering why he kept to himself so much. He surely must have a feeling for mankind, since he chose a profession dedicated to saving lives. What could have happened to make him withdraw into himself so completely? He did enjoy his work. The light that flashed in the intense blue eyes at his success with the old woman and again yesterday with Consuela told her that. She remembered the tender concern he had shown for Barney. Maybe if I break my leg, he'll show the same to me. She shook her head at her foolishness. Forget it, she told herself. You are on your way to find Donald. You have no interest in Dr. Alexander, and why he acts the way he does is none of your affair.

But she need not have worried. Once they returned to the ship, he scarcely noticed her. Beyond a brief, "Thank you for your assistance, Miss McGuire", he did not refer again to their adventure. He disappeared below deck.

Mrs. Griffin, however, bursting with curiosity, demanded a full accounting of Susan's experiences. The captain's wife knew of their mission, since it was she who had gone into Dr. Alexander's cabin and taken his medical bag for the seaman to deliver ashore. She seemed a little appalled at what Susan had been called upon to do, but, in response to Susan's obvious joy at the accomplishment, said, "Perhaps you should consider taking up nursing, Susan." She gave Susan a conspiratorial smile. "Perhaps the good doctor would like a permanent assistant."

Susan groaned inwardly, but only said, "We'll see."

* * *

Late in the afternoon of that same day, to Susan's astonishment, Josue returned to the ship accompanied by Armando, Consuela, and the baby.

"Josue," she gasped, "should Consuela be traveling so soon after the birth of her baby?"

He grinned. "Here, the women often go back to the fields the day after. Consuela only rides the cart."

"She really has to come with us?"

"*Si.* I spoke with Captain Griffin and he say yes, I may bring them. The other women, already they call Consuela the *puta*, a bad woman, for the priest, he tells them only a *puta* would allow a man who is not her husband to touch her." His eyes darkened. "I can not leave her here to be so abused." He handed the infant to Susan and turned to help the seamen lower a sling to bring Consuela aboard.

Susan looked down at the tiny bundle in her arms. He yawned and stretched his little arms above his head and blinked in the bright sunlight. Susan could not understand any culture that would condemn something so precious. She shook her head. She was discovering there were a lot of things in the world she had to learn.

The next morning, Tuesday, May 31, Captain Griffin ordered the anchor weighed, and the ship started its slow progression out of the harbor under a light breeze from the southwest. The sun had not yet cleared the skyline above the city, but the sky glowed pink above the purple of the mountains. Susan rose early. She wanted a last look at the city before their departure. Mrs. Griffin joined her. As they stood side by side at the rail and watched the rising sun, the *Even Tide* cleared the point and began her battle against the swell rolling down from the northwest.

Suddenly, without warning, the wind died completely. The sails hung limply from the yards, and the ocean began moving the ship slowly but inexorably back towards the rocks on the point.

Susan froze in horror as the crew scrambled for the longboats. First Officer Thomas even pressed some of the able-bodied passengers into service in the emergency. Susan watched in fear as Barney scrambled down into one of the boats. She wanted to cry out to him to take care, but refrained, knowing he would be embarrassed beyond endurance if she did so. She bit her lip. You're no better off than he is, she told herself. If the ship goes on the rocks, we'll all be in trouble. She thought of Consuela and the baby. Did we save them just to drown them in the harbor? Would the priest say this was a retribution from God for breaking one of his taboos? She laughed, a little shakily. Probably.

Four boats, with the men rowing with all of their strength, managed to stem the progress towards the rocks, but, in spite of their combined efforts, they were unable to move the ship forward out of danger. Mrs. Griffin joined Susan at the rail. Her eyes showed her fear, but her face remained a fixed calm.

"The men will tire," Susan said to her companion. "Then what?"

"Pray," Mrs. Griffin responded. "Pray the wind returns."

Susan did not find much comfort in Mrs. Griffin's words. She watched the scene before her with growing apprehension. She thought of going below deck to get her small cache of money, but found herself so hypnotized by fear she could not force her limbs to move.

A shout from the starboard side caught her attention, and she saw three more longboats approaching, each with a sailor poised in the bow to throw a line. She almost wept with relief, and heard a long sigh escape the lips of her companion. Susan smiled wryly at Mrs. Griffin. "Were you praying for wind or for more boats?"

"For help, my dear," she laughed. "I'll take it from any quarter."

Men on deck quickly secured the additional lines, and three more boatloads of strong rowers were added to the *Even Tide's* complement. To her relief, Susan felt the ship begin to move forward against the power of the waves, slowly at first, then more rapidly. Ten minutes later, the breeze returned and the sails billowed into great white globes. Susan let out her breath in a long, tremulous sigh, and turned to her companion. "That was close!"

Mrs. Griffin nodded in agreement. "Too close."

The lines to their saviors were thrown back and the three boats rowed off to a chorus of shouts of gratitude from the men of the *Even Tide.* The crew and passengers who had been on the longboats climbed thankfully back aboard. Some collapsed on the deck with exhaustion and relief. The First Officer promised an extra ration of grog to all hands for their valiant efforts. The breeze increased in strength, and soon the ship sliced her way through the waves at a brisk six knots, promising a rapid trip for the last leg to San Francisco.

Chapter 11

THEY COVERED THE 800 miles from Valparaiso to the islands of St. Felix and St. Ambrose by June the fifth, averaging 160 miles a day, but they rejoiced prematurely. Susan woke on June sixth to the feel of the ship slowly rocking from side to side, a very different feeling from when the *Even Tide* cut through the swells. She climbed to the deck to find the vessel barely moving in a calm, glassy sea. Their speed slowed to one or two knots, and for the next week the ship rose and fell on the long, rolling swells that bore down upon them from the northwest.

"Maybe we're not making much speed," she laughed to Mrs. Griffin as they enjoyed a cup of tea on their sanctuary on the poop deck, "but at least the weather is pleasant. And it's so nice not to be bouncing around!"

Mrs. Griffin smiled and nodded in agreement. "I do like to make good speed, but I confess I also enjoy these little interludes." She handed her cup to the young man hovering by her side. "Thank you, Charlie. That was delicious." She turned back to Susan. "There will be a full moon tonight. Perhaps you and the good doctor can take a midnight stroll."

Susan shook her head. "I'm afraid he prefers his own company. I've barely seen him. I don't think he likes me."

Mrs. Griffin smiled. She cast a shrewd glance at her companion. "On the contrary, I suspect he finds you very attractive."

Susan laughed. "He sure has a funny way of showing it." Besides, she thought, although she had no intention of telling Mrs. Griffin or anyone else, I'm in love with Donald.

Why did she have to keep reminding herself? Could she be having some doubts? Surely she could not be falling in love with the reclusive and aloof doctor. She sighed. Of course not.

She looked back at Mrs. Griffin to see her companion's bright eyes looking at her in speculation. Susan forced a laugh. "I don't think he likes women at all, unless they are a patient.

Mrs. Griffin nodded. Her silence said far more than words.

That night, Susan did take a midnight stroll, partially to escape the stuffy heat in her cabin, but chose Barney for her companion. For all of his lack of formal education, the boy possessed a sensitivity to nature she found appealing. The evenings were beautiful, calm and pleasant. Little points of light sparkled and danced in the wake of the ship. The moonlight reflected on the glassy waves, making a silver path that led off into the horizon.

As the moon sank into the west and the light faded, the stars came out, so she and Barney watched the stars and the phosphorescence.

Barney gazed in awe. "Never knew they was so many stars, Miss Susan," he said, shaking his head with wonder. "How many do you reckon there is?"

Susan laughed and shook her head. "I've no idea, Barney. I don't think anyone knows. They are just beginning to find more and more as they build stronger telescopes. We may never know for sure just how many there really are."

She looked down at the water to see what looked like three underwater tubes heading for the bow, with bubbles glittering around them. "What on earth is that?" she gasped.

Barney chuckled. "Porpoises, Miss Susan. They come to play in the bow wave all the time. They's real playful. They's comin' so fast, they make more of the little sparkles than the ship can."

Susan just shook her head in amazement. Every time she thought she had seen everything, nature handed her yet another marvel.

The days passed. Lazy days of slowly gliding over the smooth sea, the heat below decks driving everyone topside where the breeze from the northwest provided some cooling to overheated bodies. She heard some grumbling among the passengers, for with the heat, the boredom, and the length of the voyage, patience began to wear thin. Susan spent her days strolling the deck or sitting on the poop deck with Mrs. Griffin.

On the morning of the Fourth of July, as the day of their arrival in San Francisco grew closer, Susan decided she had better start making some preparations. A wave of panic washed over her as she realized how little she knew of what lay ahead of her. What did she plan to do? She had heard many stories about the lawless country she would be entering, although as far as she could hear, ladies were rare and treated well.

Still, she had to make a living, and somehow locate Donald. She smiled to herself as she remembered Barney's declaration of loyalty, swearing he would protect her and never leave her. But she had studied a map one of the passengers shared with her. The vastness of the area they approached appalled her. Growing up in Boston, she had no concept of such wide open spaces. Donald could be anywhere.

Her concern must have shown on her face, because Mrs. Griffin said, in her soft voice, "You must be thinking of what you will do when we arrive in California."

Susan laughed. "Am I that obvious? Yes, I guess I was. There's probably not much call for governesses in a country where the majority of the men are single, or who have left their families in the East."

Mrs. Griffin nodded. "Yes, that's true. Children are few and far between, even though San Francisco is gradually becoming more civilized. Some women who came out with their husbands have been widowed, and run small shops or boarding houses to survive. Perhaps a small eating establishment? From what I hear, few miners have very discriminating taste in food, so they should be easy to satisfy."

Susan shook her head with a rueful smile. "I've never so much as boiled an egg. As long as I can remember, Bridgit did all the cooking."

"Perhaps you can persuade the good doctor to hire you as his assistant."

Remembering Dr. Alexander's scorn of her as a high society lady, that seemed unlikely. Susan noticed Mrs. Griffin's all too perceptive eyes fastened on her and she sighed. "I suppose I might as well tell you why I decided to come to California." She took a deep breath and began her story, twisting her hands nervously on the table in front of her.

Mrs. Griffin listened to Susan's halting recital without interruption. When she finished, the older woman patted Susan's hands. "I think you are very brave, my dear. I do hope young Donald is worthy of you. Probably your best chance of finding him is an advertisement in the *Alta California*. The newspaper is published in San Francisco, but is very widely read in the mining community. Someone will be able to direct you."

Susan's eye filled with tears. "I feared telling you, thinking you would consider me foolish." Or worse, she thought, remembering how Mr. Andrew had called her a slut, accusing her of running after Donald.

With a gentle smile, Mrs. Griffin looked at the small watch pinned to her bodice and rose to her feet. "You may be foolish, but if you never find out what happened, it will haunt you the rest of your days. There are some things which must be done, no matter how foolish the rest of the world may deem them." She extended her hand to Susan. "Come. It's nearly ten o'clock. The Fourth of July festivities are about to begin."

Captain Griffin opened the celebration by reading the Declaration of Independence, his booming voice rolling across the assemblage of men, reciting the familiar words.

"He does this every year," Mrs. Griffin whispered to Susan. "He really seems to enjoy it, though he insists he is only doing his duty as Captain."

Several passengers followed with speeches, some short and some droning on until the audience stirred restlessly. When the last speaker finally said his piece, the cook served as elegant a dinner as his meager and dwindling stores would allow.

The afternoon passed slowly in the heat, but towards evening, the breeze picked up, the ship moved with greater speed through the water, and spirits revived. One sailor brought out a mouth harp, a passenger produced a fiddle. The cook provided the percussion by banging on a pan, and soon everyone not on actual duty joined in dancing and singing to the impromptu concert. Armando carefully brought Consuela on deck. She sat holding the baby, watching the activities with obvious pleasure. Susan wished she knew some Spanish so they could have a chat, but knew she should not pull Josue from his duties to translate.

Barney seized Susan, and they did a fair representation of an Irish jig, much to the amusement of the audience, who gave them a round of applause when they finished.

As Susan returned to her seat by Mrs. Griffin, the ship lurched, throwing her off balance. She bumped into Dr. Alexander, who had been standing to the side of the revelers. He grabbed her arm to steady her and their eyes met. She knew the dancing had shaken her hair loose, and was suddenly conscious of her disheveled appearance, for the blue eyes seemed to mock her.

"Really, Miss McGuire. You should show a little more dignity." Turning on his heel, he walked away and disappeared below decks.

Susan watched his retreating back, trying to keep her seething fury from showing on her face. You don't like society ladies, she thought, gritting her teeth, but you don't like it when I'm undignified. Well, you can just go back to your cabin and stay there.

She turned and saw Mrs. Griffin watching the interplay, her eyes bright with speculation. When Susan sat down again, the older woman observed, "Yes, I do believe our good doctor is far more interested in you than he wants to admit, even to himself."

Susan flushed. "Nonsense. He despises me."

Mrs. Griffin nodded in disbelief. "If you say so."

Chapter 12

SOON THEY WERE far enough north that the wind shifted to the northeast. On Saturday, July 16, Susan stood on the starboard rail enjoying the light breeze that wafted over her, cooling her overheated forehead. She carefully stood where the shade from the sails protected her from the fierce rays of the tropical sun.

Barney came by and grinned at her. "Almost makes a body fergit how cold it were comin' round the Horn, don't it, Miss Susan?" He wiped his forehead with his red kerchief and retied it around his head.

She laughed at how quickly he had learned to imitate his fellow sailors. "Yes, but I prefer this kind of weather. I've no desire to go back to huddling under the blankets in a smoky cabin!"

He laughed with her. "Or slidin' across the deck on a layer of ice! I'd . . ."

A yell from the lookout interrupted them. "Derelict comin' up on the starboard bow. Look sharp!"

"Three degrees larboard," came the order from the deck officer to the helmsman. The ship responded, and began a graceful turn to change course. Barney and Susan hurried forward along the rail, trying, along with everyone else on deck, to get a glimpse of the small craft just coming into view.

"Longboat offen a ship, Sir," a sailor reported to Captain Griffin, who had come out to check on the report. "Looks to be empty."

All eyes remained riveted on the open boat as it slowly drifted by, close enough for everyone to see no one was aboard her.

"Shall we attempt to put a hook on her, Sir?" the First Officer asked the Captain.

Captain Griffin shook his head. "No, Mr. Thomas, it's not worth the risk. If anyone was aboard, they have been gone long ago. Let her continue to drift." He returned to the chart house.

When the excitement passed, the crowd dispersed. Susan stood at the rail and watched the boat continue on its way, slowly widening the distance between them. She found herself wondering what had happened to the people who had been on board. Had their ship sunk in a storm, forcing the survivors into the open boat? Had one of them perhaps fallen into the water and the other drowned trying to save him?

Susan could not shake the feeling that a tragedy was associated with the little vessel. She tried to tell herself the boat could easily have been blown off a ship during a storm, that no one had ever been on it, but the feeling persisted. What would it feel like to be helpless in the sea, miles from shore, and to watch your boat drift farther and farther away? She shuddered, and shook herself with a little laugh. Stop it. You'll never know what happened, and there's nothing you could do about it anyway, so forget it.

But it took her a long time to fall asleep that night.

A week later, a gale out of the northeast struck them without warning. The ship had been on an even keel for so long that Susan had grown lax in storing her belongings. The sound of her water pitcher crashing to the deck of her cabin woke her, and she grabbed the side of her bunk with a gasp of fright. She opened her eyes to see everything piled up against the larboard bulkhead. She shook her head and struggled to her feet. Not only did the ship heel far over, the swells must have risen, for the forward plunge reminded her of when they battled the huge waves while they rounded the Horn.

She dressed with some difficulty, but as rapidly as possible, for she knew she had to get up on deck before the motion made her sick. And I thought we were past all of this, she grumbled to herself. A sudden lurch sent her flying across the tiny cabin and she struck the bulkhead with a thump. Muttering deprecations against all ships in general and sudden storms in particular, she looked with dismay at the bruise forming on her forearm.

A tap at her door interrupted her, and Barney's concerned voice came through the wooden partition.

"You all right, Miss Susan?"

She looked at the shambles of the room, at the bruise on her arm, at the tumbled mass of hair reflected in the mirror and started to laugh. "Yes, Barney, I'm fine. Wait just a moment and you can help me get up on deck." She fervently hoped Consuela had secured the baby so the sudden lurching did not harm him.

The *Even Tide* spent the next two days battling the wind and waves before the storm finally played itself out. When everything settled down, Susan spent several hours getting her cabin back into shape. She left the clothes soaked when her water pitcher overturned hanging in the cabin to dry, thankful it had been the water pitcher and not the slop jar, and returned topside. As she sat in the warm sunshine, rocked almost to sleep by the gentle roll of the ship, she shook her head at the contrast. How could this smooth expanse of water, with its gentle, rolling swells sparkling in the soft sunlight, be the same monster that had tossed them about so violently just a few hours earlier?

That evening, a southbound sailboat passed them to the west. Susan stood enchanted and watched the sun sink into the ocean behind the other vessel. She thought sunset at sea had to be the most beautiful sight in the world, and she never tired of admiring the beauty of the phenomenon. As her eyes gazed upon the scene, the yellow turned to a golden orange, drifting into reddish purple as the red ball sank slowly out of sight, seeming to flatten as it sank. Then, as the sun vanished beyond the horizon, the whole skyline erupted in a brilliant light green.

Susan gasped. "Did you see that?" she asked a nearby sailor.

"The flash o' green? Yes'm," the man nodded. "It do that, sometimes. Purty, ain't it?"

"Pretty? It's spectacular! I've never heard of such a thing. What causes it?"

The man shrugged. "Dunno. Jest happens, it do."

Susan gave up. Apparently that was all the information he could give her. Questions of others brought her no closer to an answer, so she just accepted it as another marvelous thing she encountered on this strange voyage. She thought of watching the whales and porpoises, of the huge albatross, of the beauty of the sunsets, and now, this 'flash o' green' as the sailor called it. If Donald had not decided to come to California, she would probably have spent her whole life in Boston and never seen anything of the rest of the world and all the wonders of nature she had witnessed.

A little voice popped up in her mind. And Dr. Alexander?

Be quiet, she retorted. I'm going to find Donald.

The journey grew tedious after that. Even watching the sparkles in the water and beautiful sunsets began to pall. She noticed the unrest among her fellow passengers as well. Supplies began to run short, and she heard many grumbles after the cook announced he had to ration molasses. It seems the crew relished the unappetizing pudding they called 'duff'. To Susan, it was just flour boiled in water and flavored with molasses, but sailors considered it a delicacy.

Fresh fruits and vegetables had long since disappeared. Susan wrote a lengthy letter to Abby, describing the trip and her experiences. She chuckled as she wrote about delivering the baby, for, although she barely mentioned Dr. Alexander, she knew Abby's lively mind would immediately conjure up a romance. Abby had never approved of Susan's relationship with Donald.

Near the end of July, more than six long months since sailing out of Boston Harbor on that long ago cold, January day, the Captain assembled the passengers and announced a shortage of fresh water, and that everyone would receive only two quarts a day for their personal use.

"Two quarts!" roared one of the more vocal passengers. "How's a man supposed to shave with such a limit on his water?"

Other rumbles passed through the crowd in a wave. Susan felt a stab of fright. She saw First Officer Thomas nod to one of the sailors, and the crew moved into positions so they surrounded the passengers. Finally one man shouted, "Guess we're all gonna hafta grow beards!"

The laughter that followed broke the tension, although grumbling continued for a few minutes. The Captain raised his hand for silence. "I know this will be an inconvenience, but it is better than the alternative, which is to risk running out completely before we reach San Francisco." With that, he turned on his heel and returned to the chart house.

Susan turned to Mrs. Griffin as they watched the passengers disperse. "Are we in real danger of running out of water?" She thought of the baby. Surely Consuela would be allowed enough water for the baby.

The older woman smiled. "My husband is always cautious. He prefers to cut back now, to make everyone aware that water on a ship is not unlimited."

Susan thought of the unwashed chemises and drawers in her cabin and sighed.

On Saturday, August 9, a shout from the deck woke her from a sound sleep. She had been dreaming she had found Donald. It was a pleasant dream, and she let it go with some reluctance. Scrambling into her clothes, after carefully selecting the undergarments that had been airing the longest, she hurried on deck.

Barney rushed to meet her, "Miss Susan, Miss Susan!" he cried. "Come quick. It's the Golden Gate." He seized her hand and half-led, half-dragged her forward to the starboard bow. "Look!" He pointed to two massive bluffs outlined by the rising sun.

Susan followed the direction of his arm. The ship, with a brisk westerly breeze behind her, seemed to sense the goal was in sight, for water rushed past her bow. Susan shivered, for the weather had grown colder and colder over the previous two weeks.

"Ain't it somethin', Miss Susan? Ain't it just somethin'?" He wrapped a smelly blanket around her to protect her against the morning chill. His eyes sparkled. "We're 'most there. We've made it!"

She caught his excitement. Wisps of fog still clung to the bases of the cliffs, but sunlight sparkled off the waves. Another ship, a mile or so ahead of them, entered the channel between the bluffs. The cliffs glowed golden in the morning sun.

She put her arm around Barney's shoulders and they huddled together under the blanket, watching the fabled passage come closer and closer. A stab of fright mixed with her excitement as she realized they would shortly dock in San Francisco. She would leave the safety of the ship and the protection of Captain and Mrs. Griffin.

What would she do next?

CALIFORNIA

1851 to 1853

Chapter 13

BY EARLY afternoon, they cruised along the waterfront in the calm waters of the bay. Susan gasped at the number of ships they passed lined up along the shore. Mrs. Griffin stood beside the girl at the rail and laughed at her astonishment.

"Oh, yes," the older woman said. "Five or six hundred ships at a time is not unusual. At least there are nine piers now. When we first came here, in '46, there were only two. That was plenty then, for men didn't start arriving in droves until '49." She waved her hand to include the clustered mass of ships. "At least now we could tie up at a pier if we chose. In '49 and '50, we never dared."

"Why ever not?" Susan asked.

"Because ships that did often lost their crews. Most of those hulks you see rotting in the harbor are all that's left of valuable ships abandoned by their crews for the gold fields. Some captains had their officers hold the men on board at gun point."

"Good heavens!"

"Oh, yes. Fortunately for the owners of the ships, very few sailors were willing to try and swim through this shark-infested bay, not even for the chance to strike it rich. Even if they could swim well enough, the currents are treacherous." She chuckled. "And sailors are very seldom good swimmers. Strange as it may seem, they don't wish to learn to swim."

"If the crews couldn't take people ashore in the longboats and the ships avoided the piers, how did passengers disembark?"

"A few enterprising locals set up a shore-boat service and charged a dollar a man. Had a thriving little business going for a while. But so many fortune hunters have come that the gold for easy pickings is gone. Men that come now are merchants and farmers and the like."

As the ship approached her anchorage, Susan looked more closely at the shoreline. "It looks like a garbage dump," she commented.

Mrs. Griffin laughed. "It *is* a garbage dump, my dear. Wait until you see the streets! They had fifty inches of rain the winter before last. The mud in the streets was so deep a wagon and a mule just disappeared."

"In the street?"

Mrs. Griffin nodded. "In the street. The bodies of three men were found last January and February buried in the mud." She twisted her mouth into a wry smile. "They probably had a little too much whiskey. These miners are a heavy drinking lot. Easy money does that, I guess. Make a lot during the week, then lose it in a weekend of drinking and gambling." She shook her head. "We were fortunate, though. We arrived in April of '50, after the rains had stopped. But I understand they had a terrible winter."

"Why don't they put wooden planks across the street? Or at least across the sidewalks?"

"The expense. Wood cost $400 for a thousand feet. When they finally did get some in, the damp climate rotted it out so fast it hardly paid."

"So what did they do?" Susan thought of the cobbled tree-lined streets and carefully manicured walkways along Commonwealth Avenue, and, for one brief instant, almost regretted leaving. She dismissed the thought at its inception. She would never go back to Boston, no matter how neat and clean the streets.

"They threw in rocks, brush, old clothes, boxes and barrels, even unused merchandise. Anything to make a solid enough bottom to drive a team on."

Susan looked out at the bustling city and saw buildings in every stage of construction. Men scurried around like ants. By late afternoon, the *Even Tide* had dropped her anchor in the bay, a short distance from one of the crowded piers, and close enough for Susan to see the activity. Fog slowly crept around the corner from the direction of the Golden Gate.

Susan shivered and pulled her cloak around her more securely. "Why is it so cold?" she asked. "This is August, but it feels like winter."

Her companion laughed. "Actually, summer in San Francisco is the coldest time of the year. We were here in February one year and it was quite pleasant. Of course, this wretched fog penetrates to one's very marrow." She held out her hand to Susan. "Come, my dear. Nothing more will happen here until morning. Let's go have a nice hot cup of tea in my quarters."

They settled into their chairs in the Captain's Quarters. While Charlie poured the hot tea into the delicate china cups, Mrs. Griffin smiled maternally at Susan

"Now, my dear, you must tell me your plans. We are going on to the Sandwich Islands, but I suppose it is useless for me to try and persuade you to remain with me." She laughed softly. "As dearly as I would enjoy your company, I know you are anxious to get on with your quest."

Susan nodded. "I suppose there are hotels . . . ," she began.

The older woman shook her head. "Hotels, yes. You stay at one? Never," she stated firmly. "Although I understand they have some nicer ones now. I hear the *Union* and the *Oriental* have satisfactory accommodations. A couple of others on Sansome Street are fairly decent. But proper facilities are still scarce. Men are sleeping six or eight to a room." She paused as Charlie refilled her cup, then continued, with a smile at Susan. "And while I understand the prices are now more reasonable, I would feel better if you stayed here on the *Even Tide* until arrangements can be made for your passage to Sacramento City."

Susan hesitated, then nodded. She took another sip of tea. Her mind raced as she considered her options. She knew only too well her funds were not unlimited. It would certainly be to her advantage not to spend any more money here in San Francisco than absolutely necessary.

Mrs. Griffin continued. "Steamers ply the river between here and Sacramento regularly. Dr. Alexander may go there, if he is unable to find a suitable position here in San Francisco. If he does, he has promised to see you as far as Sacramento." She smiled. "And Mr. Thomas has informed me you wish to keep young Barney with you, so you will not be unaccompanied, even should Dr. Alexander remain in San Francisco."

"Oh, yes," Susan agreed promptly. "I've become quite fond of Barney. I can't imagine giving him up." She suddenly thought of his obligation to work off his passage. Would that be a problem? She hesitated, then posed the question to Mrs. Griffin.

"I can pay off any additional passage, if he hasn't worked long enough," she added, peering anxiously into her companion's face. "I know he couldn't do much while laid up with his broken leg."

The older woman smiled. "My husband is kind and generous, almost to a fault. He has no intention of making a slave of the boy. Other captains might not be so lenient, so Barney is fortunate he selected the *Even Tide* when he stowed away."

Susan laughed. "I don't think he gave it a conscious thought. I'm sure the only thing on his mind at the time was to get away from that cruel master. The *Even Tide* just happened to be the first ship he could get aboard without being seen." She smiled. "But he will be a great comfort to me. I am very glad to have him."

"The fog has cleared sufficiently to see the pier, Miss Susan. When you and young Barney are ready, I will escort you to visit the city."

"Thank you, Mr. Thomas." Susan smiled at the young officer. "It's kind of you to offer to accompany us."

"The pleasure is mine, Miss Susan." The warmth of his smile dismayed her. Oh, dear, she thought. I hope he has not become infatuated with me.

Barney had just assisted her to a seat in the boat when Dr. Alexander swung his long legs over the rail. Susan chuckled to herself. So he decided to join us after all.

The blue eyes met her green ones. "I have to decide whether to set up my practice here or in Sacramento," he said. "My initial plans were to go on to Sacramento, but my fellow passengers assure me San Francisco is much farther ahead on the road to respectability."

"So you will be staying here?" She posed the question in her most polite tone of voice, angry with herself for the wave of desolation that swept over her at the thought of never seeing him again. As though he ever gave any indication of caring whether he sees me again or not, she thought. The knowledge made her even angrier.

"That is my plan if I find a place I consider suitable. I am sure young Barney can see you make it safely to Sacramento."

"Sure will," Barney avowed, so stoutly Susan had to laugh. She pulled her shawl more tightly about her shoulders. They had cleared the lee of the ship, and a surprisingly cold wind swept over them.

A short, chilly ride brought them to the dock, where they had to climb up a steep ladder to reach the pier itself. Smells from the rotting garbage assailed their nostrils, and Susan wrinkled her nose in disgust.

Mr. Thomas offered her his arm with a shy smile. "The tide is out, Miss Susan. The smell is not as bad when the tide covers the mud flats again."

"I certainly hope not. I can't imagine living in a place that smells like this all the time." She took his arm and smiled, very aware of Dr. Alexander's presence behind them. Let him see that some men thought her attractive, even though she had no interest in them. Mr. Thomas had been the most attentive of the officers. Knowing the scarcity of women in California, she did not doubt she would attract a number of suitors. But she had come to find Donald, and nothing would sway her from her purpose.

Not even Dr. James Alexander, a little voice whispered in her mind?

No, she retorted silently. Not even Dr. James Alexander.

They walked up Sansome Street. The first thing Susan noticed was the trash. It seemed everyone just threw the garbage out of the door. Bottles, cans, and old clothing of every description protruded from the dried mud along the edges of the planks that lined the street.

"Careful, Miss Susan," Mr. Thomas cautioned, guiding her around a gap in the boardwalk. "Wood rots quickly in this climate, so there are many holes." He chuckled. "Usually a hole means someone has fallen through."

Taking more notice of where she put her feet, Susan looked at the plank walkway and noticed many such gaps. She shook her head. If each one represented a fall through the planks, it was a hazardous walk indeed. As she watched, a huge rat poked his head out of a hole almost in front of them.

Susan clung a little tighter to Mr. Thomas' arm. "Did you see the size of that rat?" she gasped.

He chuckled. "Yes, they have many rats here. And you're right. Many of them are very large. Another reason why Captain Griffin prefers not to tie up to the wharf. He wishes to make it as difficult as possible for them to board his ship."

"I think you can attribute the size of the rats to the fact that they are so well fed, if the amount of garbage I see lying about is any indication," remarked Dr. Alexander from behind them.

Barney laughed. "Got a good point, he does, Miss Susan," the boy agreed, with a vigorous nod of his head.

"Why are there so many clothes thrown into the street?" Susan asked. "Bottles and boxes I can understand, but why old clothes?"

The young officer chuckled. "Two reasons. First, it cost a whole dollar back in '49 to get a shirt washed. The miners figured that was too much to pay just to get a shirt laundered, so when a man bought a shirt, he wore it until it was too dirty and ragged to wear, then threw it away and bought another. Cheaper to buy a new one."

Susan shuddered. She could imagine what the man had smelled like before he finally discarded the shirt.

"Second," he continued, "mud was so deep in the streets in the winter of '49 to '50 that they threw in anything they could to keep from sinking. Some even threw in whole crates of brand new merchandise."

"What a waste!" Susan exclaimed.

Mr. Thomas shrugged. "Many merchants sent vast amounts of goods totally unsuited to the city at the time. Miners had no use for good linen, fancy suits, and fine china. Now that the citizens are becoming more civilized, there is more place for those kinds of things." He waved his arm to indicate a gentleman strolling down the opposite side of the street. The man wore a suit of fine broadcloth with a starched shirt and stiff collar, in marked contrast to his fellow strollers.

"See more men dressed like that now," her escort continued. "Easy gold is a thing of the past, so bankers and lawyers and farmers are going back to their original professions. They are also bringing out their wives and families. The city is getting more churches and schools, and fewer saloons and gambling houses."

"Are there many physicians?" Dr. Alexander asked from behind them.

"A few, but the city can certainly make use of your skills, Dr. Alexander."

"Then I will make some inquiries about lodging and surgery space. Shall we meet, say, in three hours?"

"Meet us at Winn's Fountain Head, on Clay Street," the officer suggested. "That is a genteel establishment where gentlemen take their ladies for refreshment. I understand they make very good tea, and serve an excellent apple pie."

Dr. Alexander looked at his watch. "Very well. Two o'clock at Winn's." He turned at the next corner and headed for a group of buildings.

Three hours later, Susan sank thankfully into a chair at Winn's Fountain Head. As interesting as it was to see the city, an unbelievable collection of the wildest assortment of buildings imaginable, everything from tents and lean-tos to splendid two-story hotels with fancy front porches, her legs ached from walking up and down the hills. Some of the edifices were combinations, with wooden walls and a canvas roof. Also, she had seen enough rats and garbage to hold her for a long time. Mr. Thomas assured her the city was much better than a couple of years previously, making her grateful she had not come when Donald did.

Also, some small creature had bitten her on the ankle, and it itched ferociously. She tried to surreptitiously scratch it under the table. She knew ladies were not supposed to lift up their skirts and scratch a leg, but she certainly wished she had the freedom to do so.

As she removed her shawl, she saw a small insect hop from the shawl to her arm. With an exclamation, she swatted it away.

"Fleas, Miss Susan," Mr. Thomas told her. "Sand fleas. The whole city is built on one huge sand dune, and sand fleas are everywhere. They are a wretched nuisance."

"I can believe that," she said dryly, thinking of her itching ankle. "Evidently the cold doesn't bother them." The wind had increased in velocity and blown away the fog, but it also decreased the temperature markedly. "I had never imagined," she laughed to Barney, "that any place could be so cold in August! It's almost as bad as rounding the Horn. It's supposed to be summer."

She looked about her. She saw a few ladies in stylish dress, and men dressed in dark suits. None of the men wore the typical miners garb: flannel shirt, loose trousers held at the waist with a belt or sash and tucked into tall boots, heads topped with a slouch hat.

"Mr. Thomas . . . ," she began.

"Please," he interrupted, taking her hand in both of his, "call me Peter. We're no longer on board the ship and have no need to be formal."

"Peter," she obeyed, hastily extracting her hand, noticing Barney's bright eyes on the action, "do none of the miners come here? Why? Is this place expensive?"

"No, most of the miners prefer less elegant places and the company of ladies who are, shall we say, less than genteel?" He laughed. "In fact, a ship brought a whole load of lovely senoritas from Mazatlan in '49 to provide just that sort of entertainment."

Susan blushed. "I see," she murmured. The waiter brought a pot of tea to the table and poured the steaming liquid into delicate china cups. She picked up her cup and savored the warmth. Mr. Thomas ... Peter ... is right, she thought. They do serve an excellent tea.

Barney sat staring open-mouthed at the elegance surrounding him. "Gee, Miss Susan," he whispered. "I ain't never been in a place like this. Look at them lights!" He pointed to the large chandeliers. "Must take an hour to light all them candles." He picked up the tea cup gingerly, as though fearing it would break. "You sure they let the likes o' me in places like this?"

Susan laughed softly and patted his hand. "Relax, Barney. You don't have to whisper. And the cup won't break unless you drop it. This is California, not Boston. You are perfectly welcome here. Oh, look at this!" she exclaimed, as the waiter set a large wedge of apple pie in front of her. A slab of golden cheese lay on top of the flaky crust.

Peter Thomas smiled. "I told you they made a good apple pie." He glanced towards the door, over at Barney, then at his watch, back at Barney, and then to Susan.

Susan noticed his strange behavior and said, "Is the doctor late?"

"Oh," the young man looked flustered. "No, no, it's just, well, er, uh ..." he glanced at Barney who, with sudden insight, jumped to his feet.

"I'll go check an' see if Doc's about here." He headed for the door.

Mr. Thomas again secured Susan's hand, and it dawned on her what he had in mind. Oh, no, she thought. Surely he can't be serious! She tugged, trying to free her hand.

But his seriousness quickly became apparent. He held the hand tighter. "Susan," he said in a solemn voice, "Please, may I call you Susan?" She numbly nodded her assent and he continued. "I have come to admire you very much in the six months of our voyage. I know it is probably too soon to speak, but if you leave the ship, I fear I may lose you." He hesitated. "I know Mrs. Griffin would be very pleased to have your company for the rest of the voyage, if you can be persuaded to come to the Sandwich Islands with us. Captain Griffin can marry us if you wish, or we could wait until our return to Boston."

"But Mr. Thomas . . ."

"Peter, please," he interrupted.

"Peter," she said, obligingly. "No, I left Boston for good. I'm never going back."

"Then wait for me here," he begged. "I can arrange lodging at the Portsmouth House, a very fine establishment. I will be back next August or September. Then I can resign from my position with the *Even Tide* and remain here."

She shook her head. "You love the sea. I've heard you speak of the sea like most men speak of a beloved woman. I can't ask you to give it up." She had to think of something to dissuade him.

"I can get a position on a coastal ship and never be gone more than a few months at a time."

"Peter, I'm sorry," she finally said. She wasn't about to tell him of her search for Donald. "Perhaps when you return, you can look me up."

"You will wait for me?"

"Let's just see how you feel when you return, shall we?"

"Well! I see you and Mr. Thomas are becoming good friends." Dr. Alexander's icy voice penetrated her consciousness and she yanked her hand free. She looked up and met the blue eyes that stared into her green ones with disdain. Her dismay turned to anger. He had no right to dictate her behavior. How dare he imply she had no right to . . . what?

She didn't know herself. She glanced at Barney, whose face showed plainly he had tried to delay the doctor's arrival on the scene. She struggled to pull her emotions back under control. Taking a deep breath, she forced herself to say, in a calm voice that only shook a little, "And what concern is it of yours?"

"None at all," he said, his voice as frigid as his eyes. "Absolutely none at all." He changed the subject. "I have located suitable lodgings near the Portsmouth House on Clay Street. The proprietor says he will recommend me to all of his clients, since I will be close by." He met Susan's eyes and she felt her heart thump against her ribs. "I will be removing from the *Even Tide* when the fog lifts in the morning." He picked up his fork. "Now, let us enjoy this excellent pie and return to the ship before the fog forces us to remain here for the night."

Chapter 14

BY MID-MORNING of the following day, the wind had blown enough of the fog away to allow the longboat to go ashore without fear of becoming lost. The sun had not yet succeeded in breaking through the gray slate that covered the sky. It hung over the bay, a glowing, cold, red ball.

The seamen loaded Dr. Alexander's gear on board the longboat, and he said his good-byes to the officers and Captain and Mrs. Griffin. Susan stood a little apart from the group of well-wishers, trying to get her mixed emotions under control. After all, she thought, I am in love with Donald, and have come all these miles to find him. Why am I so affected by this strange, aloof man?

He stopped in front of her and offered his hand. She placed her hand in his, feeling her pulse race as she did so. Their eyes met, and her heart gave that same leap it always did when those blue eyes pierced hers.

"Good-bye," she managed to stammer, through vocal cords so tight they threatened to choke her.

He smiled, a perfunctory motion of his lips. The smile did not reach his eyes; they remained as cold as ever. "Good-bye, Miss McGuire. You are a remarkable young lady. I wish you and Mr. Thomas every happiness." He turned on his heel and walked away before she could say a word.

She stood, dumbfounded, unable to speak. He thought she had accepted Peter Thomas' offer! How could he think that? Remembering the scene he had witnessed at Winn's, she realized he could easily have misinterpreted what had transpired. But you're wrong, she wanted to scream after him. You're wrong! I have made no pact with Peter Thomas. But he was over the side and gone.

Susan stared at his back as the boat slid through the water, leaving ripples in its wake, then watched him climb to the pier and walk away. She stood, unmoving, unable to understand her feelings. Barney joined her, and stood beside her with his arm around her shoulders. He seemed, somehow, to know the turmoil that raged within her, but he said nothing.

Finally, he tightened his arm around her shoulder and turned her toward the companionway. "Come below, Miss Susan. You'll ketch yer death o' cold, a-standin' here in this wind."

The following morning, she sent Barney to book passage for them on a steamer to Sacramento. Mrs. Griffin said the *Even Tide* would be in San Francisco for another week, but Susan, anxious to get on with her quest for Donald, also wanted to get away from the eager Mr. Thomas. Although a nice young man who would probably make her an excellent husband, he aroused no romantic feelings in her at all. She felt it unfair to him to remain any longer than necessary.

Barney returned shortly after noon, his face alight. "Got us booked on the *Sea Witch*. She's a steamer. Makes seven knots. Takes her twelve, fifteen hours to make Sacramento City, dependin' on the tides." He hesitated. "Only problem is, she leaves at dawn. Means we hafta stay on 'er tonight, or at a hotel close. Won't be able to cotch 'er iffen fog won't let us go ashore afore ten, like it's been doin' the last couple o' days.

"Cost thirty dollars fer a cabin fer you," he continued. "Figured you'd be a-wantin' a cabin. Twenty for me, 'cuz I kin stay on deck." He chuckled. "And it's five dollars extra if you sleep in the bunk."

Susan thought of her meager purse. Paying for Barney in

addition to herself would use up the money much faster. But she was determined to take care of him, so she just smiled and said, "That's fine, Barney, you did very well. Thank you." The boy beamed under her praise. "And since we have paid for the cabin, we may as well use it. I'll get my things together and bid our farewells to Captain and Mrs. Griffin. We'll leave at four this afternoon, before the fog comes in."

The next morning, while Susan still slept in the small cabin, Barney on the floor beside her, the thump, thump, thump of the pistons as they began to turn in response to the head of steam building up in the boiler awakened her. As she listened, a cry of "Cast off!" rang out and she felt the movement as the ship eased away from the dock.

Susan had slept in her dress, so she pulled on her shoes, then washed her face and brushed her hair, stepping carefully over the still sleeping Barney. She refused to allow him to sleep on the deck as he had planned. He twitched in his sleep and his eyelids flickered. He's dreaming, she thought. As she watched him, a fond smile hovering on her lips, his face twisted, as if he were in pain.

"No . . . ," he muttered. "No . . . , don't . . . , no . . . ." With a jerk, he awoke. His eyes flew open and fell upon Susan's anxious face.

For a second he looked startled, then, with a shamefaced laugh, he said, "Sorry, Miss Susan. The dream come agin. It do, sometimes, and I think I'm back in Boston." He jumped to his feet, his red hair sticking out in small spikes all over his head. "It's all right, Miss Susan, really it is," he tried to reassure her, for she still looked at him with concern. "Ain't bad. Jist wakes me up sometime, is all."

She smiled. He's still not ready to confide in me, she thought. Some day he will. "Come," she said, sensing he did not wish to discuss the nightmare. "Let's eat a bite and get up on deck. We don't want to miss anything." Since Susan had not wanted to pay a dollar and a half for meals on board the *Sea Witch,* she had persuaded the cook on the *Even Tide* to prepare a food basket for them. He readily complied, and packed the basket so heavy with comestibles that she had been obliged to ask Barney to carry it.

After a simple breakfast of ham, biscuit, compote and fruit, during which Susan longed for a cup of hot tea, they hurried out on deck, already crowded with other passengers. The boiler had a full head of steam, and the boat churned across the waves, its wake eddying out to the stern in a wide V. In response to Susan's query, a nearby gentleman advised her the time was six o'clock.

"Tide's with us, Miss," he smiled. "Be dockin' by six tonight at Sacramento, if that's where you're headed. Goin' farther, m'self. Goin' up to Marysville." He chuckled. "Hope I hev better luck this trip. Last August I were on the *Fawn* when she burst her boiler, 'bout four miles upriver from Sacramento."

"Burst her boiler!" Susan exclaimed. "Didn't she sink?"

"Yup," her jovial companion replied. "Like to drowned, I did. Lucky thing 'twas end o' the dry season. River way low, so she only sunk to just above her deck. I hear they raised her off the bottom and patched her up." He shook his head. "Some of the river captains, they just push real hard to make their run faster'n the next boat. Put too much pressure on the boiler."

"Was anyone killed?"

"No, but some as was close to the boiler when she blew got real bad hurt. Most, like me, got blown overboard. Managed to get to shore, I did, along with most o' my fellow passengers, thankin' our lucky stars, let me tell you."

"Thank you," Susan murmured. "Come, Barney. Let's go stand by the bow. If this boiler blows, I want to be as far from it as possible."

In the bow, the sharp wind blew over them, and Susan shivered as she huddled deeper into her coat. The fog grew wispier as they progressed, towards what a crewman told her was San Pablo Bay.

"Got to be real careful from now on, Miss," he said. "Get out of the channel, can hit a snag or go aground right easy." He grinned, revealing yellowed teeth. A long scar ran from his hairline across his right eye and down to his chin. The eye was open, but unseeing. White scar tissue covered the pupil. Susan shuddered inwardly. He must have been terribly injured at one time.

She did not realize she stared, but the left eye twinkled as he said, "Knife fight, down Panama City way, back in '46. Got inta a fight with a limey and he pulled his dirk on me."

"I'm sorry," Susan murmured.

"Oh," he said airily "don't bother me much no more. I got even, though. Next time I saw that limey, I had my own knife. Got 'im right in the gullet." He grinned. "That's why I work the river now. Cain't never go back to Panama. They're a-layin' for me."

"I see," Susan said, inanely, unable to respond to his recitation.

"You have a nice trip, Miss." He saluted her and returned to his duties.

Susan began to realize what a sheltered life she had led, and felt a surge of gratitude for the boy standing beside her. Although he had never admitted it, she knew in her heart he had killed once to protect a woman. She felt sure he would do it again. As appalling as it sounded, somehow the knowledge comforted her.

The sun swept away the last of the fog as they entered San Pablo Bay. The mountains of the north peninsula loomed on the left. To the right lay the mainland. The *Sea Witch* passed two small islands off-shore, which the friendly gentleman en route to Marysville advised her were called The Brothers. A lighthouse stood on the larger of the two. Seagulls soared and swooped around the stern of the boat where the cook threw the scraps from the meals. The graceful white birds squabbled and bickered and screamed as they fought over the tidbits. Susan and Barney watched, laughing at their antics.

The temperature rose markedly as the boat progressed inland, and by noon, Susan was obliged to send Barney to the cabin to exchange her coat for her parasol.

"Thank you, Barney," she exclaimed when he opened it and handed it to her. "Heavens, what a change in the weather!"

"Oh, yes, Miss," a nearby passenger volunteered. "It be over ninety degrees in Sacramento City now."

"Ninety?"

"Often tops a hundred in the summer. Cools off at night, though. Never as bad as in the East."

"Thank you," Susan murmured. "That's a comfort."

The rest of the voyage passed pleasantly. She and Barney stood on the deck leaning against the rail and watched the river banks glide by. Tall, slender reeds rose from the surface, creating a sea of waving strands. Susan wondered how in the world the pilot knew where the channel ran. All of the twists and turns looked alike to her, especially after they left the main river and took a side slough called, appropriately, 'Steamboat Slough' that cut almost ten miles off of their journey. Thousands of water birds dotted the river in front of them. The birds took to the air in front of the boat, only to settle down again as soon as the noise of the passing vessel faded.

Susan had to laugh to Barney. "It's like they regard the boat only as a temporary nuisance. Have you ever seen so many ducks?"

"Sure would like to get me a duck dinner," Barney grinned. "I suspect duck is on a lot of supper tables in these parts."

"I suspect you're right." She sighed. "I suppose it means I'll have to learn how to cook one!"

True to the prediction of their unnamed acquaintance, the little vessel pulled up to the pier in Sacramento just before six in the evening. The sun still hung high in the afternoon sky, and the heat remained. Susan's skin burned, for the perspiration dried as quickly as it formed.

She sighed to Barney, "This must be what they mean when they say the heat here is dry!"

He grinned. "Better'n Boston."

Susan remembered the damp, clinging, oppressive heat and nodded. It did make the heat easier to bear, and a delightfully fresh westerly breeze had begun. She turned her face thankfully into the welcome coolness.

They watched the activity with interest. The seamen from the *Sea Witch* threw lines to the men on the dock, who swiftly wrapped them about the bollards lining the pier. They then pulled the vessel up to the side of the dock and secured her. The moment the lines were tied off, passengers streamed over the side, yelling for carts and wagons. Susan stood and watched the chaos for several moments, unsure of quite what to do next.

The gentleman who had described the boiler accident, apparently noticing her uncertainty, took pity on her and said, in a kind, fatherly voice, "You will need to disembark quickly, Miss. The Captain is making very good time, and will only stay here until he has taken on his upriver passengers. His destination, as I have said, is Marysville."

"Of course. Thank you. Barney, please gather my trunks from the stateroom."

"Yes, Miss Susan." The boy hurried to obey, and in a

few minutes both of her small trunks lay at her feet. She had put his scant belongings in with hers, to make transportation easier. Of course, all he owned were the spare pair of pants and two extra shirts his fellow sailors had pressed upon him. With the assistance of Barney and one of the seamen, she found herself and her belongings deposited on the pier in short order.

"And," her new friend continued, calling across from the boat, "I assume you have no place to stay?"

When she admitted this was the case, he added, in the same fatherly tone, "Then, may I suggest the *Southern House?* It is a comfortable and reputable establishment on 'J' Street. Get one of the carts to drive you there, but don't let the scoundrel charge you more than a dollar, for it's but a few blocks."

Moments later, the dock hands cast off the lines and the *Sea Witch* continued her journey upriver.

"Best of luck to you, Miss," shouted her friend from the boat, calling across the widening expanse of water.

"Good-bye, and thank you for your help," she cried back, waving to him as the boat moved away.

"Now," she turned to Barney, "suppose you find a cart to carry us to the *Southern House.* And find one who will do it for a dollar."

"Yes, Miss Susan." With a broad grin, Barney scurried off.

In less than five minutes, the boy returned, the grin even broader. "Found two of 'em who wanted my business, so I got one to take us for seventy-five cents!"

Susan had to laugh at his ingenuity. "I can tell you are going to be a big help to me, Barney."

Chapter 15

SUSAN ENGAGED two adjoining rooms for herself and Barney in the *Southern House,* a large, wood-frame hotel with some pretensions at grandeur, but not enough to make it beyond her meager purse. At least not for a while, she thought, rather grimly, knowing full well that she would have to find some means of income before very long.

Barney tapped lightly at her door. "Ready for some supper, Miss Susan? They tell me they's only gonna serve it for another half hour, so we got to git down there."

"Coming." She joined him and they descended the single flight of stairs and crossed the lobby to the dining room. A loud argument between the proprietor and a large gentleman in a black, broadcloth suit immediately caught their attention. The other diners wore miners garb, and watched the discussion with grins on their faces. Susan and Barney skirted the dispute and found seats at a small table by the wall.

A young girl approached, a frightened look on her face. "Supper, Miss? For you and the young gentleman?"

"Yes, please," Susan replied. "What on earth is going on?"

"Oh, Miss, that gentleman, he don't like the grub, and he blamed me. But me and the cook, she's my ma, we can only fix what we got, and . . . ." The girl burst into tears.

"Come, child, sit a moment. Barney and I aren't that hungry. Sit until you feel a little better. I'm sure the man didn't mean anything against you personally."

"Yes, Miss, I mean, no, Miss." The girl controlled her sobs with some difficulty, "It's just that, we'm is so scared. What if he fires us? Ma and me and my sister, Maggie, we wouldn't have no place to stay. Pa died last fall in the cholera epidemic, along with our little brother and baby sister. We managed to get on here, helpin', but . . . " A fresh spate of tears interrupted the narrative. "Ma's a good cook, but she don't know nothin' about buyin' and bargainin', and . . . ."

The proprietor, his face red from his argument with the irate customer, marched over to the table where Susan comforted the girl. "Peggy," he roared. "Don't set there blubbering! Get the supper for the lady and the young gentleman! I swear, you try my patience beyond what a man should be called upon to endure with your constant wailing!" He waved his hand. "Begone with you."

He turned to Susan and bowed politely. "Please don't let her upset you, Miss. It's so hard to get good help, and Mrs. Dolan, she come to me as a widow lady, her and the two girls, twins, they are, though why anyone with a whit of sense would name both girls 'Margaret' as she done, calls one Peggy, the other Maggie, if'n you can believe, anyway, they come to me, a-needin' a place and me with my soft heart, I takes 'em in, that were a terrible time we had with the cholera last fall, and all, and . . . ."

Susan held up her hand to stop the flow of words. "Please, say no more. We understand perfectly." She smiled at Barney as the proprietor turned on his heel to deal with another customer who had come to complain that he had no towel in his room. "I think I have just thought of how we can make a living in this town. How would you like to help me manage a hotel?"

He grinned. "You just tell me what to do, Miss Susan, and I'll do it." He flexed his right arm to show her his muscle. "I'm real strong, I am."

"I think I will make more use of your wits than of your muscles." She rose to her feet. "Come. Let's catch him while he is feeling the need for help."

The proprietor, his face flushed redder than ever, turned from berating a weeping Maggie for not putting clean towels in the rooms. He apologized to Susan, apparently thinking she also had a complaint to register. "I'm sorry you don't have a towel. Seems as though the linen never come back from Ah Fan's laundry, and no one thought to check why! I declare, I'm at my wit's end. I got to get some decent help, or . . . ."

"That's what I wish to discuss with you. I believe I can provide your employees with the direction they need. Can we come to some sort of an arrangement?"

An hour later, Susan and Barney retired to their rooms in triumph. They had a place to stay and three meals a day in return for seeing the customers were properly fed and the rooms cleaned and supplied with fresh linen. The proprietor, in a generous mood at the thought of being relieved of the headaches of constant complaints from the clients, even offered her a percentage of the profits, should they rise under her guidance.

Concern tempered some of Susan's elation. She had absolutely no experience in hotel management, and, as she had told Mrs. Griffin, could not so much as boil an egg. But she had learned a lot about bargaining with merchants from Bridgit, and she had Barney's shrewdness on her side. He had learned a lot in his rough and tumble life.

She yawned and picked up the pitcher to pour some water in her basin to wash her face and hands, only to discover the pitcher contained no water. She chuckled softly. So, she thought, I'll go to bed without washing. It looks like Barney and I have our work cut out for us, she smiled to herself. We'll start tomorrow with fresh water in all of the pitchers.

* * *

She awoke the following morning to the clanging of alarm bells, and started with fright. She quickly pulled on her robe and ran to the window to locate the source of the excitement. The bright red fire truck from the Mutual Hook and Ladder Company, a big '#1' painted on its side, raced past the hotel. Pulled by four sturdy horses, it headed east on 'J' street. Smoke curled in the distance. People poured out into the street and ran after the fire truck. Susan sighed with relief when she realized the fire was some distance away. She hoped the fire truck could keep it from spreading.

Barney pounded on her door a few moments later. "Miss Susan, Miss Susan, are you awake?"

She shook her head. As if anyone could sleep through all of this, she thought, with some amusement. "Yes, Barney. Come in."

He burst into the room, full of excitement. "It's the *Tehama Theater*," he reported. "And some are a-sayin' it were set a-purpose, 'cause there are some as say the plays and such are sinful."

Susan just shook her head. Apparently Boston's strict code of morality was not as far behind her as she had thought.

Three days later, her plans were moving with remarkable success. Mrs. Dolan and the two girls were hard workers, and eager to please. Once they realized she would not shout and bully them, they accepted her direction. Mrs. Dolan did have a knack with food. As soon as Susan, with Barney's help, procured the necessary ingredients, the woman made a wonderful Irish stew. To relieve Maggie and Peggy of the chores of washing dishes and preparing vegetables, Susan hired a young Chinese boy to help in the kitchen. She could not pronounce the boy's name properly, so he just grinned at her and said, "Call me Johnny Lee. Everyone else does."

"Thank you, Johnny Lee. I'm just glad you speak English so well. If you don't understand anything, or if you have a suggestion, please come to me."

"Yes, Miss Susan."

She set up a routine for the girls to follow, and assigned Barney the task of seeing all the supplies they needed were available. As she had suspected, Barney had no difficulty in getting the linen back from the laundry when it was promised.

By the end of August, Susan had the hotel operations running smoothly. The proprietor smiled and beamed upon everyone, the meals were good and on time, and customers had ceased to complain. Susan decided the time had come to begin her search for Donald.

As Mrs. Griffin had advised, she placed a small notice in the *Alta California,* and in the *Sacramento Union.* After that, she could do nothing else but wait for a response. She forced herself to be patient. The first day the *Sacramento Union* came out after she placed her notice, and as Susan scanned the pages searching for the small advertisement, Mrs. Dolan suggested she look in the Sandhill Cemetery.

"They's over eight hundred new graves out there, Miss Susan," Mrs. Dolan told her. "Most of 'em as died of the cholera last October." Tears sprang into her eyes. "My man and two of my young 'uns is buried there. Mayhap your young man is too." She shook her head and banged the kettle she held down hard on the table. "Sad thing, it were, many so young. And some as didn't even get a name on a marker." The tears rolled down her cheeks and she wiped them off with the dish towel. "Only lasted twenty days, it did, but seventeen doctors were among those who died, that's how bad it were."

"Where is Sandhill Cemetery?"

"Out on Mormon Island, in the American River. Takes a rowboat to get there, it does, but there's them as be willin' to take ye. Fer a fee o' course."

"Of course," Susan agreed.

"They was a-rowin' coffins out there all day long for a while. Those as didn't have money or kin to buy coffins, the Odd Fellows bought coffins for 'em. Coffins were runnin' from $60 to $150 dollars at the time. I didn't have that kinda money, so the Odd Fellows bought me two, one for my son and one for my man. We buried my baby with her da, seein' as how they died just a few hours apart, and her bein' so little." The tears flowed freely.

Susan put her arms around the woman and held her closely as she wept. She wondered if the poor soul had ever been given any opportunity to vent her grief.

It seemed to make Mrs. Dolan feel better, for after a few minutes, she pulled back, wiped her eyes, and blew her nose loudly into the well-used handkerchief she pulled from her ample bosom.

"Thanky, Miss Susan. You're so kind. Sorry for the weeps. Where was I?"

"Ferrying coffins out to Mormon Island."

"Oh, yes," she nodded. Then she chuckled. "One Dutchman, who never trusted nobody, he kept all of his gold, about two thousand dollars worth, in a belt around his waist. He an' a lad went to take a coffin over and the boat set to careenin' and sank. That there Dutchman, he tried to swim ashore."

"With all that weight around his waist?" Susan gasped.

Mrs. Dolan nodded. "Drowned, he did. Gold kept pullin' him under until he drowned. Never had the sense to let it go." She shook her head. "Lad with him floated ashore on the coffin."

Susan smiled. "I'll try not to emulate your Dutchman's example. Barney, let's see if we can find ourselves a boatman with better sense."

The following morning, they borrowed the hotel buggy from Mr. Perkins and Barney drove to the south bank of the American River across from Mormon Island. There Susan engaged the services of a boatman and they crossed to the island without incident.

The magnitude of the task they had undertaken almost overwhelmed Susan when she saw the large number of graves. A few stone markers were interspersed among the wooden ones. Some mounds bore no marker other than a rude cross with no name inscribed. Most gave just the name and the date of death.

Susan and Barney methodically passed up and down the rows of markers, carefully reading each one. Susan printed Donald's name on a piece of paper and gave it to Barney, who laboriously compared each inscription with the paper.

Tears sprang into her eyes at the thought of so many. How many left families back East, with no one to tell them of the fate of their loved one? Many of the names had faded. Was one of these Donald? If so, how would she ever know?

"Here's one as was only five years old." Barney shook his head. "Real sad, Miss Susan. Real sad."

It took them until the sun hung low in the afternoon sky before they had looked at all of the markers. Susan stood lost in the thought of so much death when she felt Barney take her arm.

"Come, Miss Susan. Time we was a-headin' back. Be sunset soon. Boats quit runnin' after sunset." He grinned. "And I don't fancy spendin' the night here, no way. Besides, we got an hour's buggy ride to get ourselves back to Sacramento."

Susan roused herself from her reverie and smiled into the boy's anxious face. "You're right, Barney. Let's go."

Chapter 16

THAT NIGHT, AFTER THEIR VISIT to the cemetery, sleep eluded Susan for a long time. She tossed and turned on the narrow bed. The straw in the tick she lay on rustled and crackled. With a deep sigh, she realized she had turned twenty just a short time before. So much excitement had driven all thought of the date from her mind. Heavens, she thought, turning over for what she felt must be the thousandth time, I'm an old maid. Where would her life go if she could not find Donald? The thought that he could very easily be among the many graves that bore no name, or where the name had been obliterated, would not leave her mind. How would she ever know? No one had kept any records of the burials.

As she lay there in the semi-darkness, for the light from a full moon cast a bayonet of light across the foot of the bed, she heard Barney cry out in his sleep. Frightened for him, realizing he was gripped in the throes of another of his horrible nightmares, she pulled on her robe and hurried into his room.

He lay on his back with his hand across his face, muttering, "No . . . no . . . not dead, not dead!" With a startled cry, he sat up in bed. Susan crossed quickly to his side and took him in her arms.

"Hush, Barney," she soothed, stroking the damp hair back from his sweaty forehead. "It's time we laid that ghost to rest." She continued to stroke his head as he cried against her shoulder. Her heart went out to him. Poor boy, who had never been allowed to be a child. "Won't you tell me what it is that bothers you so?"

"You won't . . . you won't . . . hate me iffen I do?" The words came in a long, shuddering sob.

"Barney, I could never hate you. You know that. Sometimes circumstances drive any of us to do things we regret later."

"All right." He drew a deep breath and began. "I told you how Master was always a beatin' on me, so I already hated him for that. But the missus, she were real kindly, a gentle, helpless kinda soul, as were trapped into marriage with that monster. In Boston, I guess onct yer married to a man, he owns ye."

Susan grimaced. "Yes, unfortunately, that is all too true."

Another long shudder ran through the boy's frame. "Then, the day it happened, Master, he were roarin' drunk, an' started to pound on me for sumthin'. I ain't even sure jest what set him off that time, but he knocked me down and started kickin' me. Missus, she tried to stop him, and he grabbed her by the hair and started slammin' her face against the wall, cussin' at her for a-interferin'."

He took a deep breath. "Sumthin' in me snapped, Miss Susan. I got to my feet and grabbed an iron bar and hit him across the back of the head." He shuddered and stopped a moment, then cried out, "And I kept on hittin' him. I couldn't stop myself. I just couldn't stop! I kept poundin' and poundin', and all the times I'd wanted to hit him, all the times I'd hated him fer a-poundin' on her jest kept me a-poundin'." He fell silent. Susan held him close and said nothing, not wanting to break the spell.

Finally he stirred restlessly against her shoulder. "The missus, she finally got me to stop, but blood was everywhere. And the first thing she said was, 'Thankee, Barney. Thankee for a-givin' me back my life.' Ain't that a funny thing fer her to say?"

Susan smiled in the semi-darkness. "I think I understand her perfectly, Barney. Then what happened?"

"She cleaned all the blood offen me, give me clean clothes to put on, then burned the bloody ones in the furnace. I stood there and watched, kinda stunned, for I know they hang apprentices who hit their masters. The missus, she fixed me a bag with some food, hugged me and kissed me, and told me to skedaddle. 'Walk casual,' she said, 'so's you don't attract no attention. Real important no one takes no notice of you. I'll go back into the shop in an hour or so and find him.' She give me a faint smile. 'There's enough as hate him that I think I can persuade the constable someone came in and killed him. But you've got to be gone, just in case. He's got a brother as lives here in Boston, and he's a mean 'un too. He jest might make a fuss if you're around. Get on the first o' the ships in the harbor as is goin' somewhere a long ways from here, an' never come back.'

"I took her at her word, Miss Susan, and sauntered casual-like down to the dock and snuck aboard the *Even Tide.* I hid behind some crates in the hold until the sailor found me, safe out to sea. Thought I was a goner, though, when Mr. Thomas suggested tossin' me overboard."

"You were fortunate you picked the *Even Tide.* Captain Griffin is a fine man. He would never have allowed you to be harmed. And I'm sure Mr. Thomas knew that. He just wanted to frighten you."

"Well, he sure did. I were right scared, I tell you." Barney lay back against the bed and smiled at Susan. She could barely make out his face in the dim light. "So now you know what I done. I'm a murderer. I killed the Master. What scares me the worst is, I let the rage take holt of me like that. I couldn't stop a-hittin' on him. Understand?"

"I understand very well, Barney. You were driven beyond endurance. But you didn't do it to protect yourself. You did it to protect your mistress, who was a good woman. I am inclined to agree with her. You did her a favor." She patted the hand that lay on the sheet. "Now, I want you to do *me* a favor. This will remain our secret, and you will stop feeling you are a bad person for what you did. It's over and behind you. Do you understand?"

"Yes, Miss Susan."

"And another thing. Johnny Lee says his brother's dog just whelped, and he's got a half dozen puppies to find a home for. Do you think you are ready to have your own dog?"

"Oh, Miss Susan! Do you mean it? Can I really have my own dog?"

Susan laughed softly at his eagerness. "Yes, I mean it. Johnny Lee will take you to his brother's tomorrow so you can pick the one you want."

"Oh, Miss Susan, you're so good to me. And," the boy declared fervently, "I'm gonna call him Jake."

A week later, as Susan relaxed with a cup of coffee while Peggy and Maggie cleared the tables from the breakfast rush, a man dressed in miner's garb entered. He held a copy of the *Sacramento Union* in his hand. Susan felt the blood rush to her face. Could he be here in response to her ad?

Maggie greeted the man. "Be ye here for breakfast, sir?"

"No," he responded, and added with a smile, "though I hear this be the best place in town fer grub now. No, I come a'lookin' for a Miss McGuire."

Susan rose, pleased to hear his comment about the quality of the food, but much more interested in his reason for coming. "I'm Miss McGuire. Can I help you?"

He grinned. "Looks more like I kin help you. This here your notice?"

Her vocal cords tightened. Could he have the answer? Unable to speak, she just nodded.

"Met a young feller in Placerville 'bout a year ago, gave his name as Donald Andrew. Tall feller? Dark hair, hazel eyes? Dimple in his chin?"

"Yes," Susan managed to say, forcing her throat to relax. "Yes. Is he still there?"

"Dunno. My claim ran dry, so I left Placerville and went up Bidwell's Bar way. Been up there 'til I come back here last week. Friend o' mine as were travelin' with me, he reads right good, an' he seen your notice in the paper." He looked at her intently. "Andrew kin o' yourn?"

She flushed. "In a way," she answered, not wanting to discuss the real reason she sought Donald. "Friends of mine in Boston asked me to look him up. He's kin to them. They've never heard a word from him, so when they learned I planned to travel here . . . ." her words trailed off as she found herself unable to continue the lie under his scrutiny. Although it's not completely a lie, she defended herself. Mary and Elizabeth did ask me to find Donald for them.

"Spent a lot of time at the *Empire* Hotel, he did. A lot of time," he repeated dryly. "George Henry were a-runnin' the place then. Andrew usta board there when he were in town an' had enough dust to pay his shot. Stay 'til he used it up, then go back to the diggin's." He hesitated, and Susan felt sure he wanted to say more, but she did not ask. "Anyways, that's what he were a-doin' last time I seen him."

"Thank you." Susan offered the grizzled miner her hand. He clasped it in his own, a huge hand with gnarled fingers, and their eyes met. She saw the sympathy in the deep, brown eyes, and wondered what he withheld from her. But he had nothing to add. He had completed his mission.

"Good luck to you, Miss." He turned on his heel and strode from the room, leaving Susan tongue-tied. She wanted to offer him a meal, at least, but before she could find her voice, he had vanished from her sight.

"Golly, Miss Susan, do you suppose he's right? Are we gonna go to Placerville to look for Mr. Andrew?" Barney's eyes grew round.

"No, Barney, we are not. I will go. I need you to stay here."

"But Miss Susan, Placerville is a long way, an' I hear they's a rough bunch as hangs out there, and . . . "

"I will be fine, Barney," she said in the firm voice which said the discussion had ended. "You have to stay here and see the hotel continues to run smoothly." She smiled at him. "We don't want to come back and find ourselves out of a job, do we?"

Barney grunted, mollified. "Yer prob'ly right. Mrs. Dolan and them two girls, they ain't got a whit of sense between 'em."

Susan laughed to herself. "Now," she told him. "Get over to the Pioneer Stage line and get some information on the schedules. I would like to leave next Monday."

"Yes'm." He scurried out the door, Jake at his heels. She watched them go with a smile. The puppy had been a stroke of genius on her part. Tears sprang to her eyes as she remembered watching him pick the puppy that most closely resembled the unfortunate shipboard Jake. The two quickly became inseparable. The proprietor of the hotel, who felt quite firmly that a dog's place was outside, conceded to Susan's wishes with great reluctance and allowed Jake to sleep with Barney in Barney's room.

Her thoughts reverted to the words of their visitor. More than what he said was what he did not say. She remembered his references to Donald spending all of his gold before returning to the diggings. Could that be why he never wrote? Could he have been embarrassed to admit he did not get rich? Or was there another reason? She tried to ignore the nagging doubts that assailed her. Did she really know Donald as well as she thought she did? She remembered the whiffs of brandy on his breath that had bothered her so often back in Boston and felt a stir of uneasiness.

She sighed. Only one way to find out, she thought. I just have to go there. And I'd better get started if I plan to be gone for a while. She strode back through the swinging doors to the kitchen. "Mrs. Dolan," she called. "Maggie, Peggy, we have something to discuss."

That evening she wrote a brief letter to Mary and Elizabeth. "News at last," she wrote. "A man came by and said he saw Donald in Placerville." She did not say it had been a whole year since the man had seen him. "I am leaving Monday to see if I can locate him. I will give him your love and scold him for not writing to you."

Chapter 17

ON THE FOLLOWING MONDAY, October 6, 1851, Barney accompanied Susan to the big staging area from which the coaches departed north, south, east, and west, to Marysville, Stockton, Placerville, and San Francisco. Barney carried her satchel on one arm, Jake on the other. Men and animals milled about, shouting and jostling one another. Piles of baggage lay strewn about with no apparent order.

"Heaven above, Barney," she sighed, staring at the confusion in front of her. "How does anyone ever figure out which stage to take in the middle of all of this chaos?"

He grinned. "The driver, he hollers out where he's a-goin'. The Placerville stage leaves from over here." He led her unerringly to a Concord coach that, though magnificent in its day, would be improved with a bit of paint and leather polish. Time and weather had sadly tarnished the once elegant brass fittings. Four men sat on the black leather seats, but there were seats inside for nine, so she anticipated no difficulty in obtaining a place. She watched another stage leave with all of its seats filled and a dozen men clinging to the top.

"I'd better get aboard while there are still seats," she told Barney. "I certainly have no wish to be forced to ride on top."

"I'd like to see the man who wouldn't give you his seat, Miss Susan," Barney growled, clenching his fist. "I'd teach him some manners right quick."

Susan laughed. "I don't think it will come to that, Barney. Stow my bag for me, please."

The clerk approached to collect her fare. As she carefully counted out the coins, he invited her to have breakfast in the small dining room before departing.

"Venison and beans and right good coffee, Miss," he said. "Mr. Stevens, him as runs the stage, he used to have a hotel and restaurant, so he knows what he's about. Makes some mighty fine grub, he do."

"Thank you," Susan declined with a smile, "but I have dined. When does the stage depart?"

"'Bout half an hour. Soon's the driver gets here. He's on time most days, when he ain't a bit under the weather, so to speak."

Great, Susan thought wryly. A half drunk coachman is just what I need. The clerk went off shouting. "Stage for Placerville now loading!"

Twenty minutes later the driver strode up and smiled at Susan. "Mornin', Miss." He doffed his rumpled hat. "Ain't offen I git to carry a charmin' young lady like yourself." He opened the door. "You," he ordered, waving an imperious arm at the miner seated on the center bench, "move over an' let the young lady hev thet seat."

The miner hastened to obey, and the driver offered Susan his hand to help her climb into the coach. "This here seat's the most comfy ridin'. You jest set back an' enjoy the trip. Gonna take right good care o' you, I am."

He strode to the front of the carriage and began a methodical check of the rigging and the four sturdy horses in the traces. Barney looked relieved. Susan had to laugh.

"See, Barney," she told him, leaning out the window to clasp his hand in farewell. "I told you I will be fine. You take care of the hotel and Jake." Jake, held securely under Barney's left arm, tried to lick Susan's hand and Barney's chin at the same time.

Apparently satisfied with the hostler's work, the driver climbed up to the high bench and shouted, "All aboard for Brighton, Mormon Island, Mud Springs, and Placerville!" He waited a moment, and, when no one else appeared, yelled a loud "Gee-up." The hostler released the bridle on the lead horse and jumped clear. Susan's head jerked back as the horses took off on a run, amidst shouts and cracks of the whip, and the creak of the harness.

"Goodbye, Barney," Susan cried, her voice drowned by the clattering of hooves, the shouts of the drivers, and the rattle of the stages rolling out of the yard. She sat back against the seat and tried to relax as the motion of the coach rocked her back and forth. She grimaced. It was going to be a long nine hours.

But she soon began to enjoy the ride. The miner in the seat beside her had not bathed for an indeterminate length of time, so she tried to keep her head as close to the window as possible. Fortunately, the breeze came from her side, so most of the dust raised by the horses' hooves blew to the opposite side. Her fellow passengers included a well dressed gentleman and another miner who smelled like he had spent the weekend in a saloon. This man slept peacefully, if somewhat noisily, with his head resting against the side of the coach. Susan marveled at how he could sleep so soundly when every rut sent his head bouncing off of the metal bar.

The gentleman seated across from her smiled as he noticed her watching the sleeper. "Much booze as he had, no wonder," the man said with distaste. "He could sleep through an earthquake."

The stage rumbled past Sutter's Fort. She noticed with dismay how badly it needed repair. Mr. Sutter, she had been told, had abandoned the fort and retired to Hock Farm, his home on the Feather River. She thought of him with some sympathy, for she knew his vast holdings had been usurped by settlers, some of whom he had helped rescue. She had also heard his pleas for reimbursement from the United States Government had proved futile. Thinking about Mr. Sutter's plight, she recalled reading a recent article in the *Sacramento Union* that said someone, she had forgotten who, had presented a bill in the State Legislature to provide some recompense to Sutter in recognition of his humanitarian efforts. Maybe he would eventually get something. She hoped so. It only seemed fair.

The stage stopped briefly at Brighton, where they gained four more passengers who climbed up on top, and proceeded to Mormon Island. There two more miners joined them. After the stop at Mormon Island, the stage rolled out across the plain for several hours at a steady pace. The road, to Susan's relief, proved relatively smooth and level and allowed them to make good time.

About one o'clock, the stage pulled up to an unprepossessing roadside inn where the driver announced they would stop for a meal and to change horses. He opened the door and, with great dignity, assisted Susan to alight. She could barely suppress a giggle at his solicitude. As if I might break, she thought. But she did have to admit his care made her feel more secure, taking off on this wild adventure all by herself.

The tough beefsteak, boiled potatoes with no gravy, and stewed beans did not tempt her appetite. The chunk of steak she tried to chew grew larger and larger in her mouth until she finally surreptitiously hid it in her handkerchief. The potatoes, while at least not tough, had been boiled almost to mush, leaving the resulting mass watery and tasteless. The beans stuck in her throat, and required large amounts of water to wash them down. She gave up on the nasty looking compound of dried apples. She noticed her fellow travelers managed to get the apples down by pouring over large amounts of molasses. She assumed the proprietor kept the jug on each table for that purpose.

Leaving the dining room, she took a short walk outside to stretch her legs before the afternoon's ride. During a brief visit to the outhouse, she disposed of the unchewable chunk of beef she had hidden in her handkerchief. She spent as little time in the facility as possible, holding her breath the whole time, for it smelled bad even for an outhouse. She tried to ignore where previous occupants had aimed with more enthusiasm than skill.

While waiting for the journey to resume, Susan looked towards the mountains. Surrounded by oak trees whose leaves had just begun to change to a golden yellow, she marveled at the beauty of the scene before her. The distant mountains tumbled over each other, each one rising higher than the one before it. No wonder they needed fresh horses.

An hour after their arrival at the stage stop, a shout from the driver summoned the passengers and they started on their way again. The horses began their struggle up the gradual ascent. As the elevation rose, each mountain increased in magnitude. Oak trees became more scraggly, and soon began to be interspersed with pines.

By late afternoon, they stopped at Mud Springs. There several of the passengers riding on the top disembarked, and fresh horses were again hooked up to the coach. Susan took advantage of the brief respite to walk around a little and get the cramps out of her legs.

The last stretch into Placerville took longer, for the road grew progressively steeper. The scent of pine trees surrounded them, mingled with the smell of pine smoke from cooking fires in the camps of the numerous miners who studded the area.

The stage pulled up in front of the *El Dorado* Hotel where the hostlers ran to tend the horses. Susan looked around. The main street slanted downhill, with numerous wooden buildings staggered up and down the thoroughfare. As she pondered on where to stay, the driver approached her. He held her satchel in one hand. With a shy smile, he offered her his arm.

"Miss, unless you got other plans, I think you ought ta stay at the *Empire.* Friend o' mine runs it, and I kin tell him to keep a' eye on you."

"Why, thank you." She accepted the proffered arm and they walked the short distance to the *Empire.* Susan had hoped to stay at the *Empire* anyway. Since Donald spent his time there, perhaps someone would remember him. She noticed a chill in the air, and commented on how much cooler it seemed here than in Sacramento City.

"Higher in the mountains. Even get some snow here, time to time. Melts quick, but nights get pretty chilly. My friend George, now, him as runs the *Empire,* he'll see you got plenty o' blankets. And iffen you need sumthin', you just tell 'im."

"Thank you, Mr. . . . er . . . ," Susan began

"Charlie. Just Charlie. Everyone knows ol' Charlie. Remember now, iffen you need anythin' at all, Miss, you jest tell George to tell Charlie."

"Thank you, Charlie. You have been so kind to me. I hope you will be my driver on my return journey."

With a smile that Susan could have sworn was wistful, he tipped his hat and opened the door for her to enter. Handing her satchel to the clerk, he turned on his heel and left.

Evening found Susan settled in her little room after agreeing upon a price for a week's room and board. She stood at her window and stared out over the main street at the traffic passing up and down. Placerville was a busy place. Miners with burros mingled with neat buggies of the more well-to-do citizens, and with carts carrying all shapes and sizes of boxes, barrels and bales. She watched a nondescript dog chase a cat up onto the roof of a nearby shed. The dog set up an excited barking. The cat looked down on the noisy animal with disdain from the safety of her elevated perch. The dog kept up his strident chorus. A loud shout from the interior of the shed, followed by a boot sailing out to strike the unfortunate mutt, ended the cacophony.

Susan laughed at the scene, then sobered as she thought of the task before her. Where do I begin? She sighed. All I have to show is this one small portrait. The clerk at the desk, when she inquired, had said Mr. Henry was out of town. He himself had only been in Placerville a few months, and had never heard of Donald Andrew.

She finally decided the best thing for her to do at the moment was go to bed. Her day had begun at daybreak, and she had to confess to her exhaustion. I'll start my search tomorrow, she thought, and burrowed under the blankets in the surprisingly comfortable bed. For a few moments the voices and clatters from outside kept her awake, but she soon drifted into a deep, dreamless sleep.

Chapter 18

"HERE, YOU YOUNG-INS, you git along outta there, y' hear me?"

The shouting woke Susan from a sound sleep and she blinked in the unfamiliar surroundings, trying to orient herself. Memory flooded back. I'm in Placerville, she thought. Excitement surged through her. Today I begin my search for Donald! To think they could be in the same town, after all those weary miles of travel, and that today could be the day she would find the answers that had eluded her for so long. She sat up in bed as the racket continued outside her window.

"I'm sick to death of you gol-durn kids a-diggin' under my sidewalk. Last time you left sich a hole the boards teetered and Mr. Tunney like to fell on his keester, he did."

Susan's curiosity overcame her reluctance to leave the warmth of the blankets. She wrapped her robe about her and hurried to the window. Looking out, she saw a half dozen rag-tag boys who stood just out of range of the broom wielded by the indignant clerk. Apparently he had been doing the shouting. Each boy carried a small wooden pail laden with dirt.

She wondered what all the fuss was about until she remembered. Of course. The miners all carried little bags of gold dust. When they came into town, especially when they got to drinking and carousing, they probably spilled some of the dust. She chuckled at the enterprise of the boys. The dust would filter between the boards on the sidewalk. The dirt underneath those walkways probably had as much gold as the miners' original claims.

Hunger pangs reminded her she had not eaten supper the night before. On the trip up, she had eaten only those watery boiled potatoes and sticky beans. The smell of bacon frying reached her nostrils. Washing quickly in the icy cold water on the stand, she dressed and joined her fellow boarders in the dining room.

The seven men sitting around the table looked up as she entered, and conversation ceased as they quickly rose to their feet. One man hurried to pull out a chair for her. She stifled a giggle.

"Please, gentlemen, don't let me interrupt your meal."

The waiter brought her a plate stacked with bacon, fried potatoes smothered in grease, a slab of dark-colored meat she could not identify, a runny egg, and a huge chunk of bread. She looked at the pile with dismay. Surely he didn't expect her to eat all of that! She would be lucky to get around half of it. A tin cup of coffee placed in front of her gave off a welcome steam in the chilly room, but when she tasted it, she found it so vile she could barely swallow the sip she had in her mouth. She smiled to herself. Mrs. Dolan's cooking has spoiled me for the usual California fare. No wonder our restaurant is so popular.

The conversation seemed stilted after she joined the group. She wondered how long it would take them to adjust to her presence. Women were no longer the oddity they had been in '49 and '50. She had even seen a couple of ladies walking along the street when she arrived the previous day, but apparently young women who traveled alone were still rare.

Well, she thought, if I'm going to find Donald, I had better begin. She smiled at the gentleman seated on her right, a kindly looking man of indeterminate years, with grizzled hair and fleshy jowls that covered his starched collar. Susan found herself wondering what brought him to town. Taking out the miniature painting of Donald, she showed it to him.

"Excuse me," she said, continuing to smile. He looked a little flustered. "I am seeking the whereabouts of this young man. His name is Donald Andrew, and he came in '49. I have been told he lives here in the Placerville area."

The man studied the picture, then looked at her shrewdly. "And why be ye a lookin' for him, if I may be so bold?"

She knew this question would come, and had carefully rehearsed her plausible story in her mind. "I worked for his father as governess to his two younger sisters. When they learned I planned to travel to California, they asked me to seek his whereabouts." She smiled again. "He has not written, and they are understandably concerned."

The man harrumphed, and conceded he could see where this might be the case, "there bein' so much cholery and sich among them as come." He studied the picture again and shook his head. "Don't know as I've ever seen 'im. 'Course, I ain't from these parts. Hail from up Kelsey way, I do. Only been here since day before yestiddy."

Her heart sank as the picture passed from hand to hand around the table with the same discouraging shakes of the head. Apparently this would be harder than she thought. With a shrug, she tucked the picture back in her reticule and thanked the men for their help. Realizing she would have to go farther afield, she returned her attention to her breakfast.

The meat had a strong taste she could not identify, so she asked one of her fellow diners what kind of animal it came from.

"Why, that's grizzly b'ar meat, ma'am. Mighty fine eatin', long's you get off a quick shot. Otherwise, 'stid 'a you eatin' the b'ar, the b'ar'll eat you!" He laughed at his own sally.

Susan managed a small smile in acknowledgment. Her appetite disappeared. She excused herself and departed the dining room.

Back in her room, she stood and stared out of the window at the activity in the street for a long time. She shivered and pulled her shawl more closely about her shoulders. The sun slowly warmed the room, and promised a pleasant day. Fall approached, and, even though the weather in California was supposed to be much milder than in Boston, she could not depend on the good weather lasting forever. A rainstorm could wash out the roads and trap her here for weeks. She had to get started on her search.

Besides, although she trusted Barney's business acumen, she did not have too much faith in his tact. His patience with Mrs. Dolan and Maggie and Peggy ran short very quickly. She had visions of him getting the girls so distressed they would sit and cry instead of working, like the owner had done before Susan took over the management. She dared not be gone longer than the week she planned. Besides, she thought with a chuckle, if she took any longer, Barney just might get it in his head to come up here looking for her.

But where to start! At the beginning, she told herself. Start on one end of the street and stop in every shop and speak to everyone you meet. If only she had a larger picture, or enough pictures to spread around. Well, I don't, she thought with a heavy sigh at the prospect of the job ahead of her, so I will have to make do with what I have.

She tied her bonnet under her chin and picked up her reticule. Might as well get on with it.

When she returned to the *Empire*, late in the afternoon, the sun already dipped low behind the hills to the west. It would be dark in another hour. She threw her bonnet and reticule on the table and collapsed onto the bed. Her feet hurt, her legs ached from walking up and down the hilly streets, and dust covered her from head to foot. She knew she should clean up and go down to supper, but the thought of the greasy food from breakfast left her with no appetite.

She chuckled. At one small cafe where she stopped to question the patrons, the proprietor took pity on her and offered her a piece of pie and a cup of coffee. The coffee, although so strong she felt it would take the enamel off her teeth, had not been so bad, and the pie had actually been pretty tasty. That, combined with her fatigue and discouragement, convinced her to skip supper.

She managed to get her shoes off before she fell asleep.

Susan woke in the middle of the night with a start, shivering from the cold. She had fallen asleep without even pulling a blanket over herself. She got off of the bed and walked to the window, wrapping her shawl around her shoulders. Moonlight bathed the quiet street. She had no idea how long she had slept, or how close it was to daybreak. No hint of pink showed in the east, so it had to be at least an hour away.

A yawn forced its way past her lips. I really should try to get some more sleep in order to walk all over town again tomorrow, she thought. Or later today. Whatever. She shook her head. Was there something else she could try? She yawned again. I'll think about it in the morning, she told herself.

She took off her dress, crawled under the blankets and fell asleep within moments.

The second day was a repeat of the first. This time, she started her return trip sooner, and reached the hotel in time to rest for a while before supper. She was ravenous, for she had skipped breakfast, and no one had offered her anything. She had read the menu at the El Dorado when she stopped there, and the rice pudding with brandied peaches tempted her palate, but she was not about to pay two dollars for it, especially when she had already paid for her board at the *Empire*.

A very depressed Susan presented herself at the supper table, and, hungry as she was, did very little justice to the codfish balls and baked beans placed in front of her. How she would have loved a nice cup of tea! She sighed. Memories of the leisurely afternoons seated on the poop deck of the *Even Tide* with Mrs. Griffin, and the companionship they had shared, flooded her mind. She wondered how the *Even Tide* fared on her trip to the Sandwich Islands. At that moment, she almost regretted not continuing with the bark on her voyage across the Pacific. What an adventure that would have been!

Dr. Alexander's blue eyes intruded into her memory. She closed her eyes and again saw him as he left the ship. Why can't I forget him? Here I am searching for Donald, hoping to marry him, and I can't get Dr. Alexander out of my mind. She remembered the thrill she felt when she helped him deliver Consuela's baby. Susan could still feel the touch of his hand as he bid her farewell that cold morning in San Francisco Bay. He thinks I'm marrying Peter Thomas, she thought glumly. No wonder he has dismissed me from his mind.

She shook her head and smiled brightly at the gentleman on her right. He had said something to her, although she had no idea what. "I'm sorry," she said. "I'm afraid I was wool-gathering. What did you say?"

He smiled back. "You did seem to be miles away. I asked how your search progressed."

"Not well," she sighed. "Hardly anyone seems to have any memory of seeing a Donald Andrew, and the few who do remember him deny all knowledge of his present whereabouts." She did not mention the hesitancy with which some of these responses were given, but they made her uneasy. She smiled brightly at her companion to cover her own mixed feelings. "And I have to return to Sacramento soon."

"I have a friend," her companion offered, "a young man named David Burnside, who is a very talented artist. He can do wonders with a piece of charcoal. I spoke with him of your search, and he has offered to sketch several larger portraits for you. Perhaps if you post them about the town, someone will come in from some of the outer diggings who has a more recent memory of the young gentleman."

Susan's hopes resurged. "What a wonderful idea!" Then she hesitated. "But I cannot afford to pay him very much . . . ." Her voice trailed off.

Her new friend raised his hand. "Davy has offered his services for no charge. He makes more than enough from the miners." The man chuckled. "He tried his hand at placer mining, but decided a lot easier way to get the gold was to let others dig for it. He has done quite well for himself. He goes into the saloons, and, while the miners are drinking, sketches their picture. By then, they are so drunk they pay him whatever he asks."

Susan laughed. She could see Donald doing just that.

"He will be here this evening," the man continued. "I took the liberty of asking him to drop by."

"Thank you. I will be pleased to meet him."

David Burnside turned out to be a delightful young man. He took Susan's miniature of Donald with him, and returned the following morning with a life sized sketch that looked so much like Donald it took her breath away.

"What a marvelous likeness, Mr. Burnside," she exclaimed. "You are very talented."

"Thank you, Miss McGuire," he said shyly. "I'm glad you like my work. Now that I got this one, I'll make up a dozen or so more and we can post them. Where can folks contact you if they recognize him? I'll make a note of that information on the back of each one."

"At the *Southern House* on 'J' Street in Sacramento City,"

she said. "I live there, and manage the housekeeping services. Everyone knows me."

"I'll be back tomorrow. By then I'll have at least a dozen of these. We'll go 'round and post 'em." He offered her a shy smile. "I'd be right proud if you'd allow me to buy you supper at the *El Dorado* tomorrow evening. They make pretty good grub."

"Thank you. That will be lovely." She owed him that much, and the greasy food at the *Empire* was becoming too much to bear. "I will plan to return to Sacramento the following morning."

Young Mr. Burnside proved a charming companion. He did not look much older than Barney. She found herself wondering what had brought him clear out here all by himself. Another runaway apprentice? She did not want to ask, and he volunteered no personal information. But although reticent to discuss himself, he grew quite voluble on the local history. As they walked the streets posting the portraits in the different saloons and cafes, he told her stories of the early days of the town. He pointed out an oak tree near the northeast corner of Main and Coloma Streets.

"That's the old hang tree," he said, "where a mob hung three men accused of attempted robbery and murder."

Susan looked at the tree and shuddered. "When did that happen?"

"Back in January of '49. Wasn't much law in those days. Mostly by vigilante committee. Placerville's original name was Dry Diggings, named by young William Daylor, the feller who first found gold here in the creek sometime in '48. He called it that because the creek is almost dry in the summer." He shook his head. "Fine young man, Daylor was, from what I hear. Died of the cholera in the epidemic of '50. Took it from a stranger he found dying, and was trying to help."

"How sad. He must have been a good man, to risk his

life to help a stranger. It must have been a terrible time. I know my cook lost her husband and two of her children." Susan returned her attention to the weathered oak in front of her. "I wonder what the tree would say if it could speak?"

"Plenty, I'm sure. It all happened before I came. I got here in August of '49," the young artist continued. "Mr. Buffum, the editor of the *Alta California*, he was here at the time as a lieutenant in Stevenson's New York Volunteers. He told me all about it. Said five men as were caught robbing a Mexican gambler were ordered flogged. Flogging was a common way to treat thieves then, since there were no jails."

"I hope they don't do that any more."

"Not around the settled areas. Sometimes out in the camps. Anyway, since it was Sunday when the flogging was scheduled, a whole mob come to town to watch. Some of them got pretty liquored up. After the floggings, someone yelled that three of the men had attempted to rob and murder someone down on the Stanislaus River. Whether they did or not, no one seemed to care much. The mob demanded they be hung to rid the community of such evildoers."

"Without a trial?"

"Well, they had a trial of sorts, a pretty informal one. None of the three could speak enough English to defend themselves."

"Oh, Davy, how dreadful! To hang those poor men with no evidence at all."

Her companion chuckled. "That's what Mr. Buffum tried to say. He got up on a stump and protested the action, but the crowd threatened to hang him too if he did not cease his complaints. He said they were drunk enough to carry out the threat, so he quietly got down from the stump and said no more."

"And so they hung all three of them?"

"Yes, still bleeding from the flogging and pleading for an interpreter. From that day on, everyone called the place Hangtown. It was Hangtown until February of '50 when the State Legislature decided that was too undignified, and changed the name to Placerville."

"I think I like Placerville better," Susan declared. In her mind she could hear the cries of the doomed men and the shouts of the angry mob. She shivered and took Davy's arm. "Let's go."

Chapter 19

POUNDING ON HER door woke her from a sound sleep the next morning. At first, Susan covered her head to shut out the sound and tried to recapture a fading dream. But the pounding persisted. Finally, her dormant senses aroused and she remembered telling the clerk to awaken her before dawn, since she planned to catch the early morning stage for Sacramento.

"All right, I'm awake! Thank you," she shouted to the unseen person hammering on the door.

"When your bag's packed, Miss McGuire, tell me and I'll come up and git it," the voice on the other side of the door responded. "Charlie, he's already tol' me he won't go 'til you're ready."

Susan chuckled at Charlie's determination to take care of her. She found herself looking forward to the return trip. She lighted her candle and hurried to dress in the chilly room. She had packed her bag the night before and hastily tucked in her nightgown. Descending to the lobby, she dispatched the clerk to fetch her bag. Charlie stood by the counter waiting for her, a welcoming smile spread across his broad face.

"How nice to see you, Charlie," she greeted him. "I am so glad I will be riding with you again."

"You're lookin' mighty pert for so early in the mornin'," he grinned down at her, the tobacco-stains prominent on his teeth. At least, she thought, he is always clean shaven. He doesn't have the usual yellow stains most men have in their beards. He picked up her satchel and offered his arm.

She looked with dismay at the number of men crowded in and around the stage. The thought of being crushed among all of those unwashed bodies did not appeal to her at all. I wish I could ride in front with Charlie, she thought. On an impulse, she decided to ask and approached him. "Charlie, can't I ride in the box with you? I love the feel of fresh air in my face, and you can point out the sights to me as we go along."

"Why, shore, little lady. I'd be right proud to hev yer company. Jest let me get a blanket to pad the seat fer ye a bit."

Susan watched with amusement as he fussed around making a comfortable seat for her, then assisted her to climb to the elevated perch. The passengers stuffed themselves into the body of the big Concord coach, and those left over climbed up on top.

Charlie walked around, scanning the equipment with a critical eye, then bellowed, "Mud Springs, Mormon Island, Brighton, and Sacramento City! Board!" He finished checking the gear on the horses, then climbed up beside her and gathered the reins. "Let 'er go," he ordered the hostler who stood holding the halter of the lead horse. The hostler stepped back, and the horses took off. Susan grabbed the rail and held on for dear life as they clattered down Main Street, soon leaving Placerville well behind them.

As the day grew warmer and the horses settled into a steady pace, she relaxed and watched the trees go by. Three deer grazing in a little meadow looked up as the stage passed, but did not move. On several occasions, large rabbits scurried across in front of the horses, stopping on the other side and raising their big, long ears. Susan laughed at the sight of them and asked Charlie what they were called.

"They are so much larger than the rabbits I've seen in the East," she said. She had seen one rabbit, once, when her parents took her on a drive from Boston to Concord.

"Why, them's jack-ass rabbits," Charlie informed her. "Call 'em that because they got ears like a jack-ass. Make pretty good eatin', they do." Susan remembered the listing on the menu at the *El Dorado*, and decided that creature must be the rabbit they served.

A sudden jolt almost threw her off, and she decided she had better pay closer attention to the road. It seemed to be a series of precipices the stage kept leaping over with crashing and thumping sounds. But she was never frightened. Charlie handled the team so well she had every confidence in him.

"Do any of the stages ever crash?" she finally ventured to ask. "Are people ever hurt?"

"Oh, yeah, kill 'em quite lively on some routes. But Mr. Stevens, now, he won't keep a driver as gets drunk or reckless. Bad for bizness, mashing up passengers and stages. Get alang, my beauties," he called to the horses as they reached an open stretch.

A cloud of dust enveloped them and Susan shut her eyes and coughed. "How can you see the road in all this dust?" she asked.

"Smell it!" Charlie replied. "Traveled these roads so often I kin tell where the road is by the sound o' the wheels. Rattle good on hard ground. Don't hear no rattle, got ter look over the side and see where she's a'goin'."

He grinned over at her. "An' when I git a little skeered, I chaws more 'backy."

"Don't you get tired of going over the same road time and time again?"

"Ain't never the same, Miss McGuire. Road conditions, passengers, horses, everthin's a little different each time. Keeps it interestin'." He pulled back on the reins as the settlement of Mud Springs appeared in the distance. "Ready for a bite o' breakfast?"

"Reckon I am," she replied. Heavens, she thought. I'm beginning to talk just like him. I might even be able to bring myself to eat some of the so-called food they serve at this establishment.

As much as she enjoyed the trip and Charlie's company, Susan greeted the outskirts of Sacramento City with a sigh of relief. Dust clung to her, and she felt it chafing where it worked its way into her clothing. She looked forward to getting back to the hotel and soaking in a warm tub. All the bouncing and jostling left her sore and aching.

As the stage pulled into the yard, she immediately spotted Barney, waving and shouting in his pleasure at her return. Bless him, she thought. He has come to meet me. Love for him swept over her. He who had never known a mother had accepted her in the role with unvaunted enthusiasm.

"Miss Susan, I'm so glad you come back early. I kinda felt you might. Any luck?"

"Not much, I'm afraid," she sighed, accepting his hand to alight. "I never dreamed the population of the town changed so fast. Most of the men there were not even around a year ago." She hugged him. "How on earth did you know I would be coming in on this stage?"

"Didn't," he grinned. "Been a'meetin' the stage from Placerville ev'ry night since you left. Charlie's been tellin' me how you fared. Seems he were a-keepin' a' eye on you. I felt better, knowin' he was a-lookin' after you."

"Well. I'm glad you are here. I have to confess I did not look forward to carrying my satchel back to the hotel." She turned to Charlie. "Thank you so much, Charlie, for your care and for your company." She offered him her hand. "I certainly did enjoy the trip. You are an excellent driver. I must drop a note to Mr. Stevens and tell him what an exemplary employee you are."

Charlie looked a little confused, but he pumped her hand with enthusiasm. "My pleasure, Miss. Any time you got to go back, you just ask fer ol' Charlie." He tipped his battered hat and turned to check on his other passengers, one of whom demanded to know what Charlie had done with his baggage.

With a laugh, Susan turned back to Barney and accepted the arm he offered. He's getting so grown up, she thought with a smile. And he is learning beautiful manners. "And how did things go while you were in charge?"

'Ev'rythin's fine. Them two girls is as flighty as ever, so I hadda keep an eye on 'em or they'd a forgot half the things you told 'em to do." He snorted in disgust. "If their ma wa'n't such a good cook, I'd be for chuckin' 'em." He took the satchel Charlie handed to him and grinned down at her. "I'm right glad you're back. Let's go home."

Life settled into a routine after her return from Placerville. Week after week her little notice ran in the *Sacramento Union* and the *Alta California*. The leaves turned color and the days grew short as fall faded into winter. Susan often stood by her window watching the activity in the street. She found herself studying the face of every man who passed. Where was Donald? Was he still alive? Did he still love her? Or had he ever loved her? Had the love only been one-sided? Or did she really love him as she once thought she did? She found herself asking that question more and more as time passed.

She managed to get a letter off to Mary and Elizabeth, telling them of her abortive trip to Placerville. She knew they would wonder if she had been successful.

"My trip to Placerville, while very interesting, was, unfortunately, fruitless," she wrote. "I could find no one who could tell me where Donald is now."

She did not mention the feeling she had gotten from the

miner who told her he had seen Donald in Placerville, or the wariness she had sensed among some of the Placerville residents who remembered him. Nothing had really been said, but her sense of uneasiness persisted. She felt it best not to say anything to the girls until she actually found him, or at least determined if he still lived.

In mid-November, the rains began, turning the dusty streets into seas of mud, which men then tracked in, getting mud all over the floor Maggie and Peggy were forced to scrub regularly. The fog rolled in, and some days she did not see the sun except for brief periods in the afternoon, if at all. On such gray days, her discouragement deepened. Sometimes she felt her soul as bleak as the fog. At such times, only Barney's cheerful good will and open adoration for her kept her from giving in to the despair and desolation she felt so deeply.

On occasion, a passer-by would remind her of Dr. Alexander. At those times, the memory of those incredible blue eyes intruded into her mind, and she would think again of the pain that had stabbed through her as she watched him walk away from her. His last words wishing her and Peter Thomas every happiness echoed in her mind. Why could she not forget him? He had obviously forgotten her.

Two days before Christmas, Charlie appeared at the hotel with a small pine tree from the forests of Placerville.

"Felt ye should have a wee tree for the Yule, ma'am," he smiled, with the same wistful smile she had seen on his face before. She wondered if perhaps he had lost a daughter, or someone dear to him whom she resembled.

"Thank you, Charlie. It was sweet of you to remember me. Could you perhaps join us for Christmas dinner?"

His face beamed. "Why, thankee, ma'am. Tha's right neighborly of ye, ta think o' ol' Charlie."

* * *

After Christmas, time dragged. The proprietor of the hotel proposed marriage, but Susan declined with thanks. She thought more and more of Dr. Alexander, reliving the experiences they shared in Valparaiso and Saint Catherine's. She took Donald's picture out often, for she found him fading from her memory.

You are never going to find him, she told herself at last. And you are probably never going to see Dr. Alexander again either. Why should he come to a backwater town like Sacramento when he had a thriving practice in the sophisticated city of San Francisco? With a deep sigh, she realized she had better get on with her life. But what should she do? Life stretched out before her in one long, unvarying round of serving meals and changing linen. She just knew it would never change.

Until one dreary cold February morning.

Chapter 20

BARNEY RAN INTO the kitchen, breathless with excitement. "Miss Susan, Miss Susan! There's a man here, miner from his dress. Got your pitcher o' Donald, he do, an' he's askin' to see you."

Hope surged through Susan's body and she quickly gave the long-handled spoon she held to the girl beside her. "Here, Maggie, stir this stew. Don't let it burn." She tucked in an errant curl that had strayed out from under her snood, wiped her hands on her apron, and, not without some trepidation, followed Barney back to the restaurant.

A grizzled miner stood by the counter, his battered hat in one hand, the portrait of Donald in the other. Although folded and frayed from being carried, she recognized it immediately as one of the charcoal sketches she and Davy Burnside had distributed among the hotels and saloons in Placerville.

"Miss McGuire?" He held out his work-worn hand. She placed hers in it, conscious of the rough skin and gnarled fingers as he enveloped her hand in his. "Seen this in the *El Dorado Hotel*, where the barkeep sez you were a'lookin' for this young feller."

"Yes, yes," she gasped. "I am. Do you know where he is?"

"Wal, been 'bout a year since I seen 'im. Told me he was gonna move to Marysville, gonna hang out his shingle as a lawyer." He grinned. "Said diggin' for gold was too much work." He shook his head. "Course, any gold he did get he spent at one o' the saloons. 'Scuse me if that gives offense, ma'am."

"No, thank you, that's fine. I'm not offended." Susan remembered similar comments she had heard before that she tried to ignore. "I appreciate you coming to tell me. Won't you sit down and have a meal, as my guest?"

"Don't mind iffen I do," the old miner grinned. "Hear tell this here place makes the best Irish stew this side o' the old country."

Susan smiled. Mrs. Dolan had told her Irish stew was unheard of in the old country, having been developed by the Irish who had migrated to New York. She did not disillusion him. She only said, "Please. Sit down. We are glad to hear our fare is so highly regarded. Maggie," she called to the girl in the kitchen. "A plate of stew for the gentleman."

After the man finished his meal with gusto, he thanked Susan profusely and departed. Barney watched the big man's retreating back disappear out the door, then turned to Susan. "Now I 'spose this means you're gonna go traipsin' off up to Marysville."

"Monday. Please check the stage schedules for me, Barney, there's a good lad."

"And you won't let me come along to take care o' you." It was a statement, not a question.

Susan smiled. "I need you here, Barney. You know no one else can keep the hotel supplies coming in and Ah Fan on time with the laundry."

Barney only grunted.

Susan could not resist teasing him. "And both of the girls work so well for you. I do believe Peggy is getting sweet on you. Or is it Maggie? I forget which."

She managed to repress her smile and escaped to the kitchen in the midst of his tirade about what he would like to do with both girls.

Charlie had developed the habit of eating supper at the hotel whenever his schedule kept him in town. The following evening, when he appeared on her doorstep as usual, Susan asked him about the stage to Marysville. "Is it a safe line?" she asked, remembering his comments about some of the other stage companies.

"'Tis now," he declared. "Farmer name of John Sharp, he started 'er up, and it were run real crude like in them days, but Hall and Crandall bought 'er last year. Run it real good, they do. Friend o' mine, Alf Parker, he's the reg'lar driver. You go on Monday, you'll be a'ridin' with him. I'll tell 'im to take right good care o' you." Charlie mopped the last of the gravy from his plate with a biscuit and sank his teeth into it with a sigh of pleasure. "Miz Dolan, she shore is a mighty fine cook."

Susan smiled fondly at him. "I'm glad you enjoy it, Charlie. I do plan to go next Monday, and I'm sure Barney will be happy to learn Mr. Parker will take care of me. He frets so when I go off by myself."

"An' you take along somethin' to eat. The slop they serve at the stage stop on the road to Marysville ain't fit for man nor beast."

"Thank you. I'll remember that." Susan thought of the food she had tried to eat at the stage stop on the trip to Placerville. She remembered watching Charlie eat the tough beefsteak and watery potatoes with gusto. If he thought what they served at the Marysville stop inedible, she shuddered to contemplate how bad it must be.

The following Monday found Susan en route to Marysville in a brand new Concord coach. Mr. Parker had greeted her cordially and settled her into the most comfortable seat in the coach. He assured Barney he would take good care of her for, as he said, "Ol' Charlie'll have my hide iffen anythin' amiss happens to Miss Susan."

As she rode along, she could not help thinking how different attitudes were here, what a change from Boston. There, as the daughter of Irish immigrants, she had been shunned and ignored, and would never have been accepted into polite society. Here, the men treated her like royalty, and pampered and protected her every step of the way.

The roadway followed the course of the American River. Susan remembered how low the level of the river had been the previous August when she and Barney had visited the Sandhill Cemetery on Mormon Island. As the stage rumbled along the riverbank, she noticed the water at the present time reached almost to the top. Memories of stories she had heard of the floods in Sacramento before they built the levees flashed unbidden into her mind. Susan stared eastward, where the line of the Sierra Nevada mountains loomed. Masses of snow remained piled high on the peaks. It probably hasn't even begun to thaw, she thought, since today is only the18th of February. Charlie had told her the snow melt often began as early as the first of March.

Susan looked with some apprehension at the already high water in the river. Would this be a potential threat? Her fellow passengers dozed or chatted. None of them seemed particularly worried. She dismissed her concerns and dug out the fruit pie Mrs. Dolan had tucked into her reticule. She savored the aroma, compared it with the food served at the stage stop en route to Placerville, and bit into it with a satisfied smile.

The sun had long since disappeared in the short winter day, and Susan shivered with cold by the time the stage reached Marysville. Exhausted by the trip, she did not even notice the name of the small hotel where Mr. Parker led her. Her teeth chattered as she undressed quickly and snuggled under the blankets, trying to get warm. Not even the thought that tomorrow she might find Donald and end all of her uncertainties could keep her awake. As soon as she stopped shaking, she fell into a deep and dreamless sleep.

Susan woke early the next morning and sat up in bed with a start, then recalled her whereabouts. Whoosh, it's cold, she thought. Her breath made little clouds in the frigid air in the small, cheerless room. Thinking of her cozy room back in Sacramento, she washed her face in the icy water from the pitcher on the table and hastened to dress. She descended to the dining room before the cook had begun breakfast, so she took advantage of the time to talk to the desk clerk.

"Donald Andrew?" The clerk frowned when she asked. "And why would a young lady like you be a-lookin' for him?"

Susan sensed his disapproval. "I have heard he is a lawyer here."

"Oh, that he is, all right." He hesitated, then shrugged his shoulders expressively. That shrug told Susan more than his words. "Got his office over on Main. Lives in the back, so he's there most times when he's . . . . Well, he's there a lot."

"And how do I get there?"

"Turn right outta the hotel, cross two streets, turn left on the next 'un. About four, mebbe five houses down on yer left. Can't miss it. Got a sign out front, he does."

"Thank you." Wondering what he did not tell her, Susan turned and started for the door. She hesitated, feeling a little faint. She stopped and clung to the back of one of the over-stuffed easy chairs in the lobby to catch her breath.

The clerk observed her and came around the desk with remarkable speed. "Not 'til you've had a bite o' breakfast. You look ready to drop. You never ate nuthin' last night, and I know the stage stop serves nuthin' but swill. You'll be a-fadin' away iffen you don't eat." He took her arm and guided her to the dining room. "Jest let me roust out the cook. Pretty good cook, he is. Some bacon and biscuits and taters'll fix you up. Stick to your ribs all day."

Susan shook her head. He could be right. She thought the dizziness due to the eminence of finding Donald, but it could easily be from lack of food. The giddiness passed, and she allowed the clerk to seat her at a small table with a none too clean cloth. She just hoped the food would not be as greasy as the usual California fare.

The man hurried back with a large mug in his hands and placed it in front of her. She stared in dismay at the thick dark liquid. She shrugged. At least it emitted a pleasant steam. "Breakfast be along in a minute," he promised, beaming down on her. "You just relax and enjoy your coffee."

"Thank you." Susan ignored the chip in the mug and managed to suppress her laughter. Charlie's admonition to Mr. Parker to see she was well cared for apparently extended to also seeing her well fed. She shook her head. I've waited this long, I can wait until after breakfast, she thought. It would never do to faint on the street.

An hour and a half later, so full of eggs, bacon, potatoes, and biscuits smothered in marmalade she could hardly move, she ventured out to find Donald's house. As she walked, she considered if she should even have come. If he had a law practice, he obviously still lived, and surely could have written to her. The old doubts assailed her. Was she making a fool of herself? What if she came face to face with Donald and he rebuffed her?

She flushed with embarrassment. Had she come on a wild goose chase? Abby was probably right. He had not written because he came out here and forgot all about her. She should just turn around and go back. But she had promised Mary and Elizabeth to find out what happened. If he had no interest in her, she would say she traced him because the girls had begged her to find out how he fared. She would emphasize that the girls were concerned about him, not Susan herself.

She reached the gate of the ramshackle house. The gate, missing a hinge, bore a sign that read, "Donald Andrew, Esq., Attorney-at-Law". She read and re-read the sign, trying to build up her nerve to enter.

You owe it to Mary and Elizabeth, she finally told herself, and pushed aside the creaky gate. Donald certainly had not done very well for himself, judging from the condition of the house and the fence. She walked slowly up the walkway, mounted the two rickety steps, and found herself on the porch.

Susan stood staring at the closed door for several moments before she could force herself to raise her arm to knock. The sound echoed in the silence surrounding her. She felt she stood in a bubble where time itself stood still. Her heart pounded so rapidly she felt dizzy, and for a moment feared she would faint.

To steady herself, she put her hand on the door jamb. At that moment the door opened. A girl about seventeen or eighteen years old stood there, a baby in her arms, a frightened look on her face.

Susan gaped at the girl. The baby, about a year and a half old, smiled and cooed in delight. She met the baby's eyes. She would know those eyes anywhere. She also recognized the dimple in the baby's chin and the little widow's peak on his forehead.

Donald's child, she thought. This baby is Donald's child.

As Susan stood, staring at the baby, unable to speak, the girl stammered, "I . . . I'm so sorry. Mr. Andrew is . . . he's . . . well, he's . . . out of town. He can't see no one." She stopped, then said in a rush, "But we do need the business, if you're lookin' for legal work done. Could you maybe come back tomorrow, or . . . ?"

A bellow from the back of the house interrupted her. "Missy, who's there?" Susan recognized Donald's voice at once. She also did not mistake the slurring. My God, she thought, he's drunk at nine o'clock in the morning. "Goddammit, Missy, I've told you . . . " A loud crash, like a body falling, reverberated through the house. The baby's smile faded and the girl looked more frightened than ever.

Susan knew then. Knew what she had tried to deny all along. All the hints of Donald's drinking. The concern on the face of the miner who told her his whereabouts. His failure to write. He had never loved her. He only used her to defy his father. What a fool she had been!

But the baby's eyes captivated her. And this poor frightened girl was just a child. She wanted to help them, but how?

She wrote her name on a piece of paper and tucked it into the girl's hand. "Don't let Donald see the name," she said, "but if you ever need help, write to me, General Delivery, in Sacramento. I will come."

Suddenly, Dr. Alexander's long face and piercing blue eyes rose in her mind, but she rejected him. Never again would she let a man make a fool of her.

She walked quickly away from Donald's house and from all the dreams and plans she had built up around him. The next morning, she took the stage back to Sacramento.

Chapter 21

THE RETURN TRIP to Sacramento seemed endless. Susan huddled in a corner of the stage, lost in her misery and disappointment. How could she have been such a fool? All of the signs were there for her to see. In her anxiety to believe Donald the man she wanted him to be, she had ignored them. Well, she resolved, it would never happen again.

She glanced out the window at the water in the American River as their vehicle approached the bank. It seemed to rage higher than it had just two days before on her trip up, eating away at the banks with frightening ferocity. She certainly hoped the levees surrounding the city of Sacramento itself would hold. If the water reached this level in February, how much higher would it get as that mass of snow on the mountains melted?

As the sun slid towards the horizon, the fog rose from the surrounding fields, growing thicker and higher until the dense mist obscured the road. The stage moved more slowly in response as the visibility vanished in the rising cloud. She found herself listening, as Charlie had advised her, to the crunch of the wheels rolling over the road. As she listened, she heard the sounds change from a hard rattling to muted. In response, the driver pulled the team to the left, and the noisy clatter began again. She chuckled softly. It works. Charlie was right. That's how they can stay on the road even when they can't see it. Her admiration for the skill of the drivers increased.

But the slow pace at which the fog forced the coach to

travel made the trip last even longer. They did not pull into the stage yard in Sacramento until nearly ten o'clock. Susan, exhausted by the trip and by all of the strain she had endured, could barely pull herself out of the seat.

When she reached the hotel, everyone slept except the night clerk. He hurried to help her with her bag, and when she reached her room, she fell into bed without even washing off any of the travel dust.

The next morning, she told Barney briefly of the outcome of her trip. Barney wanted to go to Marysville immediately and beat Donald to a pulp.

"I can't let him treat you thataway, Miss Susan," he declared.

Susan smiled and patted the hand he had clenched into a fist. "I appreciate your loyalty, Barney, but I can't help but feel he did me a favor. I keep seeing myself in the place of that poor child he married. She was frightened to death of him."

Barney scowled. "Jest like the Master's wife. Allus scared o' what he'd do if she crossed him." He shook his head. "Can't see why any man acts like that."

"It's the drink, Barney. I know now that Donald always drank too much. I just never let myself believe it before." She smiled into the earnest green eyes so like her own. "Besides, if I had not come to California, I would never have found you, so perhaps it was destiny."

"You shore been good to me, Miss Susan. Wan't fer you, I dunno what mighta happened to me."

"As clever as you are, Barney?" Susan laughed. "I'm sure you'd have done very well. Come, now, let's go over the list of supplies for next week. Before we do, please go by the *Sacramento Union* office and tell them to stop running my notice." She handed him a letter. "And mail this to the *Alta California*."

Barney ran off, and Susan took out her note paper. She somehow had to compose a letter to Mrs. Andrew to let Mary and Elizabeth know she had located Donald. What in the world should she tell them?

She decided to be as brief as possible. "I have located Donald," she finally wrote, "although I did not see him." That's true enough, she thought. I didn't actually see him. Might as well spare them as much pain as possible. "He has a wife and a lovely little boy. You are a grandmother! I hope he writes to you himself. I understand he has a thriving law practice in Marysville." Perhaps that stretched the truth a bit, she told herself, but after all, they are three thousand miles away.

She poured out her feelings in her letter to Abby. Abby's "I told you so" rang in her mind, for Abby had never liked Donald. "I suppose running off to California was a foolish impulse," Susan finally wrote, "but I have been happy here in Sacramento. I have never felt any of the snobbishness so prevalent in Boston. Everyone is so open and friendly. I have even received several proposals of marriage." She did not add that she had no intention of marrying any of the eager strangers, but she did find it flattering to be asked so often. "In fact," she continued, "American ladies are so scarce in California that men come into the restaurant just to meet me."

Susan found it difficult to put her feelings on paper. Barney and Mrs. Dolan and the girls adored her and depended on her. That gave her a feeling of satisfaction she could not explain even to herself. Maybe because, for the first time in her life, she felt really useful, similar to the feeling that filled her when she helped Dr. Alexander save Consuela and her baby in Valparaiso.

And Dr. Alexander? The little imp in her mind persisted in spite of her attempts to ignore him. Be still, she retorted. You're never going to see the man again, she told herself firmly, so forget about him. Besides, he never even liked you anyway. She rose to her feet and crossed to the linen closet to count the number of towels. Business had been brisk of late. Good. She wanted to be busy.

Two weeks later, Charlie came by for supper and reported the American River at a record high.

"High as she were early in '50 when she went over her banks. Higher'n the levees. Shore hope they hold."

Susan, startled, but not surprised, remembered her own feelings as she had watched the raging river on the trip to and from Marysville. "And if they don't?"

Charlie shrugged. "Guess some folks'll be a-gittin' their feet wet." He laughed. "Don't you worry none, Miss Susan. Water comes in, it'll come in slow. Jest be ready to git everthin' to the second floor right quick."

The following Saturday afternoon, she sent Barney to check the condition of the levees. He came back to report that whole crews of men were busy reinforcing the beleaguered dikes.

"Puttin' in everthin' they can git their hands on, Miss Susan, from timber and hay to plain dirt to bags of barley to build 'em up. River's awful high. Eatin' away at the bank right ferocious-like."

Susan thought for a while. Should they wait, or should she start preparing for the flood waters? She considered the amount of work it would require to move everything vulnerable to water damage to the second floor, and the amount of time involved. How much time would they have if she waited until the levee actually broke?

She made her decision. "Barney, get Mrs. Dolan and Johnny Lee and the girls and any men you can find to help. We are going to move as much as we can up to the second floor."

Barney started to protest. "Now, Miss Susan? That's a lotta work. Do we hafta? Can't we do it tomorra?"

"Tomorrow may be too late. Come, let's get started."

Barney sighed in resignation. "Yes, Miss Susan."

At ten o'clock that evening, after six grueling hours of toil, Susan collapsed on her bed, worn out from her exertions. The proprietor of the hotel and the night clerk had helped, although under protest, and most of the perishables that could be easily transported to the second floor were stored in two empty rooms. Susan thought with dismay of the piano in the saloon, but knew it would be impossible to move upstairs without stronger help. "Tomorrow," she murmured into the pillow as she drifted off to sleep. Tomorrow she would enlist the help of a few sturdy men and get the piano and the carpet moved upstairs.

Before seeking the haven of her little room, she had praised them all for their hard work. "Go to bed," she ordered. "We're all worn out. Perhaps the levees will hold after all."

Susan had barely closed her eyes when the wild clanging of the alarm bells awakened her. She quickly lighted her candle and checked her clock. One A.M. No wonder she felt she had not slept. Only three hours had elapsed since she had crawled into bed. She scrambled into her clothing, not wishing to have to evacuate in her night dress.

While she dressed, Barney pounded on her door. "Miss Susan, Miss Susan," he called through the flimsy panel, "do you hear the bells? The levee musta broke."

Susan shook her head with a wry smile. He must think she slept very soundly, for the bells still echoed through the whole building. "Yes, Barney, I'll be right out. We'll have to get everything else moved upstairs. Aren't you glad we started yesterday?" At the time she had some doubts, fearing everyone thought her overly cautious, but the clanging bells proved the wisdom of her decision.

Candle in hand, she hurried from her room to join Barney. They started down the hall and met Mrs. Dolan, looking like a great white ghost in her voluminous nightshirt. The candle she carried in her hand cast eerie lights on her frightened face.

"Oh, Miss," she gasped. "Do you suppose we'll all be drowned?"

"I doubt it," Susan reassured her. "The second floor of the hotel is higher than the level of the river. But we do have to get the rest of our supplies moved upstairs. Where are Maggie and Peggy?"

"In their room, a-blubberin'," Barney reported in disgust. "Them two bubble-witted females is wuss than useless. I say we leave 'em drown."

Susan smothered her impulse to laugh. "Mrs. Dolan, please try to calm them and have them come down to help." Guests emerged from their rooms, some with offers to help, others in need of reassurance. She ordered Barney to enlist their help in moving heavier objects to the second floor. "Especially the piano," she called after them. "The water will ruin it. And the carpet from the lobby!"

She opened the door to another empty room, then hurried down the stairs. By three in the morning, everything movable had been transported to the second floor, even the carpet that covered the lobby floor. As the men collapsed from their exertions, Charlie burst in through the front door.

"Jest wants to be sure ye're in good hands," he said. "Levee broke right where the American comes inta the Sacramenta. They're a-throwing in ever'thin' they kin, but the water jest washes it down the river. Brooks' warehouse, on the levee, it went inta the river about an hour ago. All the trees an' stuff a-washin' down the river piled up agin the Third Street bridge, snapped it right offen its pilin's. River's pourin' inta town at a terrific rate. Whole town's gonna be under water soon."

By six o'clock, Susan stood at her window in the predawn light and looked out over the street, and found it under several feet of water. She shuddered as the body of a mule drifted by. She hoped no humans had been trapped by the raging flood. Muddy water reached part way up the stairs, and stood two feet deep in the lobby. They were trapped, along with their guests. Susan wondered vaguely how they were to feed people, with the kitchen knee deep in water. The pies and beans she had ordered Mrs. Dolan to prepare for just such an exigency would not last very long. She wondered how much bread they had. Bread and jam would serve if they had nothing else.

She thought with sympathy of those who had not had the foresight to move upstairs, and of the people who lived in tents, or in one story buildings. She wondered what they would do.

A hail from the street reached her ears and she saw a boat rowing towards her, several feet below the level of her window. She lifted the sash and leaned out.

"Yes," she replied. "We are safe, thank you."

"Can you take some folks in?" the voice called back. "Got a family of young'uns as is half drowned and half froze."

"Of course. Row up to the front door. I'll send some men down to help ferry them in." She turned from the window. "Barney, Johnny! Get some of the men to help you carry the women and children across the water. We have to get them warm and dry or they'll get inflammation of the lungs."

That was the first of many such boats to appear. Susan found herself ministering to dozens of shivering, waterlogged men, women, and children from the makeshift camps about the city. She set Mrs. Dolan and the girls to heating water for tea and making stew on the two small

Topsy stoves that stood, one at each end, of the long hallway. She had persuaded the proprietor to install them to take some of the chill off of the upstairs, and thanked her lucky stars she had done so. They proved a Godsend.

Johnny Lee went out to reconnoiter at mid-day and reported the water still gushed through the burst in the levee. "Got another problem now, Miss Susan," he reported with a grin. "Break in levee on north end let water in. Levee on south end keep water in." He broke into giggles.

Susan just shook her head. "In that case, Johnny, I think we had best prepare for a long siege. We are using the Topsy stoves for heat and cooking, but we only have a small supply of wood available. When that runs out, I have no idea what we will do. I'm sure there is not a dry piece of firewood in the city. When you go out next, watch for a passing boat selling firewood. I'm sure someone will recognize the opportunity to make some money."

Johnny Lee's grin widened as he picked up a chair. "Made of wood," he said.

She laughed. "Well, I guess it could come to that. But I'm afraid that won't make the owner of the hotel very happy." She thought of another problem. Water to drink. She shook her head. If she knew her enterprising fellow citizens, it would not be long before someone would be selling water as well. "Johnny," she said, "also keep an eye open for someone selling water."

Monday night, she fell exhausted into bed only to be awakened by Barney a short while later.

"Miss Susan, Miss Susan," he said, his voice husky with fatigue and strain, "I hate to wake you, bein' as you're so worn out an' all, but . . . "

"It's all right, Barney. I know you would never call me unless it's important. What is it?"

"One o' the babes. The one as was a-coughin' earlier.

He's a-runnin' a fever now an' all his ma can do is cry. Drivin' me straight up the wall, she is."

"We need a doctor. I so feared the chilling would bring on inflammation of the lungs, especially in the little ones. I just wish one of these boatloads of people we keep taking in contained a doctor." Susan struggled into her robe and stuck her feet in her slippers. So, she thought, the sickness has begun. How many will we lose? The poor children! Her heart ached.

By Tuesday morning they had lost one baby and several others were ill. One old man raved, out of his head with shock and fever. A few started complaining of the flux. As evening approached, Mrs. Dolan approached Susan, a lugubrious expression on her face.

"We got all these chamber pots. We got to dump 'em out the winder. The miasma's gonna make us all sick. Mebbe even bring on the cholery." Her face paled. "We sure don't want the cholery, Miss Susan."

The thought of dumping the contents of the noxious pots out of the window into the water streaming past the building nauseated Susan, but the smell had become overbearing. She finally nodded her assent, wondering what the water must soon smell like if everyone in town did the same, as they no doubt already did. She shrugged and turned her attention to another baby with not only fever, but the flux as well.

Dipping a rag in the sweetened herb tea she had been told was a febrifuge, she tried to persuade the infant to suck.

"Come on, baby," she murmured in encouragement. "Just take a wee sip. You'll feel better." When the infant made no effort to suck, she tried dribbling a few drops onto the blue lips. As she held the moist rag to the child's mouth, a convulsive jerk wracked the tiny body. She put the rag back on the plate and felt for a heartbeat. Nothing. The body lay still in her arms.

It was so unfair! Poor tiny mite, its struggle for life so hard. She sat, unmoving, rocking the baby back and forth in her arms. Tears ran unchecked down her cheeks.

Barney found her there half an hour later, still numbly rocking the lifeless body. He took the infant from her arms and placed it on the bed, carefully covering it with the small sheet. "Come, Miss Susan," he said gently. "Come and rest. You got to git away from this fer a spell." He led her to her bed and took off her shoes. Her last memory before sleep enveloped her was Barney tucking the blanket around her shoulders.

Susan rose in the predawn light Wednesday morning, feeling much refreshed by the rest, but she dreaded the thought of facing another day. She looked out of her window, as she had each morning, to check on the flood conditions. To her relief, the water had at last begun to recede, and was down to the level of the porch. Some parts of the street emerged above the waterline Thank heavens it's finally going away, she thought grimly. But she also knew, shuddering to think of the filth in that muck, that the streets would be seas of mud for some time to come.

She pulled her shawl around her shoulders and went to check on her patients. Barney looked up as she entered the first room. Johnny Lee smiled serenely and handed her a cup of tea. He, too, had proved a pillar of strength in the past terrible days. Affection for both boys washed over her.

"Bless you, Johnny," she said, gratefully sipping the tea. "Good morning, Barney. How are our patients?"

Barney hesitated. "We lost the little Martin girl a little while ago, but ev'ryone else seems to be a-holdin' their own."

Handing her cup back to Johnny, she said. "Guess I'd better get to work."

The proprietor of the hotel marched in, shouting. "This

here Chink cook o' yourn, he says you tol' him to go ahead an' use the chairs for firewood." Behind him, Johnny Lee smiled and rolled his eyes heavenward.

Barney hid his grin. Susan turned to the irate gentleman with a sweet smile. "Perhaps, Mr. Perkins, you would prefer he use the walls?"

The man looked as though he might explode. His face grew red, and his eyes bulged. He sputtered wordlessly for a moment, then turned on his heel and stalked from the room.

She called after him, "Possibly you could use some of your leisure time looking for a source of supply?" He vanished from her sight.

Barney could no longer contain his laughter. "Miss Susan, ain't a man born as could match wits with you."

Susan had to laugh herself. "Thank you. Now let's get back to tending our sick.

Later that morning, as she changed the bedding for a sick woman, she heard a voice she immediately recognized.

"I understand you have requested assistance, Miss McGuire."

She turned and met the one set of blue eyes in the world she would never forget.

Chapter 22

SUSAN could not believe her eyes. He's here, she thought. He's really here. You've been wishing so hard your wish came true. She shook her head at her nonsense. He probably had a very valid reason for appearing on her door step, and she was sure it had nothing to do with her.

"Yes," she managed to say calmly, when, with some difficulty, she got her heart rate back under control. "We have a number of very sick people. They really need a doctor." Tears sprang into her eyes. "We've done the best we know how, but between inflammation of the lungs and the flux, we have lost three children already."

The ghost of a smile touched on his lips. "I am surprised you have not lost more. You have done very well, considering the chill they no doubt received during the flooding and the circumstances under which you were working."

The depth of her response to even this faint praise dismayed her. She pulled herself together. After all, he had often made it quite clear he had no interest in her other than as a casual acquaintance.

"I heard of the flooding," he continued, "and assumed there would be illness. I also wished to see how young Barney fared. When I arrived yesterday, I made some inquiries and was directed here." The blue eyes met hers with an intense stare. He hesitated, then asked, "Is your husband at sea? Is that why you choose to reside at this establishment? I would think you would want to stay in San Francisco, as that is much closer for when he returns."

"Husband?" Oh, she thought. Of course. Peter Thomas. For the moment, Susan had forgotten all about the unfortunate incident the doctor had witnessed in Winn's Fountainhead. "I have no husband," she stated in a firm voice, forcing it not to quiver, "nor am I promised to anyone. I assure you, there is nothing between myself and Mr. Thomas except in his imagination."

Did he show just a little reaction of pleasure to the news? If he did, he hid it well, she thought with some dismay. He removed his coat and handed it to the hovering Maggie. Rolling up his sleeves, he said, "Enough idle chatter. Let's get to work. We have patients in need of care."

The moment Dr. Alexander took charge, things moved smoothly. Mothers verging on hysteria calmed at the sight of his confident face and obvious capability. Even the raving old man grew quiet and subdued. At the doctor's order, Maggie and Peggy boiled all of the water Johnny had purchased from an enterprising boatman. Susan had been forced to pay $1.50 a barrel for the water because it had, supposedly, been strained. She shuddered to think of using unstrained flood water, knowing the number of slop jars emptied into it from all over town, to say nothing of the dead animals.

"Boiling takes out the deleterious properties," Dr. Alexander explained to Susan. "In Edinburgh, they told us the steam carried the same miasma as the air from other noxious waters, and we were careful to avoid contact with it. But I have never accepted that." His face thoughtful, he continued. "I have always felt there was some other agent at work. But I have also noticed that using the boiled water to clean a wound results in fewer cases of suppuration. And persons who drink the boiled water seem less prone to flux and fever."

"Are you going to stay in Sacramento?" she asked, more interested in his future plans than his theories of medicine.

"Perhaps. Many physicians have been coming into San Francisco, and the city is becoming quite sophisticated. Those with money to pay for care have already formed an upper society group. They have more interest in physicians who are using the latest fads for the treatment of various nervous disorders than in any who can cure real illness." The bitterness crept back into his tone.

Susan shook her head. "You need not be concerned about that here. I'm afraid Sacramento still has a long ways to go before it reaches that stage." But it will get there, she thought. It will get there sooner than we think. Already some bankers and merchants scorned the casual miner's garb for suits of broadcloth and stiff collars. Will I be scorned as the daughter of Irish immigrants again?

She dismissed the thought at its inception. The original settlers would become the "upper crust". The late comers will be the immigrants. With a little shake of her head, she turned her mind from the whole subject. They had no time for philosophical discussions on society. They had work to do.

"Good thing you had us haul that carpet upstairs, Miss Susan. Can't imagine tryin' ta git all that mud outten the carpet."

Susan recalled the grumbling that had greeted her decision and hid her smile. "Yes, Barney, wasn't it lucky?"

Three days had passed since the arrival of Dr. Alexander. The water had finally released its hold on the city, and Susan and Barney stood at the foot of the stairs and surveyed the damage. Susan eyed the thick layer of mud on the warped floors. "What a job it's going to be, cleaning out all of this smelly muck." She wrinkled her nose. She suspected the contents of some of the slop jars they dumped out of the windows had returned to haunt them. If not their own, then someone else's. "But we have to get the restaurant open again or we'll be out of business."

Mrs. Dolan stood behind them, repeating, "Oh, dearie me, oh dearie me," as she viewed the sight.

"We're not going to do it alone. Johnny, go get some of your friends. Tell them we will pay them to help us clean up."

"Yes, Miss Susan."

A week later, life had returned to reasonably close to normal. The restaurant reopened, the carpet and piano again resided in their usual positions, and all of the non-paying guests had departed. Some offered to pay, some only gave their heartfelt thanks, and some sneaked out without even saying good-bye.

"Musta been skeered we was gonna ask 'em to pay," was Barney's assessment of this last group. He offered to run them down. "They oughta at least thank you, Miss Susan, for all you done fer 'em."

Susan shook her head. "Forget it, Barney." She sighed. "What an experience we have had! I hope they build sturdier levees this time. I never want to go through anything like that again."

Bright sunshine streamed through the window and the open door. They sat in the restaurant enjoying the fresh air and a bowl of Mrs. Dolan's stew and fresh biscuits. Peggy served them. Susan could barely keep a straight face when Peggy simpered over Barney as she placed a second plate of fresh biscuits beside the one he had already emptied. Barney looked at her with his usual scorn. Susan wondered how soon he would begin to notice that Maggie and Peggy really were pretty girls, even if they were a year or so older than he. The girls had turned sixteen in January. Barney must be about fifteen. Another year, she thought with a smile. Heavens, I sound just like his mother.

A sudden fondness for the boy surged through her. She

reached over and patted his hand. As she did so, she looked up and saw Dr. Alexander enter the restaurant. Her heart gave the same unwelcome leap at the sight of his tall figure. Annoyed at her reaction, she met his eyes and he smiled, a smile she felt all the way to the tips of her toes. Why did she react this way to him?

"Miss McGuire, Master Barney," he nodded. "May I join you?" He pulled out the chair next to Barney and seated himself with an easy grace. "I will have some of your mother's delicious stew, Miss Dolan," he said to Peggy as she set a steaming cup of coffee in front of him, along with a bowl heaped with sugar. "And biscuits with honey." Peggy, like Maggie, stood in some awe of the distinguished doctor, and scurried to obey.

Dr. Alexander sipped his coffee and excitement showed in his eyes. Susan wondered what could have inspired such an appearance. Usually nothing stirred him.

"I have just returned from a visit with the good Doctor Morse," he said. "A fine man, who feels as I do about medicine, that it should be available to all." He grimaced. "And he shares my scorn for those who spend their lives dancing attendance on society ladies and all their vapors just to make themselves rich."

"Are you going to join him in his practice?"

"No, I am going to open a small hospital myself. Dr. Morse agrees that Sacramento is one day going to be a large city, and there will be business enough for all." He paused as Peggy placed a large bowl of simmering stew in front of him. "Thank you, Miss Dolan." He savored the food for a few moments before continuing.

"He and I agree that the county should provide a hospital for the indigent, and that all of the community's doctors should donate some time to the free facility. Thusly doctors can make a decent living and at the same time serve those without funds."

"That sounds like a wonderful idea. Have you presented it to the city fathers?"

He grinned. "Not yet. We decided to let them fix the levees first."

Susan laughed. "Good idea."

"I am, however, looking into property which should be a satisfactory place to set up my hospital. It's a few blocks from here." Their eyes met and he looked at her for a long time. He seemed about to say something, then, with a little shake of his head, rose to his feet.

"I am returning to San Francisco tomorrow, to close out my practice there. That will probably require a month or so. I plan to return to Sacramento towards the end of May, at which time the property should be ready for occupancy." He smiled at Barney. "Young man, I have need of someone to oversee the preparation of the building while I am gone. Do you suppose you could do that for me?"

"Sure, Doc." Barney's face beamed at the prospect, obviously flattered to be entrusted with the responsibility. "You just tell me what you want an' I'll see it gits done."

"He can do it, if anyone can," Susan laughed. "A very capable lad, our Barney."

Barney blushed at the praise, and Dr. Alexander smiled.

"Then I will instruct you. Come along." He bowed slightly to Susan. "I bid you good day, Miss McGuire. As with our previous encounters, it was an interesting experience. I look forward to seeing you again." He strode out of the door, Barney at his heels.

Susan watched them go with mixed feelings. She did not want to commit herself to any man and risk the disillusion she had suffered with Donald. Yet she could not help feeling that any commitment James Alexander made he would keep.

Did he care for her or didn't he? He had seemed glad to see her, yet he made no sign that his interest in her was any more than that of a casual acquaintance. Still, he did come from San Francisco when he thought she might need him. Or had he really come, as he said, to check on Barney? She shook herself to cast off the feelings. Maybe he came just to see about moving his practice, since he appeared disillusioned by his experience in San Francisco.

She sighed and rose to her feet to start her check of the inventory. The extra guests had sadly depleted their stores. She would just have to wait until he returned to see what would happen next.

Sacramento returned to life with remarkable rapidity. Susan never ceased to marvel at the vitality of the town. Animal carcasses, victims of the flood, were quickly cleared away. Tents sprang up again, and every day she woke to the sounds of hammers and saws. The city grew around her as she watched.

A brief rainstorm in the middle of May signaled the end of the rainy season, and the sun came out to stay. One day, towards the end of the month, as Susan sat in the restaurant enjoying a second cup of coffee, she found herself thinking, as she often did, of a pair of striking blue eyes, expecting any day to see him walk through the door.

She looked up as the door opened, halfway expecting it to be Dr. Alexander. But it was not. Charlie stood there, a bit of paper in his hand.

"Miss Susan, Alf Parker brung me this note down from Marysville last night. Says a young lady there ast him to see ye got it. Bein' as how he knows I allus come here fer supper when I'm in town, he figgered I could give it ta ye."

"Thank you, Charlie." She thought immediately of Donald and the note she had left with Donald's wife. She stared at the crude letters spelling her name on the outside of the folded paper.

What had happened?

Chapter 23

THE NOTE was brief, obviously written by someone with little schooling. It said simply, "Pleeze kum. Missy."

Charlie watched her closely, a look of concern on his weathered face. "Ain't bad news, is it Miss Susan? Alf said the little lady were real anxious fer you to get it. Said she din't know how ta write. Alf, he never had much schoolin' neither, so they jest wrote what you see . . . ."

"Thank you, Charlie. I am grateful to you and Mr. Parker for seeing I received this so promptly. I must return to Marysville at once. Are the roads safe now?"

"Yep, bridges all back in place. Alf din't have no problem his last run." Charlie grinned. "He did git hisself stuck in Marysville for a few days after the floods. Couldn't git back. Me, I wuz lucky I got caught here 'stid o' Placerville."

"Then I will plan to leave in the morning."

Barney objected to her going by herself, as she knew he would. "What if he's a mean-un like my old master? Don't want you a-facin' 'im alone."

"I don't feel that will be the problem, Barney." She smiled to herself. She knew that would be his reaction, wanting to protect her. "I need you here at the hotel, plus Dr. Alexander is due back any time. He planned to return the end of May. He will expect a report from you."

Barney grumbled and muttered, but in the end she wound up going alone as she planned. Mr. Parker had again installed her in the best seat in the big Concord Coach, and they left Sacramento at dawn.

As she rode along, she admired the landscape. All of the rain had brought out droves of wildflowers that covered the fields with a riot of color. White and lavender wild radish, which the local Indians gathered for food, yellow mustard, which made tasty greens she used herself, and interspersed through them all were the lovely golden poppies for which California was noted. In the afternoon, purple four o'clocks added their touch to the tapestry.

She knew the heat from the relentless sun would soon dry everything to a dull brown, but could not help comparing the beauty of a California spring with the drabness of the dry season. Sun glittered on ponds of water left standing by the last rains of the season, sending little diamonds sparkling across the surfaces as they rode past.

The day seemed endless. In one way, she was eager to arrive, to solve the mystery left by the cryptic note. Further queries of Mr. Parker shed no further information. He only knew that Missy had wanted very badly for Susan to receive her message. He had not questioned her.

"T'warn't none o' my bizness iffen she din't wanna tell me, Miss Susan," he had told her simply.

Susan had been in California long enough to understand the code. If a man wanted you to know about his past, he would tell you. Otherwise, his business was his own. In a way, she appreciated that. Mr. Parker and Charlie had both honored that code, and neither had questioned her motives for her trip to Placerville and the first trip to Marysville.

On the other hand, she dreaded what she might find. What had driven the girl to write that desperate note? For desperate it was, from all she could glean. She sighed, leaned back against the seat and closed her eyes. Worrying would gain her nothing. She would find out, all in good time.

* * *

Alf Parker pulled the team to a halt in Marysville at sunset. Susan took a room at the same hotel she had utilized on her previous trip. She did not plan to face whatever Missy had to tell her hungry, fatigued and unwashed. It had waited this long, it could wait until morning.

The clerk greeted her as a long-lost friend. "Miss McGuire! We are so pleased to have you as our guest again. I hope you are in good appetite, for one of our hunters brought in a fine, fat doe this afternoon. The cook is serving fresh venison tonight." He handed her the quill pen so she could sign the register. "What brings you back to our fair city? How long will you be staying?"

Susan laughed grimly. "I'm not sure, to either question. I'm going to wash up and go eat. Fresh venison sounds marvelous. I'm half starved." She still could not bring herself to eat the so-called food at the stage stop, and had left in such a hurry Mrs. Dolan had not had the opportunity to prepare anything for her to take.

After supper, to which she did full justice despite her worries, Susan returned to her room. She opened her window to let in the cool evening breeze and to blow out some of the smells from the previous occupant. She stood looking out over the street for a long time, gripping the red velvet curtain. Judging by the grease on the material, many other fingers had gripped that same spot, but Susan did not even notice. She did not realize how tense she was until her fingers began to ache.

With a deep sigh, she turned from the window and crawled into bed.

The next morning, a loud crash from out in the street, followed by a string of curses, brought her out of bed like a shot. She pulled on her robe and hurried to the window. Looking out, she saw a cart had apparently tried to turn the corner too sharply and upset. Barrels falling from the cart created the crash that had awakened her. As she watched, one rolled slowly down the street and came to rest against the wooden curb. Another had broken open and scattered its contents, an assortment of nails, into the thick dust of the roadway.

"Would ya look at what ya done, ya stupid mules?" The obviously uninjured driver let out another string of invectives at the mules, who stood quietly, still hitched to the overturned cart, swishing the persistent flies with their tails. They seemed undismayed by the incident, and looked totally unrepentant.

The clerk from the hotel ran out and berated the driver. "I got me a lady a'sleepin' in this room up here," he waved in Susan's direction, "so watch yer language. And iffen you had half the sense God gave geese, Jeb Larson, ye wouldn't stack yer cart so high."

A small crowd gathered while the clerk and the driver argued, and several men returned the cart to its upright state, apparently little the worse for the unfortunate incident. Small boys appeared like magic, gleefully scooping up nails from the broken barrel. The driver then vented his wrath upon the boys.

"Git! Stop a-stealin' them nails!"

Susan could restrain herself no longer. She sat back on the bed and laughed until her sides ached. She stopped laughing, took a deep breath, and shook her head. "That's just what I needed," she murmured to the silent room. "A little levity to even things up a bit."

By the time Susan dressed, ate the usual huge breakfast the cook insisted upon heaping on her plate, and emerged from the hotel, the morning's excitement had dissipated. A few boys still sifted the dirt, seeking for any remains of the bonanza of nails from the broken keg. The cart and its driver had disappeared.

Susan remembered the directions to Donald's house from her previous trip and shortly found herself at the gate, the hinge still missing. Not, of course, she thought with a grim little laugh, that she had expected to find it repaired. An ominous stillness surrounded the house and made her shiver in spite of the warmth of the morning sun.

Blaming an overactive imagination, she forced herself to cross the weed-strewn walkway and mount the three steps to the dilapidated porch. As she raised her hand to knock, she listened again. Nothing. No sign anyone still lived there.

Had she come for nothing? She shook her head to dispel the feeling. Her knock sounded loud in the morning stillness. She still heard no sound from within, but suddenly the door opened and she stood face to face with Missy.

Susan almost gasped aloud in shock at the sight. Missy's hair had not been combed in days. Her eyes were red and swollen, her skin blotchy, her nose chapped and cracked. But Missy's swollen and purple left eye caught the most of Susan's attention. A cut on the eyebrow still had not healed.

"Oh, Miss McGuire, I'm so glad you come." Missy threw herself in Susan's arms and wept. It took Susan several minutes to calm the girl down. She led her into the kitchen and seated her at the small table.

Susan glanced around, half afraid Donald might suddenly appear. "I'll make us a cup of tea. It should help make you feel better." When Missy did not respond, Susan crossed to the rusty stove and managed to find everything she needed to build a small fire. A bucket of water stood in one corner. Susan filled the tea kettle, put it on to boil, then sat down beside the still weeping girl and took the cold hand in both of her warm ones.

"Now," she said, "tell me what drove you to send for me. Where's the baby?"

"Sleepin'," the girl gasped out between sobs. "He'll be a-wakin' up any time now."

Susan gently dabbed the tears from the girl's cheeks with her own handkerchief. "And Donald?"

"Dead."

"Dead?" Susan could not keep from gasping. "Dead? Donald is dead?"

The girl nodded. "Six days ago. He . . . he were ragin' drunk. Got mad at me fer, fer . . . ." Her words trailed off with a glance at Susan. Realizing Missy had decided not to tell her what she had been on the verge of saying, Susan did not press her.

Finally Missy blew her nose and continued. "He punched me . . . ." She touched the swollen, purple eye gingerly. "Then he jumped on his horse and tore off. Horse hit a cart about three blocks from here and throwed 'im." She lowered her head. "Couple men come by later to tell me."

"And?"

"That's all. The landlord come that night and told me Donald hadn't paid no rent, and . . . and . . . while he felt sorry for me, bein' a widder an' all . . . ." She broke out into fresh sobs. "I didn't know what I was gonna do 'til I remembered the note you give me, that you told me to tell you iffen I ever needed help." She smiled shyly. "I never learnt to write, but I figgered you musta come up from Sacramenta on the stage, and Mr. Parker, he helped me with the note, and said he'd see you got it."

In the momentary silence, the teakettle reached a boil. Susan rose and made a pot of tea. After extinguishing the fire so as not to dispel the welcome coolness of the morning, she searched the meager cupboard and managed to find two cracked cups. She poured the tea and placed one cup in front of Missy. "And when did you eat last, child?"

The girl looked startled. "I didn't have no money. Neighbors give me some food for the baby, but Donald . . . ." She hesitated. "Donald had a way o' drivin' folks off, so we didn't have no real friends, to speak of . . . ."

Susan remembered the Donald she knew back in Boston. Handsome, suave, charming, with droves of friends. Could the drink have altered his behavior so much? Or had it been something else? Bitterness, perhaps, when his plans for getting rich in the gold fields came to nothing? She sighed. Perhaps she would never know, now.

"Mama," came a cry from the bedroom. When Missy did not move, Susan rose and went to fetch the baby.

He looked at her and smiled. He hadn't been bathed in days, and his beautiful hair stuck to his head, but there could be no mistake. This child was Donald's son. She took him in her arms. He nestled close to her and she lost her heart to him. Poor, neglected baby. Poor lost Donald.

Well, she owed him this much, for the love she had once felt for him, if nothing else. She would see his son provided for. If she did not, no one else would. She returned to the kitchen with the child in her arms. Missy had not moved. She had not even touched her tea. Susan touched her shoulder and the girl jumped.

"Get your things together, Missy. We will go to the hotel for tonight. Tomorrow, I will take you and the baby with me to Sacramento."

It took four hours for Susan to get the baby cleaned up and fed and their meager belongings together. She looked at the pathetic little pile, all that remained of the man she had thought she loved so much, and all the dreams she had cherished. The dreams that had sustained her on all the hardships of the long journey to California. Silent tears poured down her cheeks. She could only think, now that he's dead, can there be so little to show that he ever lived?

But when she looked at Donny, she saw a miniature Donald. The baby had his father's dark hair and hazel eyes, and high cheek bones. The nose, while still a baby's, already showed signs that he would have his father's nose as well.

When she finally finished the task, Susan walked back to the hotel to enlist some help to carry Missy and Donny's belongings. They took only two satchels and a box. Missy did not want anything else, so the rest she left for the landlord.

Susan took Donald's watch. She knew it had belonged to his grandfather, and felt it should be returned to his father. His father! With a start, she realized she had not given a single thought to how devastating this news would be to the Andrew family. They all doted on Donald, the only son. She shook her head. She would have to write them as soon as she returned.

The following morning, they rose at dawn and took the return stage to Sacramento. Baby Donny sat on Susan's lap the whole ride back. He would be two in August, his mother told her, a bright, active child. Susan pointed out sights along the way, related all of the children's stories she could recall, and played pat-a-cake with him. She cradled him in her arms while he napped, and taught him to say, "Auntie Susan."

As they pulled into the outskirts of Sacramento, Susan suddenly thought of the reaction of her entourage to her arrival with Donny and Missy in tow.

"Donny," she said to the sleepy little boy in her lap, "I think the next thing we had better teach you to say is Uncle Barney."

"Unca Barney," the boy nodded obediently, and fell asleep with his head on Susan's shoulder.

Chapter 24

"THIS IS a friend of mine," Susan said, presenting Missy to the Dolans and Barney. "She is recently widowed, so I have brought her and her baby here to stay with us."

Barney's eyes met hers. Susan read the knowledge there, but he said nothing. She silently blessed him for his tact.

Mrs. Dolan clucked in sympathy and gathered Missy in her arms. "Poor child. I'm a widder, too, and know how hard it be. And you jest a lass yourself." If she noticed the still swollen black eye, she said nothing, so Susan had no need to resort to the story she and Missy had created between them to explain the injury.

Peggy hurried to take the sleeping Donny from Susan. Susan handed him over with relief, for her arms ached from the weight. She had not dreamed he would be so heavy.

As the girls cooed over the baby, Susan said, "We need a room for Missy. Is Number Seven still empty?" At Barney's nod, she continued. "Good. And we will need a little bed for Donny. See what you can find."

Barney scurried to obey, and Susan turned back to the girl, who sat slumped on a chair, as though no longer caring what happened to her. "That room is right next to mine, in case you need me, Missy. Come on." She took Missy's arm and spoke to the hovering night clerk. "Jeremiah, please bring the bags." Ignoring Jeremiah's muttered comments about the probable reaction of Mr. Perkins to the latest additions to his household, she started up the narrow staircase.

When Susan returned from settling Missy and Donny in

their room, Mr. Perkins awaited her, grumbling about having to give up yet another room to house permanent nonpaying guests.

"Gonna drive me to the poorhouse, you are," he griped. "Only got eighteen rooms, now I got another one I can't rent out."

Susan, knowing full well the bulk of the profit garnered by the hotel came from the restaurant, allowed him to say his piece. When he paused to catch his breath, she said, in her sweetest tones, "If you wish, Barney and I and the Dolans can accept the offer from the *Golden Eagle* to manage a restaurant there. The owner not only offered us rooms, he offered me a salary as well. I told him my loyalty was to you, since you took us in when we arrived."

Vanquished, the proprietor shoved his cigar back in his mouth with a loud "harrumph" and stalked out of the room.

Barney turned to Susan. "Really, Miss Susan? The *Golden Eagle*?"

Susan smiled. "Hush, Barney. The secret of successful negotiations is to always keep your opponent in the dark."

The next morning, Susan rose and dressed early to begin her usual busy day. She heard Donny in the next room, but no answering sounds came from his mother. Concerned, she tapped on Missy's door and entered. Donny, still wearing the little night shirt Susan had dressed him in to tuck him into bed, tugged at Missy's arm.

"Hungry, Mama," he said in a plaintive tone. Susan also noted his diaper needed to be changed. Apparently his mother had done nothing for him.

Missy's eyes were open, but she did not move.

"Missy, are you ill?" Susan asked.

"No," the girl whispered. "Jest . . . don't feel like movin', is all." The straw in the ticking crackled as she stirred restlessly in the bed. "You ever want to curl up in bed and pull the covers over your head an' jest stay there?"

Susan understood the feeling very well. She remembered the panic and desolation that swept over her when her parents died, so long ago in Boston. She thought of how she had felt at the time, but so much had happened to her since then it seemed several lifetimes ago. She smiled at Missy. "Yes, and part of the shock comes from the feeling that no one in the whole world cares what becomes of you. But we do care about you, Missy. We're going to keep you here with us. You and Donny will always have a home."

The girl closed her eyes and made no response. Donny started to cry. Susan changed his diaper and shirt, then scooped him up in her arms. "Tell you what. You just rest. I'll feed Donny and send Peggy up with a tray of breakfast for you."

"I ain't hungry. Don't bother."

"You have to eat or you'll be ill." Somehow she had to snap the girl out of her depression. "Remember, Donny needs you."

When Missy again did not respond, Susan sighed and took Donny down to the dining room. A bowl of porridge soon restored his good humor. Barney entered the room and she whispered to Donny, "Look, baby, there's Uncle Barney."

"Unca Barney," the boy cried out happily, holding out his arms.

Barney's eyes shone as he gathered the child up. Susan hid her smile. Conquest complete, she thought.

After breakfast, Susan sent Mrs. Dolan to Missy's room with a tray and orders to see that the girl ate at least part of it. Perhaps Mrs. Dolan's motherly mien would be the best for Missy right now. She assigned Maggie to care for Donny, Peggy to start dinner preparations, Barney to fill Mrs. Dolan's grocery order, and Johnny Lee to Ah Fan's to get the laundry.

Alone at last, she sat at her usual table in the corner of the restaurant and stared at the blank piece of paper in front of her.

"Dear Mr. and Mrs. Andrew." She had written that much, but could go no further. How can I deliver such devastating news? Was there any way to soften the blow?

She sighed. If there was, she couldn't think of it, and finally decided to be as brief as possible. The less said the better. No need to tell them Donald was drunk when the accident happened, or how severe his problem with liquor had become. No need to mention the poverty-stricken state in which he had left his family. She just said Donald had been killed when his horse threw him, and that she, Susan, was caring for his widow and child.

She closed with "I am so sorry to be the bearer of such tragic news. Please be assured that Missy and Donny will be well cared for." She closed with "Give my love to Mary and Elizabeth. They must be mature young ladies by now."

With a sigh of relief to have the ordeal behind her, Susan folded the letter inside of a blank piece of paper to protect it, and sealed it with a dab of wax. Barney could take it to the Post Office for her when he returned from the market.

A week went by. June arrived, and the sun rose hotter every day. Missy still stayed in her room, mostly in bed, sometimes staring out of the window. She refused to eat more than a few bites, even with Mrs. Dolan's motherly cluckings.

Donny, once clean, safe, and well-fed, turned into a delightful child. He even won over Mr. Perkins, who would come by with a sweet or a small toy for him. Barney collected some chunks of wood, and sanded and smoothed them into a set of building blocks. The two of them would patiently build a large edifice which Donny would then demolish, and, laughing with glee, beg Barney to build it again.

Two weeks after her trip to Marysville, Susan sat at her usual table going over the figures for the past week's restaurant expenses, Donny patiently piling up blocks on the floor beside her, when the door opened and Dr. Alexander walked into the room. Her heart jumped at the sight of him, though she tried very hard to maintain a casual demeanor. On the outside at least.

"Good morning, Miss McGuire. Just the person I wanted to see." He looked around. "And Master Barney?"

"He'll be back shortly." She smiled faintly, keeping her tone even, while trying to get her breathing back under control. "Ah Fan did not have the laundry ready when Johnny Lee went to pick it up, so Barney had to go." She shook her head. "I don't know how Barney does it, but he always comes back with the laundry." She laughed. "I sometimes suspect Ah Fan gives him someone else's laundry to placate him. But where have you been? We expected you before this."

"It took longer than I thought to close my practice." He smiled into her eyes and she fought to keep him from seeing how that smile affected her. "But I am now at my new building, with everything I own. I came to tell Barney he did a fine job. The work was done just as I wished."

Susan laughed. "Oh, Barney's good. I don't know how I would manage without him."

"That's what I wish to discuss with you, Miss McGuire. I will have need of a cook, a handy man, some helpers and, most of all, a good business manager." He smiled ruefully. "That is one thing I learned well in San Francisco. I know I did not collect half of the fees due me. I have no head for business." He took her hand, and his touch sent shock waves through her body. "Would you consider coming to work for me?"

"Work for you?" Thunderstruck, she gaped at him.

"As a full partner, of course."

"Oh, yes, of course, as a partner." She could see herself trying to deny her feelings for him if they worked together every day. And he just wanted a business partner. "I'll think about it," she finally said. "I just can't up and leave Mr. Perkins. He's been very good to us."

"Good to you!" The eyebrows over the magnificent eyes shot up. "He'd have been out of business long ago if it hadn't been for you. I've heard several say how poorly run this establishment was before you took charge."

"I suppose. Nevertheless, I must keep my promise to him." Even though it breaks my heart to turn you down, she thought. Or maybe if you cared just a little for me instead of my management ability.

She turned her mind from her feelings. She might as well make use of his medical skills and have him tend to Missy. "While you are here," she said with a smile, "I wish you would examine a young lady who is our guest, the mother of this baby." Donny looked up from his construction project and smiled "She is recently widowed, but refuses to rise from her bed or eat more than a few spoons of soup." She started for the stairs and he followed. Angry at herself for being so conscious of his proximity, she continued. "I so fear she may go into a decline."

An hour later, they emerged from Missy's room and returned to the restaurant. Peggy served them both a cup of tea.

Dr. Alexander shook his head. "Melancholy," he said. "She has no physical illness, but she no longer has any will to fight, no desire to stay alive."

"Not even for her baby?"

"She brought her baby to you, Miss McGuire. She has seen her child will be cared for. She has no further reason to live."

Chapter 25

JULY FADED into August, accompanied by blasting summer heat. Donny grew dearer and dearer to her, and Susan began to understand the passion that drove mothers to protect their children with such ferocity. The child responded to the love surrounding him and became a source of joy to all of them. He adored his 'Unca Barney', and tagged after him as much as he could. Barney returned Donny's affection with enthusiasm for, as he put it, "I sure know what it's like to grow up 'thout no one carin'".

Mrs. Dolan and the girls doted on the baby as well. Mrs. Dolan often said, wiping a tear from her eye on the hem of her apron, that he reminded her of the child she had lost. With Barney's help, the Dolans fixed up a corner of the kitchen as a play area for Donny's use, and arranged a blanket for his nap.

But Missy spent all of her time in her room. Susan made futile efforts to interest the girl in taking part in the activities around the hotel. She watched, helpless, as Missy slowly weakened before her eyes, growing thinner by the day until her clothes hung on her. The color faded from her cheeks, and her face grew gaunt. Susan often sat with Missy during Donny's nap time, trying to encourage the girl, hoping to bring her out of her depression, all to no avail.

Finally, when Susan joined Missy the day before Donny's second birthday, the girl sat straight up in bed, a determined look on her face.

"Are you going to get up and come downstairs, Missy?" Susan asked, encouraged, her hopes rising.

Missy shook her head slowly from side to side. The pale blue eyes looked straight at Susan for the first time since Susan and Missy had returned from Marysville. "No. But there's sumthin' you got a right to know." She stopped.

Susan waited. The rattle of a team passing by in the street sounded loud in the silence.

Missy shifted on the bed. "I come out in '49, with my folks. Ma was sickly. Weak lungs. Pa had heard the air in California was good fer them with bad lungs. We come around the Horn, in the *Capital*, outta Boston." Tears welled in her eyes. "But Ma couldn't take the cold and damp of the Horn. She got lung fever and died. They buried her at sea, jest afore we got to Valparaiso." She stared into space for a long moment. The tears ran unheeded down her cheeks and dripped off her chin. Finally, she continued her story. "Me and Pa got to San Francisco in July." She laughed, a clunky sound with no humor. "They called it Yerba Buena then, after some plant as grows there. When so many Americans came, they named the city after the bay." She again fell silent.

Susan did not move, not wanting to break the spell.

"Pa was a carpenter back in Vermont, where we come from. When we got to Sacramento City, they was payin' carpenters $16 a day, three times what he was a-gittin' in Vermont. So he decided to stay. Said it'd be easier on me, stayin' in the city 'stead o' campin'." The tears spilled over again. "Then Pa got hit by a runaway team and died three days later."

And left you all alone in a strange city, three thousand miles from anyone you knew, you poor child, Susan thought. She said nothing.

Missy wiped her eyes on the sheet. "We'd met a young gentleman on the ship. He got on in Panama, had come across from Chagres. Some come that way, as it was shorter." A slight smile curved her lips. "Name of Wheelock. Alfred

Wheelock, he were. Had lovely hazel eyes and the nicest smile. He'd read to me sometimes, as I never learnt how, and he had such a nice voice. He were from Vermont, too, though a diff'rent part from us."

She stared, unseeing, at the wall for a long moment, then shook her head. "When Pa died, I figgered maybe Mr. Wheelock would help me, so I took what gold Pa left me and headed for Placerville, as he'd said he were goin' there." She blushed.

So, Susan thought, she fell in love with him on the trip. What irony. And she wound up with my Donald.

Missy shifted restlessly in the bed. The straw in the ticking rustled as she moved. "But I couldn't find him. They was so many men there, and none of 'em knew very many names." Susan nodded, thinking of her own abortive trip to Placerville in search of Donald. "I knew the gold Pa left me wouldn't last long, so I had to do somethin' to earn a livin'. I got me a job as a cleanin' woman in the *Empire*. George, him as was a'runnin' it then, was real kindly."

Susan remembered how others had spoken of George on her trip to Placerville. She wished she had met him. Yes, thoughtful, gentle George would take the child in. "How old were you then?" she asked in a soft voice, sure Missy had to have been very young. Pity for the girl wrung her heart. She wondered how she herself would have fared if Bridgit had not been with her.

"Sixteen." Missy blew her nose on a not too clean handkerchief she pulled from beneath her pillow. "That's where I met Donald. He had a room there. I'd seen him on an' off, an' he'd always been polite and nice." She closed her eyes, and a look of pain crossed her features. "Then one night, I guess he'd been makin' the rounds of the saloons, for he come back drunk. He laughed and caught me in his arms and kissed me."

She broke into a fit of weeping. Susan waited while the

storm passed. Finally Missy blew her nose again and continued. "I don't know how it happened, but I wound up in his room. The next thing I know we were . . . we were . . . ."

The words seemed to choke her, and she stopped. When she finally continued, she said in a husky voice, "We woke up at daybreak. He was sober then, an' he looked at me like he'd never seen me afore. 'How'd you git in here?' he ast me 'I can't have you in here. I'm engaged to be married.'"

She squeezed her eyes tightly shut and took a deep breath. "I told him he'd brung me in, and . . . and . . . ." She stopped again. "He was polite, told me he musta been too drunk to know what he was a'doin', for he didn't remember nuthin'. Apologized and left the room so's I could get dressed."

"And that is when you got in a family way with Donny."

Missy nodded. "Donald, he left the next day and I figgered I'd never see him again. So when my monthlies never come . . . " Her voice trailed off and she was silent for a moment before going on with her story. "I wuz skeered to tell anyone. I'd heard tell what happens to girls who find themselves in a family way with no husband. I'd a' lost my job, that's for sure, for George's wife, I'd heard the way she talked about the girls that work the saloons. She decide I'm a tramp, I'm on the street."

"So what did you do?" Susan asked quietly.

"I went to one of them girls. She was real nice, and tried to help me. She give me some herb as was supposed to bring on my monthlies, but all it done was make me sick." She rose from the bed and walked to the window. Susan noted with horror how frail the girl had become.

Missy stood and stared out of the window for a long time. "Finally," she said, turning to face Susan again, "in March, Donald come back. I was already havin' to start wearin' my clothes a little looser, so I knew for sure I was gonna have a baby. He looked at me when I come up to him like he didn't even remember me, then he smiled and said, 'Why, hello,

Missy. Still working here? I thought you'd have a husband and a home by now.' I started to cry. He took my arm and led me into his room so's no one would see me a'cryin'.

"I'm carryin' your child, I told him. I jest blurted it out. He looks at me with horror. 'But I can't marry you,' he sez. 'I'm engaged to a lovely lass back in Boston. She's waitin' for me there.'"

Susan's heart surged with pleasure. So Donald did love me after all, she thought. He didn't just come out here and forget me.

" 'But the bairn,' I cried," Missy said. " 'You got to help me take care of the bairn.' He jest looked right through me. 'Yes' he sez. 'I must help with the child.'" Then he squinched up his eyes and looked at me suspicious-like and sez, "Are you sure it's mine? How kin I be sure one of the other fellows isn't the father?'

"That hit me like a slap, it did, and I snapped, 'I ain't never been like that with no other man'. 'How did you learn so much?', he came back at me. I told him I talked to Belle, down at the *El Dorado*. She told me ever'thin'." Missy sagged, clinging to the windowsill for support.

Susan hurried to help her back to bed. "You're getting weaker by the day, child. You have to eat. Let me help you down the stairs. Some of Mrs. Dolan's good Irish stew is just what you need."

"No," Missy whispered. "I got to tell you . . . the rest." She lay back against the pillow with a long sigh. "He decided we'd move to Marysville, where no one knew us. 'Not gettin' rich here anyway,' he said, 'and my claim don't amount to much. I'll set myself up as a lawyer. Had three years of lawyer schoolin'. That oughta be enough.'" She fell silent.

Susan waited, conscious of the stifling heat in the tiny room. She often wondered how Missy could bear it. Susan herself always left the window open in the morning and did not return to her room until the evening breeze had cooled it off.

"We rented the little house where you found us, and he hung out his shingle. We told everyone we was married." She glanced at Susan who could not repress a start of surprise. "Yes, he never married me. Donny's a bastard." She shook her head. "Not even to spare Donny would he marry me. 'I'm goin' back to Boston for my Susan,' he'd say, 'soon's I get enough money to take care of you and the babe.'"

She shifted the frail body into a more comfortable position and the voice droned on. How the money never seemed to be enough, how he started drinking more and more, his rejection of Donny.

" 'He should have Susan's eyes,' he would say," she said with a gulping sob, the tears overflowing and spilling down her cheeks. " 'My Susan has the most beautiful green eyes in the world.'" Missy stared into Susan's eyes. "When you come that day, I knew who you was the minute I opened the door and looked into those eyes of yourn. But by then . . . ." Her voice trailed off.

"By then," Susan continued the story for her, "his drinking had grown so bad he could no longer even earn enough to support you and Donny, let alone enough to ever be able to return to Boston."

Missy nodded. "And I was skeered if he knew you was in California, he'd leave me for you. So I never told him you come."

"But he found out?"

"Yes. The day he died. Someone at the hotel told him you'd come a'lookin' for him. That's why . . . that's why he were so mad at me." She wept again. "He said . . . he said . . . he wished I was dead, that I'd ruined his life, and that I didn't even tell him you was in California."

She took a long breath. "That's all. He said he was goin' to Sacramento to find you. I run after him, a-holdin' his coat, pleadin' with him not to leave us, that I could never care for Donny 'thout him to help. He turned and hit me. That's the only time he ever hit me, honest. Knocked me down, he did. I got up and run to the door, but he had already jumped on his horse and was a-tearin' down the street like the devil was after him." She fell silent for a time before she said, "I never seen him alive again. 'Bout three hours later, a neighbor come to the door to tell me he'd run his horse into a cart and got throwed and killed."

Susan took the frail body in her arms and held her closely, stroking the silken hair. "Poor child," she murmured. Poor Missy, who never found her Alfred. Poor Donald, who never made his fortune to marry his one true love. Poor Donny, a child nobody wanted. No wonder he had blossomed in the past months, with all of the love lavished on him.

"See, Miss Susan," the girl wept, "because of me, he drank too much, and because of me, he got hisself killed."

Susan remembered Donald's fondness for brandy back in Boston. "No, Missy, Donald had a problem with drinking long before he ever met you. You couldn't help having Donny, and he is such a delightful child. You should enjoy him. You are safe now, and we love you."

"You don't hate me, Miss Susan? Now that you know the truth? That I never told him you come?"

"I told you not to tell him, remember?"

Missy looked startled. "That's right. You did." She gave a little laugh. "I forgot."

"So stop feeling guilty. You can't blame yourself for any of this. Put it behind you and try to get your strength back. Come, let me help you dress. You need to get out of this heat and you need some food. Besides, Mrs. Dolan and the girls are busy planning for Donny's birthday party tomorrow. We all want you to be included."

* * *

Everyone agreed Donny's party was a huge success. Even Dr. Alexander stopped by briefly with a hobby horse, which the child immediately climbed on, shouting with delight as he rocked back and forth. Susan thought the doctor had scarcely noticed the child, but the smile on his face as he watched Donny revel in his gift could not be mistaken. He did care.

While he was there, he checked Missy, who sat quietly in a chair watching the festivities. Susan walked outside with him as he left to ask him about Missy's condition.

He looked grave. "Her melancholy has improved, but I would watch her. She seems to have made up her mind, that she has reached a decision."

"To what?"

"I don't know. Just something about the look in her eyes makes me uneasy."

Chapter 26

THE FOLLOWING MORNING, as Susan totaled the figures for the week's income and made up the grocery list for Barney, Peggy came running into the room.

"Miss Susan, Miss Susan," she cried. "I can't wake Missy. She just lies there. I shook her arm and . . . and . . . it were cold, so I come a'runnin' fer you."

Susan jumped to her feet. "Barney," she ordered, "fetch Dr. Alexander."

Barney took off on a run. Gathering her skirts with both hands, Susan ran up the stairs, her footsteps clattering on the wooden steps. Peggy had left the door ajar in her haste, and when Susan pushed the door open, she saw Missy, her eyes closed, lying back on the pillow, a slight smile parting her blue lips. Susan picked up the hand that lay on top of the sheet covering the frail body and found the fingers stiff and cold.

Susan's eyes filled and the tears slid down her cheeks. Poor little Missy, whose short life had been so harsh.

Dr. Alexander came in while she sat by the bed holding Missy's cold hand. He felt for the pulse in the girl's neck, lifted the lid of one unseeing eye and nodded.

"She's gone, as I'm sure you knew." He raised the sheet and picked up the empty bottle lying beside the still body. Susan recognized it at once. Mrs. Dolan's laudanum, she thought with horror. So that's why Missy had been willing to come downstairs. She needed to find the bottle. She must have known we would have one somewhere. Everyone kept some on hand, they used it for so many minor ailments. Mrs. Dolan, pleased to show Missy how she and the girls cared for Donny, had led her back into the kitchen. But Missy sought only the location of the laudanum bottle. She must have sneaked down during the night after everyone went to bed, gotten the bottle, and returned to her room to drink it.

Dr. Alexander pulled the sheet over Missy's pale face. Susan, still stunned, whispered, "You warned me. You tried to warn me. I should have watched her closer."

He took Susan's hands in his. "Do not blame yourself. You cannot blame yourself. She had made up her mind. That's what made her so cheerful at Donny's party. She knew then what she planned to do — and it comforted her."

Susan, tired of being strong, wanted to throw herself in his arms and beg him to hold her. The sympathy in his eyes almost broke through her reserve. Her pride held her back. Don't be a fool, she told herself firmly. He has no romantic interest in you at all, and does not want a clinging female on his hands. He had certainly voiced his scorn for vapid society ladies often enough. She took a deep breath and pulled herself together with an effort.

"Of course," she said calmly. "You're right. The poor, lonely, unhappy child. I just hope she is in a better place now. She certainly deserves to be." He released her hands and she pulled her handkerchief out of her sleeve and wiped her eyes.

"Thank you for coming so promptly. I hope Barney didn't pull you away from a patient. He can be very persuasive."

The doctor laughed. He had a wonderful laugh, Susan thought, which he used far too rarely. "I believe his words were, 'Doc, Miss Susan says come quick.' He grabbed my arm and pulled me towards the door. I trust the good lady I was examining at the time of his arrival will still be there when I return."

Susan shook her head. "Then I suppose you won't have time to stay for breakfast, or at least a cup of coffee?"

"Thank you, I must decline, but I will return for supper this evening if you wish."

Their eyes met and she smiled. "I'd like that very much."

The next day, they buried Missy in Sandhill Cemetery. The Dolans, Barney, Johnny Lee, Dr. Alexander, and Susan were the only mourners. In the absence of a minister, Susan read the Twenty-Third Psalm out of Mrs. Dolan's worn Bible. Mrs. Dolan had selected that particular passage, saying it had comforted her when her husband and child died. They stood in silence while Johnny Lee and Barney shoveled the dirt on top of the coffin. The hollow sound of the clods striking the wood echoed in Susan's head. She felt that had to be the most dismal sound in the world.

The small wooden marker that Barney pounded into the soft earth at the head of the grave read, 'Missy Andrew, age 18, died August 19, 1852.' Susan planned to order a marble headstone. She could not bear to think of Missy's marker fading like so many that surrounded her.

I don't know her birthday, Susan had thought sadly as she watched Barney and Johnny Lee lower the crude pine-board coffin into the grave. I don't even know her last name. She had decided that, as far as the world was concerned, Donald and Missy had been married. It could do no one any harm, and for the sake of Donny and Donny's grandparents, she felt it better she keep Missy's secret to herself. California was not like Boston. Here no one kept any records. It was as impossible to disprove a marriage as to prove one.

After Barney finished placing the temporary marker, Mrs. Dolan showed Susan where her husband and children were buried. The wooden markers had faded. Susan could barely make out the names. The date had already been obliterated by the ravages of the weather.

"Will have to find 'em by countin' the rows soon," she lamented.

"I am sure, Mrs. Dolan," Susan smiled, "that we can afford stones for these two graves as well as Missy's. I will speak to Mr. Luce tomorrow."

"Oh, could you, Miss Susan?" Mrs. Dolan's eyes filled. "Oh, Miss Susan, you're so good."

True to her word, the following day Susan, armed with the details of the Dolan family and accompanied by Barney and the faithful Jake, walked down to Israel Luce's Marble Works on the corner of Seventh and 'L'. Stacks of marble and granite stood piled at apparent random around the wooden platform that served as the showroom floor. A huge canvas tent covered the whole. Two workmen in dusty overalls busily chiseled on slabs of stone. Another vigorously polished a finished headstone. A boy that could not have been over eight years old swept dust off of the floor.

The voluble Mr. Luce hurried to greet her. "Fine marble, it is," he declared. "Come from Boston in '49. Got both Italian and Vermont varieties." He chuckled. "Ship a-carryin' it sank off the coast of Chili, but Charlie Minturn, him as owned it, got it raised up off the bottom, all twelve tons of it, and brung it to San Francisco. Myrick and Hoag hauled it to Sacramento City on the first trip in their new ferry boat, the *Beta*. February of '51, it were. Had my shop down between 'J' and 'K' then. Moved it to Fifth, then got this place here on the corner." He nodded. "Better spot. Easier for folks to find. Gonna be right nice, soon's I git me a permanent buildin' built."

When he paused for breath, Susan, only half listening to his ramblings, said, "Yes, your marble has an interesting history. I think since Missy hailed from Vermont, that the Vermont marble would be appropriate."

"You'll be right pleased with it," Mr. Luce babbled on "Comes from the Wheelock quarry, it does. Some of the finest pink marble in the world."

Suppressing her start at recognizing the name, Susan wondered vaguely if the quarry and the Mr. Wheelock Missy had sought could be connected. Deciding she had no way of finding out without queries that would raise more questions than she cared to answer, she dismissed the idea and selected four slabs of the exquisite marble, varying in tone from a pale pink to a deep rose. Two for the Dolans, one for Missy, and the fourth for Donald. She would have to see about transporting Donald's to Marysville, but she somehow felt responsible for seeing his grave properly marked. She could only hope the townspeople had put a name on his grave, for she somehow felt Missy had not made any effort to do so. She sighed. Well, she decided, if I can't find it, I can't. At least I will have tried.

Several mornings later, Donny asked once for his mother. Susan took him on her lap and explained to him that his mother had gone to heaven to be with his father. Donny mulled that over for a moment, then nodded.

"Okay," he said. "Donny go Ah Fan's with Barney now?"

Barney stood by the door waiting, a big grin on his face.

Susan shook her head. "Yes, go on." She stood Donny on his feet. The child hurried to Barney's side and took his hand with a happy smile.

Susan watched them go with tears in her eyes. Poor, sad little Missy. Never loved by Donald, not even missed by her own child. She thought of the young man from the ship whom the girl had loved and wondered if he ever thought about what had become of her, or of trying to find her. She shook her head. Probably not. She sighed and went to change the bedding in Missy's room. Since Missy's suicide, Maggie and Peggy refused to enter the room, saying her spirit still lingered. Susan found any efforts to dispel their notions useless, so she tended the room herself.

As she tucked the clean sheet around the mattress, she

heard the clang of the fire truck's bell. She looked out of the window and saw it head up 'J' Street. She looked for smoke. When she saw nothing, she sighed with relief and returned to her work.

The hot dry summer continued. The dried grass crackled when Susan's skirt brushed against it. She remembered the muggy heat of Boston, but at least in Boston an occasional shower of rain kept down the danger of fires. The fire department remained alert. They quickly extinguished several small fires, but Susan could not help fearing what could happen if a fire got a good start among the tinder dry buildings of the city.

She wrote again to the Andrew family to tell them of Missy's death. She said nothing of what Missy had told her, and did not mention how she died. She only assured them that Donny, a bright, happy, and intelligent child, was healthy and well cared for.

"He has Donald's eyes," she wrote, "and the same widow's peak on his forehead. I know a young man who can do a wonderful likeness. The next time he comes to town, I will have him do a small painting to send to you." She also told them that she and Barney had taken Donald's headstone to Marysville, and seen it properly installed on his grave.

Susan did not mention the emotions that wracked her as she stood by Donald's grave. She was not sure she understood them herself. She realized she had never really loved Donald, at least not with the depth of feeling she had come to experience with James Alexander, but still, Donald's tragic death seemed such a waste of a charming young life.

* * *

September passed, and October. Davy Burnside came down from Placerville and stopped by the restaurant to see her one day in October. She had the young artist paint a likeness of Donny which she sent to the Andrews. Davy took great pains with it, and it was such an adorable painting Susan could hardly bear to give it up.

Dr. Alexander became a frequent patron of the restaurant. Finally, on the first of November, he tried again to persuade her to come and help him with his hospital.

She sighed. "I'd like very much to work with you. You know that. But Mr. Perkins needs me. He took in Mrs. Dolan and the girls, and put up with all of their bumbling. Then he gave Barney and me a chance. I was an unknown to him. For all he knew, I could have been as inept as the Dolans."

"But you've made his hotel a success. And your restaurant is the best in town."

"And if I go to work with you, I would have to give it up. What about the Dolans and Johnny Lee?"

"There is more than enough work for all of you. I have not been able to find any reliable help. My cook just quit, complaining she could not serve decent meals without someone to assist her with the marketing and preparation. And I'm sure I need someone to manage my books. I know I'm not collecting half of what's owed me. I will make you a full partner. We will split whatever we make. You will probably earn more than you do here."

"And where will we live? If we have to pay for lodging, we won't be any better off."

"I thought of that. When I remodeled the building, I had lodging for the staff built on the second floor."

Their eyes met and he smiled. Her heart again gave that unwelcome lurch and she felt her knees go weak. Angry with herself for her reaction, since he sought only a business partner, she forced herself to return his smile.

"I'll think about it," she said.

The next morning, she woke to the whistle of the wind howling down the valley from the north. She looked out of the window. Dust and bits of trash blew around the street. As she watched, a teamster's hat flew off and sailed away. He cursed, pulled the team to a halt, and took off down the street in pursuit of the escaping hat.

She laughed at the scene, but immediately sobered. This was what she feared all along. The rains had not started yet. The fires that occurred thus far had been easily contained, because the wind had been calm. What if a fire got started while the winds blew with hurricane force?

She shook her head. No need to borrow trouble. She dressed and went downstairs to help with the breakfast crowd.

As they cleared away the dishes from the last diners of the morning, she heard the loud clang of the fire bell. Her heart missed a beat when it sounded not just once or twice, but a loud, continuous clanging that she had not heard since the night of the floods the previous March.

Chapter 27

SUSAN RAN to the door. Looking up 'J' Street, she saw billows of black smoke climbing to the sky, streaming out before the ferocious wind. It's happening, she thought. Just like I feared it might. She realized, with a flash of panic, that they could be in real peril. Very few buildings were brick or adobe. Most of the city had been constructed with wood, and everything was dry as tinder. In this fierce wind, a spark could easily set off an uncontrollable blaze.

Barney, behind her with Donny in his arms, gasped aloud. "Miss Susan, look at all that smoke. Must be a right big fire."

She turned and smiled grimly, recognizing their vulnerability only too well. "Yes, and we are probably very close to its path. I think we had better prepare to evacuate." She turned to Maggie who stood beside her, staring at the smoke, transfixed, twisting her hands in her apron. "Get your mother and Peggy. Go upstairs and get your belongings together. Be sure to pack no more than you can carry. And hurry," she called as the girl scurried away.

"Mr. Perkins, go knock on the doors of all of our guests and tell them the same thing." He gaped at her and she gave him a shove. "Go!"

Barney grinned at her as he watched Mr. Perkins waddle away and start his laborious climb up the steep stairs. "Packin's easy for me, Miss Susan. I ain't got nuthin'."

"I hope you can keep your sense of humor, Barney. I'm afraid you're going to need it. We may all be in the same situation soon."

Charlie appeared on her doorstep, wild-eyed and disheveled. "Miss Susan, Miss Susan," he panted, trying to get his breath back, "the fire started at Madame Lama's hat shop. That's just down 'J', t'other side o' Fourth. Not two blocks from here. You gotta git out. I run all the way to git here ta help ye."

"Bless you, Charlie. Where should we go?"

"They's a block of brick buildin's jest down the street, Mitchell's Shoes, an' Brown 'n' Henry's Wholesale. Fire should stop there. But we gotta hurry. Wind's blowin' it a bit away from here, but with ever'thin' so dry, anythin' wood's bound ta burn, and once she starts, she'll burn fast."

Susan, as always when faced with a crisis, reacted with her usual outward calm. Quelling her inner fears with an effort, she started issuing orders. "Johnny Lee, get your things together quickly and run upstairs to make sure the girls and Mrs. Dolan get organized. They're probably standing in the middle of the room wailing over what to take and what to leave. Barney, collect Donny's things and your own." Donny had insisted on sleeping in Barney's room after his mother died, to Barney's delight and Susan's relief. "We'll meet back here as soon as we can."

She ran upstairs and looked around the room that had become home to her. She dug her satchels out of the armoire and quickly tossed in her most precious possessions: Her mother's pearls, Donald's picture, the small portrait of her mother and father. Other than that, she took only her toilet articles, two pair of chemises and drawers, some stockings, and an extra dress. She returned to the lobby, astonished to discover how short a space of time had elapsed.

She found Barney waiting for her, standing in front of the desk, a satchel in one hand, holding Donny with the other, and the hobby horse under one arm. Jake cowered at Barney's feet, whimpering. "Donny wouldn't let go of Horsie," Barney grinned, "so I brung him along."

Susan laughed despite her growing anxiety that the evacuation was taking far too long. "Very well." She handed Charlie the two satchels she had packed. "Charlie, please escort Barney and Donny to Brown & Henry's. I will meet you there. I have to get the Dolans going, and I want to gather up my books. I also have to be sure everyone is out."

"I don't wanna leave you, Miss Susan," Barney protested.

"You must take care of Donny for me, Barney. I'm depending on you. Now go." She kissed him on the cheek and gave him a gentle push. "Go," she repeated.

"We – ll, okay, iffen you're sure that's what you want, Miss Susan." With obvious reluctance, Barney, with Jake at his heels, followed Charlie out the door. At the door, he called back. "And don't waste no time on them wuthless Dolan wenches. If they can't figger out what to take, leave 'em to burn."

Susan laughed and waved him off. "Don't worry about me. Just get moving!"

Patrons of the hotel streamed by. Some wore worried frowns, others seemed to accept the dislocation as just another hazard of travel. One man wailed that he needed help with his possessions. Susan turned to the clerk and ordered him to assist the gentleman.

"Got to git my own stuff together, Miss Susan," the clerk protested in response. "Ain't got time to help no one as travels with more than he kin carry."

"He's our guest, Jeremiah, and our responsibility. Enlist some more help if necessary. I must check on the Dolans. Just hurry and get everyone out. The fire must be very close by now. The whole building could burst into flame at any time."

Still grumbling, but responding to the urgency of her words, the clerk shoved the protesting man towards the stairs and hurried after him.

Gathering her skirts in her hands, Susan scampered up the stairs behind the two men. As she had predicted, she found both Maggie and Peggy in tears while Mrs. Dolan dithered over which items to take with them and what to leave behind.

A harried Johnny Lee greeted her with relief. "Miss Susan. So glad you here. Can't get girls to stop cry, start pack."

Susan sighed. I should have sent Barney, she thought. He can handle them better than anyone. But since Donny was her first concern, she had assigned Barney, the one she trusted the most, to his care.

It took her more time than she wanted to spend, but she finally got the Dolans and what belongings they could carry easily out of the door under Johnny Lee's escort. By then, she had trouble breathing in the thick smoke. Her eyes smarted. A quick check of the rooms proved to her everyone else had escaped. She returned to her office and unlocked the safe. She pulled out the stack of little pouches of gold dust and tossed them and the gold coins into a sack, tucked her ledger under her arm, and started for the door.

When Susan reached the front porch, flames crackled so close she could hear them. A stab of fear rushed through her body as she suddenly realized her own peril. Had she waited too long? She had to hurry.

As she watched in horror, the wind blew the smoke away from her and the building next door to the hotel erupted into a mass of flames. A blast of heat struck her face and she cringed. The wind picked up a burning board and carried it to the roof of a building beyond. Another shift of the wind brought the smoke back across where she stood and her visibility disappeared.

Coughing and choking, she felt her way along the side of the building, hoping she went in the right direction, unable to be sure. Her eyes streaming, she had just begun to feel dizzy when a hand grasped her arm.

"Miss Susan, Miss Susan!" Barney's voice reached her ears. She felt a second hand take her other arm and she sobbed with relief. "We got to hurry!" One of her rescuers relieved her of the heavy bag of gold, the other took the ledger, and together they hurried her down the wooden planking, their footsteps barely audible above the roar of the crackling flames.

They cleared the pall of smoke and Susan blinked. To her astonishment, her second rescuer was Dr. Alexander. He gathered her into his arms and held her. Her reaction surprised her. She felt . . . safe. She knew danger still surrounded her, but somehow, clinging to him, with his arms around her, his cheek against her hair, she felt safe.

He released her almost at once, with a murmur of apology. She wanted to cry out, don't apologize, hold me again. But she said nothing.

"Come on, we gotta hurry." Barney's urgent words finally penetrated her stupor. "Fire's still a'comin'." He tugged at her arm as he urged her along.

"Donny?" she gasped.

"Safe with Charlie and the Dolans. Charlie said he'd take care of 'em. That Charlie, he's as good with the bairn as a woman."

The memory of Charlie's smooth cheeks flashed across her mind. Could he possibly be a woman, dressing like a man? She shook her head. Don't be ridiculous, she told herself. Why would any woman want to do that?

By then, they had reached the safety of Brown & Henry's Warehouse and hurried through the doorway. They found themselves surrounded by many others seeking safety as well. The smell of smoke penetrated the building, but at least she could breathe, and ash no longer filled the air. She could not believe the amount of heat the fire generated. Taking a deep breath, Susan rubbed her streaming eyes with her handkerchief. Barney led her up the rickety stairs and into the corner where he had stowed their belongings and the Dolans. The girls still wept. Johnny Lee sat on their luggage shaking his head. Jake cowered at his feet.

Barney grinned at Johnny Lee and scooped the shivering Jake into his arms. "Tell them silly wenches they kin stop their blubberin'," he said, grimacing as Jake lavished wet doggie kisses on his face. "Me and the doc went back and got Miss Susan. Here she is, safe 'n' sound."

Susan felt herself smothered in Mrs. Dolan's embrace. Both girls tried to hug her at the same time. She laughed softly at their exuberance.

When they finally released her, she looked over at Donny astride his hobby horse. Charlie sat on a box beside him. Donny's eyes sparkled. "Looka me, Auntie Susan. Unca Charlie teached me to ride real fast!"

Chapter 28

BY LATE AFTERNOON, the fire had passed the building where they huddled for refuge, gathering headway as the wind continued to whip the flames about them. Barney went out to reconnoiter and returned to report.

"Wind's still a'blowin' burnin' boards all over. With ever'-thin' tinder dry the way it is now, 'specially with the wind a-blowin' so fierce-like, it catches any place the boards land." He chuckled. "Guess not ever'one in town wants to see 'em get it out. Hear tell they seen one man a'settin' fire to a buildin'. Shot him dead, they did."

"Good," Susan muttered, half under her breath. "Anyone who makes this any worse deserves to be shot."

Susan slept restlessly, unable to get comfortable in spite of her exhaustion. Dozens of people crowded into the second-story storage area of Brown & Henry's Wholesale where they had taken refuge. It seemed every time she drifted off, someone would cough, or a baby would start to cry. One woman awoke wailing in fear in the middle of the night, startling Susan out of the first sleep she had managed to achieve. In the far corner, one man snored lustily the whole night. Susan envied him his ability to sleep so soundly under the circumstances, and marveled he did not awaken himself.

The fire burned all night. Susan lay awake and watched the red glow of the flames reflecting through the grimy windows. They rose the following morning to the smoldering embers of the city, the wind still howling about them. At dawn, Barney, Jake at his heels, went to check on the hotel. He returned in less than half an hour, a lugubrious expression on his face.

Susan glanced up from the pile of luggage where she had attempted to sleep. One look at Barney's face told her the hotel had burned to the ground. She nodded as he shook his head sadly.

Maggie and Peggy immediately set up a loud wailing over the loss of miscellaneous possessions they had been forced to leave behind when they fled. Mrs. Dolan's face paled.

"What we gonna do, Miss Susan? We got no restaurant, no place to stay, no food, no money, nuthin'." Tears ran down cheeks already stained from previous bouts of weeping.

Susan thought of the bag of gold dust and coins that Barney and Johnny Lee protected so fiercely. The bag she had risked her life to rescue, glad she had not known at the time the enormity of the danger she had faced. She smiled reassurance to Mrs. Dolan.

"I'm sure we will manage. Please see if you can get the girls to stop weeping before they drive Barney to distraction."

When Susan rose the morning of November 4, the smoke had dissipated. The day dawned clear and cold, with not a breath of wind. Barney came for her.

"Come, Miss Susan. Come up to the roof. You got to see this." He helped her up the rickety steps leading up to the top of the building. She looked out over the city and gasped at the sight. Ninety percent of the city lay in smoldering ruins.

The girl stood and stared. "Oh, Barney," she whispered. "So much destruction. So many must have lost all or most of their possessions." Tears filled the emerald eyes and slid slowly down her smoke-begrimed cheeks. She thought of people. Had anyone been trapped? What a horrible way to die! She remembered staggering along the ash-laden street, fear rushing through her at the memory of the crackling flames and the fierce heat of the fire. Especially the heat. She knew she had come very close to losing her life, for she had been on the verge of losing consciousness. Had Barney and Dr. Alexander not returned for her . . . . She turned her mind from it.

Barney put his arm around her shoulders to comfort her. With a start, she realized he stood taller than she. How could she not have noticed how much he had grown? He smiled down at her, a soft, gentle smile, unlike his usual ear-to-ear grin. "I never thought I had nuthin' to lose." His voice broke and she saw tears spring into his eyes. "But when it looked like you was trapped in that fire, I realized I had nuthin' to lose 'cepten you, Miss Susan." His other arm circled her and he held her closely and whispered. "'Cepten you."

Touched by his concern, Susan returned his embrace. They stood together for several moments, then his sense of humor returned and he chuckled. "You ever seen two more addle-pated females than them Dolan wenches? I declare, they'd drive a man around the bend, they would."

Susan laughed. He may be a lot taller, she thought, but he's not mature enough yet to appreciate the fact that Maggie and Peggy are really pretty girls, and they both admired him in spite of his scorn. She dried her eyes, smearing the soot around on her cheeks even more. She looked at the black streaks on her handkerchief in dismay. "You're right, Barney. They don't have a whole brain between them. But they are good-hearted girls. And we are fortunate we are all alive and healthy. It could have been a lot worse." She smiled into the green eyes so like her own. "Right now, I'd pay anything for a bath!"

They descended the stairs which, to Susan's relief, did not collapse under their weight, as she feared they might.

When they reached the place where the Dolan's waited she saw Dr. Alexander standing beside Mrs. Dolan, watching Donny ride the hobby horse. A smile of genuine pleasure lighted his face. He looked up as she and Barney approached.

"Ah, Miss McGuire. You are looking as lovely as ever, if a little grimy."

"Thank you," she replied dryly. "As you can tell, I'm hard to kill."

"I'm glad." Their eyes met.

He does care for me, she thought. She remembered how he held her after he and Barney had rescued her from the inferno. He has to care for me. Why can't he say it?

"I came to tell you," he continued, "that my building was surrounded by brick edifices and spared from the holocaust." He smiled. "The offer of a partnership still stands."

Susan broke out laughing, almost hysterically. Now that we are burned out, she thought wryly, he can get us to come and work for him. She choked back her laughter and swallowed her pride. After all, six people depended upon her for their support. She had to consider them. She returned his smile and offered her hand. "Thank you, Partner. Under the circumstances, I think we will accept your offer."

Three days later, the first rains came, pouring out of leaden skies in great sheets, accompanied by rolls of thunder and an occasional streak of lightning. The ashes from the fire turned into soggy masses of black, and added to the mud in the streets. Susan could not help wondering what a difference it would have made had this pouring rain come a few days earlier. She shrugged off her thoughts as she watched the water pouring off the eaves and flowing past the window. No point in speculating what might have been.

Perhaps, she thought, continuing to stare out of the window, it was destined. Certainly everyone had settled into the rooms on the second floor of Dr. Alexander's little hospital quickly, with no Mr. Perkins to complain of how many rooms they occupied. Mr. Perkins announced his plans to return to New York. As for Maggie and Peggy, the memory of the meager possessions they had lost in the fire faded quickly in the delight of having, for the first time in their lives, a room they could each call their own.

Susan turned from watching the rain to observe Donny, still in his little nightshirt, riding the hobby horse. She was glad Barney had saved it from the fire. Of all the toys he had owned, it remained his favorite. Barney had to carry it downstairs to the kitchen for him every day.

"See me go fast, Auntie Susan," he cried. "Go faster, faster!"

Susan laughed. "Yes, you can go very fast, but now we have to get Donny dressed. Barney will be here any minute to carry Horsie down to the kitchen for you. And we have to get your shoes on. Your feet are like ice."

After breakfast, and after she had gotten everyone started on the day's chores, Susan sat down and pored over Dr. Alexander's books. Two hours later, as the doctor entered the room, she rubbed her aching neck.

She looked up at his step and shook her head. "You're right. You are a terrible bookkeeper. It's going to take me days to straighten this out."

"Thank you," he said wryly. "And you look much lovelier with a clean face."

She laughed. "Touché." She rose to her feet and stretched, trying to get some of the kinks out of her back. "I'm ready for a cup of coffee. And I had better see how Mrs. Dolan is doing."

He grinned down at her. "Much better than my previous cook. Especially since Barney is handling the procurement."

Susan nodded. "I told you he was good."

* * *

They settled into a routine. Under Susan's direction, the hospital ran smoothly, and began attracting a good clientele. In response to the demand from people who had developed a fondness for Mrs. Dolan's cooking, especially her Irish stew, they set up a special dining area and added extra tables for the use of clients other than hospital patients.

Susan persuaded Dr. Alexander of the wisdom of the move. "It will be completely separate from the hospital, and will keep her busy. Besides, I think she likes to feel she can contribute something on her own. And it will bring in a little extra money. After discovering how little you actually manage to collect from your clients, I think an extra source of income is quite practical."

The winter passed to the sound of hammers and saws rebuilding the city around them. By spring, most traces of the fire had disappeared.

One Monday morning in June of 1853, Susan stood at her upstairs window looking out over the city, still amazed at how quickly it had grown back. The vitality of Sacramento and its citizens never ceased to thrill her. She thought of Boston, with its rigid society, the division of the well-to-do areas from the poorer areas. By keeping those people down, by not realizing newcomers had a contribution to make, the city lost that vitality. People like herself, the ones that rebel, move out and start anew, building the Sacramentos and the San Franciscos of the world. She wondered if they, as in Boston, would grow rigid as society solidified into upper and lower castes again.

Somehow she did not think so. The people who built California were made of a different clay. The elite would rise to the top, but she felt sure somehow that the rest would never allow themselves to be trodden down. Not these people. Even the women had an inner strength that would have been unthinkable in Boston.

She thought of Barney's old master, and the laws in Boston that had trapped his wife into a marriage with such a cruel and abusive husband. No laws like that would survive among these women.

Barney tapped on her door. "Got the grocery order ready for me, Miss Susan? Me an' Johnny Lee jest got back from Ah Fan's with the laundry."

"Good. We're ready." She gathered Donny in her arms, Barney picked up Horsie, and they descended to the kitchen. "On your way back, please go by the Post Office. I should be getting another letter from Abby soon."

Barney returned in mid-morning, waving a letter. Susan opened it eagerly and scanned the pages. She gasped in horror at what she read, putting out her hand to clutch the table.

Barney hurried to her side and put his arm around her shoulder to steady her. He eased her into a chair. "Bad news, I take it," he said gently. "Here, you set. Want me to fetch the doc?"

"No, no, I'll . . . be all right." Tears sprang into her eyes and poured down her cheeks. She pressed her fist to her upper lip and took a deep breath. She looked over at Donny, merrily knocking down a building he had just erected from the new set of blocks Barney had made for him, the original set victims of the fire.

Once she felt she had her voice back under control, she told Barney what the letter had said. "They had an epidemic of the fever in Boston." She stopped and took another deep breath to keep her lip from quivering. The memory of her parents' deaths, as fresh in her mind as when it happened, rose before her again. "Donald's step-mother and his sisters are dead." Dead! The word echoed in her mind. Mary and Elizabeth dead? How could they be dead? The memory of the two little girls she had loved so dearly and cared for and taught for over two years again threatened to overwhelm her.

"Oh, Barney," she wept. "How can those two lovely young girls be dead?" She put her head down on the table and buried her face in her arm as the sobs overtook her. Barney stood by, awkwardly patting her shoulder, tears in his eyes.

Donny trotted over and patted her knee. "Don't cry, Auntie Susan. Wanta ride Horsie?"

Susan raised her head and met the child's trusting eyes. She gathered him into her lap. Her heart went out to Mr. Andrew, in spite of his cruelty to her. He lost his first wife, then his son, now his second wife and two beautiful daughters. No one ever deserved to suffer such losses.

"You're all he has left, Donny baby. You're all he has left." She felt a stab of fright. Would he now want to take Donny away from her and take him back to Boston? He could. She knew only too well that she had no claim to the boy at all. She thought of the portrait Davy Burnside made of Donny the previous fall, the one she had sent to his family. Any grandfather seeing that adorable little boy would want the child.

Of course, then Donny would grow up in a lovely home, with servants and expensive clothes and toys, instead of sharing a tiny room over a small hospital with Barney and Jake. He could go to the best schools. There was certainly nothing like that in California. And he would be cared for. His grandfather had plenty of money, and could see the child was well provided for. Susan knew only too well that were she to die or become disabled, there was no one she could really depend upon to care for Donny.

She met Barney's worried eyes and managed to smile. "It's all right, Barney. I'll be fine."

But the fear never left her.

Chapter 29

TWO DAYS before Donny's third birthday, the door to the restaurant opened. Susan, seated at her usual table reviewing the previous day's receipts, looked up from the papers in front of her and gasped as she recognized the man walking toward her.

"Good morning, Miss McGuire. I was told I would find you here."

Susan took a deep breath to get her heart rate back under control and managed to find her voice enough to say politely, "And how are you, Mr. Andrew? Abby Chase told me of your tragic losses. I am so sorry." She looked at him. Still a handsome man, she knew he could not be more than fifty. Strands of gray mixed with the sandy blond hair. The blue eyes held grief in them now, instead of the arrogance she had always seen before. Somehow, it saddened her. "Please, sit down. Would you like some dinner? It's a little late, but we can warm something for you. When did you arrive in Sacramento?"

"Yesterday afternoon. I took a room at the *Golden Eagle* and made some inquiries. Finally the clerk directed me here. It seems the *Southern Hotel* address you gave no longer exists."

"That's right, along with the *Missouri* and the *Crescent City* and about ninety percent of the city. It all went up in flames during a three day firestorm that struck last November."

He took the chair opposite her and sat for a long time without saying anything. She waited, until at last he spoke.

"Where is Donald's son?"

"Taking his nap." Not sure of what he wanted, Susan decided to take her cues from him. She looked into his eyes. Startled, she saw pain there so patent she felt it like a stab. Her heart went out to him and she took his hand.

He clung to her hand with both of his. "May I see him?" he whispered. The tears in his eyes spilled out unheeded.

"Of course. He should be sound asleep. We won't disturb him." She led the man up the stairs to the little room where Donny slept, his tousled curls clinging to his damp forehead. The long, dark lashes lay against his porcelain-fair cheeks. As Susan looked at him, a surge of love for him washed over her.

Mr. Andrew looked at the child for a long time. Susan watched his face. He finally turned to her. "He's just like Donald when he . . . when he . . . ." His voice broke.

Susan took the man's arm and led him back down the stairs to a secluded corner of the deserted restaurant. "He'll be awake in about an hour." She smiled. "I told him he has a grandfather. He says he'd like to meet you."

He stared at her, a startled look on his face. "You've done that? After the way . . . after the way I treated you?"

"I want what is best for Donny. He had a right to know he has kin." She rose and paced back and forth for several moments. Finally, she stopped and turned to face the silent man. "I did love Donald, you know."

"I know," he whispered, his head bowed. He looked up and met her eyes. "Would to God that I had sanctioned your marriage to him!" he cried hoarsely. "He would never have left, and probably would not have died." His voice dropped. "My stubborn pride. I so feared what my acquaintances and business associates would say if Donald married the daughter of Irish immigrants." He dropped his face into his hands.

Susan said nothing. She could think of nothing to say.

She waited in silence for him to continue.

After a moment, Mr. Andrew raised his head and met her eyes. "It seems so foolish now. You are intelligent, practical, well-educated, gracious. You would have made him an excellent wife."

She sat down beside him and draped her arm across his sagging shoulders. "You were thinking of him. You did what you thought best." Susan surprised herself with her words. After all, this was the man who drove Donald away from her. The man who would have thrown her out into the street had Mary and Elizabeth not intervened. She could not understand her sympathy for him

But he had changed. His losses had drained him. He was a broken man.

He turned to face her. The sympathy in her eyes melted the last of his reserve. He broke into tears. She pulled his head to her shoulder and stroked his hair as his grief tore at him. Gradually the racking sobs eased and he wept quietly. She continued to hold him.

The door opened. Susan looked up at the sound and saw Dr. Alexander standing in the doorway, his face stricken. Before she could speak, the mask fell back across his features.

"Excuse me, Miss McGuire. I was not aware you had a guest." He turned on his heel and stalked out. Oh, no, she thought, shaking her head in dismay. He's misunderstood again.

After the storm passed, Mr. Andrew, embarrassed by his emotional display, wiped his eyes and blew his nose. Susan brought him a cup of coffee and sat down opposite him.

"Tell me everything," he demanded. "I have to know the whole story."

She told him, as gently as she could, everything she had learned in her quest for Donald. She omitted Missy's confession that Donald had never married her. She did tell him Missy had said Susan was the love of his life. She almost withheld that bit of information, but felt he should know, if for no other reason than to strengthen her claim to Donny.

He shook his head sadly at the conclusion of her narrative. "I knew. I always knew Donald could not control his drinking. Neither could his mother. She died in a sanitarium."

Susan's eyes widened. She had been told Donald's mother died at his birth. He smiled slightly at the startled look on Susan's face. "Yes, we hid it well. I told my friends she had a nervous disorder." He smiled grimly, a perfunctory movement of his lips, with no humor. "It's all right to have a nervous disorder, but not a problem with drinking. Donald was two when she died. He never knew."

"You never told him what killed his mother?"

He shook his head. "I told him she died when he was born. In a way she did, for I had to put her in the hospital shortly after his birth. But I did try to talk to him about the drink. He just laughed. I thought maybe if I brought him home from Edinburgh, where he could be with the family . . . ." He broke off with a long, shuddering sigh.

"So that's why he came home across the Atlantic in mid-winter! It seemed a strange time to travel."

Donald's father shook his head. "That's only part of the reason. He had also been expelled from Edinburgh. I know all the young university students drink and party, but he let his studies go. They finally wrote me and told me he could no longer attend, that they did not wish to waste the space on a young man with no interest in learning." He drew a deep breath and took another sip of the coffee that had grown cold in the cup in front of him.

"I dreaded bringing him home in mid-winter, but I feared leaving him there more."

"And you still never told him about his mother."

He shook his head. "No. And now I see his son, who is so much like him." He rose. "I have taken too much of your time. I will return to the hotel. When can I meet Donny?"

He's asking me, she thought with a start. He is actually asking me. Could his losses have changed him so much? Apparently so.

She rose and offered him her hand. He kissed it gently and smiled.

Surprised at his sign of affection, she returned his smile and said, "Please come for supper at six. Donny will be so pleased to meet you."

She escorted him to the door and watched, with mixed emotions, as he walked slowly down the street in the direction of the *Golden Eagle Hotel*. At the sound of footsteps behind her, she turned to meet Dr. Alexander's intense blue eyes.

"And who was that?" he demanded. "You seemed very well acquainted."

And what do you care, she thought. Are you afraid you will lose your business manager, now that I have your hospital running smoothly? She sighed. She knew she was being unfair to him. He did have a right to know, so she said simply, "Donny's grandfather."

"Grandfather? He has come for the boy?" He nodded. "That's good. Boy should be raised by his family." He looked into Susan's eyes. "I'm sorry. You do love the child, I know." His eyes narrowed. "I feel there is more to this than I have been told. Just what is your relationship to Donny?"

Susan had known for some time that this question would eventually come, and she had her reply prepared in her mind. "Mr. Andrew employed me as governess to Donny's father's sisters after the fever left me an orphan, back in Boston in '48. Donny's father came to California to seek gold in '49. He never wrote, and no one knew what had become of him , so when I left Boston to come here, I promised the girls I would try to find out."

"And you did." A statement, not a question.

"Yes," she whispered. "I did."

She saw more questions in his eyes, but, to her gratitude, he did not ask them. He changed the subject. "I came to ask you if Mr. Aston paid his bill for his wife's last visit. He wants her to return for another few days of treatment."

She laughed. "He just wants a few more days respite from her nagging."

The doctor grinned. "Probably. But he is well able to pay for it."

"He is and he did. Tell him to go ahead and bring her in. But I warn you. I've promised Maggie and Peggy extra pay if they have to put up with her again."

Dr. Alexander nodded. "Just add it to his bill. I had hoped to get away from this kind of patient when I left San Francisco, but her sort does help pay the expenses for those who have little or no funds." He strode to the door and turned, his hand on the door jamb. He looked at her for a long moment. "And when is Donny's grandfather returning?"

"At six."

Donny woke from his nap at four. Susan bathed and dressed him carefully, combing the curls back from the widow's peak. Donald's widow's peak, she thought, meeting the trusting hazel eyes. Donald's eyes.

"Why I wearing my good clothes, Auntie Susan?"

She took a deep breath. She had to tell him. "Remember how I told you about your grandfather?" The boy nodded. "Well, he's come all the way from Boston just to see you. He's coming for supper, and he wants very much to meet you."

"He' s not gonna take me away, is he Auntie Susan? I don't wanna leave you and Jake and Unca Barney."

Susan's heart sank. Maggie and Peggy must have been chattering. They both knew Donny had family in Boston, for they had been present when Davy did the portrait Susan sent to the Andrew family. One of the girls had to have said something within the child's hearing. Why else would he think someone might take him away?

Susan looked forward to the coming meeting with mixed feelings. One side of her wanted Donny to be with his family, the other side wanted to keep him for herself. Her eyes filled. She took him in her arms and held him closely to her, resting her cheek against the soft curls. "No one is going to take you from me," she murmured. "No one."

Chapter 30

THE VISIT WENT BETTER than she had dared hope. Donny shook hands with Mr. Andrew with a polite, 'How do you do, Grandfather?' Susan felt she would burst with pride at his behavior. The child thrilled at the set of lead soldiers Mr. Andrew brought as a gift. The man returned to his hotel with a personal invitation from his newly-found grandson to attend Donny's birthday party the following day.

"I gonna be three, Grandfather," he announced proudly. "I be all growed up."

"So I've noticed," Mr. Andrew replied gravely. "I shall be delighted to attend the festivities tomorrow. Now, if you will excuse me, I believe I should set about seeking an appropriate gift for a grown up young man."

The birthday party was a huge success. Susan could not help remembering Donny's second birthday. Could it be a year already? She closed her eyes and envisioned poor little Missy sitting in the chair Mr. Andrew occupied. She sighed, still unable to accept Missy's death. It seemed such a tragic waste. Was Susan the only one who ever even gave Missy a passing thought? Probably. She shook off the melancholy and joined in the festivities.

At the end of the games, Mrs. Dolan's delicious cake eaten, Donny opened his presents. After he opened the last package, with still no gift from Mr. Andrew, the boy looked at his grandfather and said, "I guess you didn't have time to find something. But it's okay," he consoled. "Don't feel bad."

Mr. Andrew just smiled and took the child's hand and led him outside. "Your sentiments are a credit to your upbringing, my boy, but your gift is here." Standing patiently by the hitching post was a small pony, a bright red ribbon tied in his forelock.

Donny's eyes widened. "A pony! A real live pony! Oh, Grandfather. Thank you, thank you!" He threw his arms around the pony's neck.

Susan watched with mixed emotions. Mr. Andrew could give the child so much more than she could. Did she have a right to stand in his way? She sighed, then noticed Barney's bright eyes fixed on her. She smiled to cover her fears.

After that, the man returned every day to take Donny for a ride on Pony, as the boy named the diminutive horse. The two would go off, the boy riding proudly, his grandfather leading the pony. Donny started calling him Grandpa, and eagerly looked forward to his visits. Susan told herself it was only right, since Donny was all that was left of Mr. Andrew's family.

Finally one day towards the end of September, as the summer heat at last began to cede the city to autumn, and the evenings grew cooler, Mr. Andrew asked to see Susan alone.

Donny ran to him, and he scooped the child up in his arms. Donny planted a kiss on Mr. Andrew's cheek. "Go for a ride on Pony now, Grandpa?"

Mr. Andrew kissed the rosy cheek and returned the child's hug before setting him on his feet. "A little later, my boy. Right now, I want to talk to your Aunt Susan."

"Hokay. Donny go to Ah Fan's with Barney." He scurried to the door and turned to smile. "Bye, Grandpa. Bye, Auntie Susan."

Susan watched Mr. Andrew's face and her heart lurched.

It had finally come, as she knew it would. He's going to say he wants to take Donny back to Boston.

His first words justified her fears.

"Donny will be old enough for school soon," he began. "He's a bright boy. As far as I have been able to determine, there are no proper schools available here."

Susan, sinking into black despair at the thought of losing Donny, had to agree. "But," she added hopefully, "as more and more people come, there will be more demand for a proper school system. I am sure there will be one soon."

He smiled. "But not soon enough. I want to take him back to Boston where he can be properly educated. Surely you agree that would be the best for him."

Susan felt tears sting her eyes. She lowered them so he would not see. "Yes," she whispered. "It would be best for him. And he has accepted you now. He would not be unhappy."

Lost in her own misery, she scarcely noticed when he took her hand in his.

"Look at me, Susan," he said. Startled at this use of her first name, she raised her eyes and obeyed. He smiled gently. "You are the only mother the boy has ever really known. I can't take him from you."

Her eyes widened. Would he leave the boy after all? His next words startled her even more.

"I want you to come back with us, Susan."

She twisted her mouth into a wry smile. "No, thank you. I am never going back to being a nursemaid and governess. Here I am my own mistress."

He met her eyes. "I don't want you to come as his governess. I want you to come as his mother." He stroked the hand he held as she stared at him, thunderstruck as it dawned on her what he was about to say. "I'm putting this badly, Susan," he continued, still stroking her hand as she gaped at him, "but I am asking you to marry me."

* * *

Susan thought long and hard about Mr. Andrew's marriage proposal. She did not love him, of course, and would not pretend she did. But if she married him, it would mean she could stay with Donny. She had to smile at the irony of going back to Boston as the wife of one of its scions. She who had been so rejected as the daughter of Irish immigrants! And, she thought with a smile, it would be fun to see Abby again.

Then the other side of her rose in protest. What if they still did not accept her? In a few short years, Donny would be grown. Then what? Would she be content in a loveless marriage? Perhaps she could grow to love Mr. Andrew. She thought of his relationship with his wife, and what a thoughtful and considerate husband he had been. His cruelty to Susan had been to protect his family, she knew that. She could not hold it against him.

And Barney? She would have to leave Barney here in California. She did not dare take him back to Boston, even as the wife of the mighty Mr. Andrew, for she knew how harsh the laws governing apprentices were in Boston. Barney, of course, would be a man soon, and Dr. Alexander would take care of him.

And Dr. Alexander? The demon in her mind persisted.

Be still, she retorted. He doesn't care what becomes of me. He can find another business manager.

Two weeks later, when Mr. Andrew came for his daily visit, she still had not decided. He greeted her with a small box in his hand. When she opened it, she gasped at the perfection of the emerald surrounded by small diamonds nestled against the black velvet.

"To match your eyes, my dear. Please accept it."

She took the box from him, her hands shaking.

"I will return tomorrow for your answer. Good-bye, Susan." He kissed her gently on the cheek and left.

Susan stood, stunned, the small box in her hand. Suddenly, she became aware that Dr. Alexander had entered the room and stood watching her. Had he been there long? Had he seen the interchange? From the look in his eyes, she feared he had.

"Well," he said coldly. "I see you and Mr. Andrew are becoming good friends. Was there perhaps more to your relationship in Boston than as governess to his children?"

Stung at this suggestion, she lashed back at him. "No! How can you think such a thing?" She met his eyes. She had to tell him. "I was in love with his son, not him."

"Ah! Donny's father."

"Yes," she whispered. "Donny's father."

"He came west to seek his fortune and you followed him." The voice held no judgment, merely stated the fact.

"You make it sound so . . . so sordid," she said. "I had to know if he still lived."

"And now that you know he does not?"

The emerald eyes grew dark with pain. "I want what is best for Donny. I owe that to Donald, for I know he loved me, and would have returned for me if . . . if," her voice faltered. "I know Donny's grandfather can do everything for him, but I love him so much I can't bear the thought of giving him up."

"Because you still love his father?"

She thought that over. Did she still love Donald? Had she ever loved Donald? She thought of her feelings when Dr. Alexander held her after their escape from the fire in November, of the emotions that surged through her whenever their eyes met. She had never felt that way with Donald. And certainly did not feel it with Mr. Andrew.

She met the magnificent eyes fixed upon her. Why, she thought, can't you love me? Why do you keep yourself away from me? You have to care for me at least a little. That much she knew. Can't you see I love you? In her pain and anger, she lashed out at him. "As it so happens, Mr. Andrew has asked me to marry him. He wants me to return to Boston and help him raise Donny."

Did she mistake it, or did a flash of pain cross his face? It passed in seconds. The mask fell back into place.

"So now you will have great wealth and that which you sought for so long, a place in Boston society."

Stunned, she could only stare at him.

"You must do as you wish, of course." He turned on his heel and stalked out.

Susan tried to call after him, but her vocal cords tightened, making her mute. She remained where he left her, staring after his retreating back, the small box with the emerald clutched tightly in her hand. She heard him call to his horse as he rode away.

She had not moved when, ten minutes later, a frantic Barney ran in and seized her arm.

"Miss Susan, Miss Susan," he cried. "Come quick, it's Doc! He's got throwed from his horse."

Chapter 31

GATHERING HER SKIRTS, Susan raced down the street after Barney, her feet kicking up little clouds of dust as she ran. A small crowd had assembled, staring at the still body, murmuring with uncertainty. She shoved the men aside in her anxiety to reach Dr. Alexander's side.

He lay half in the dust of the street, half on the wooden walkway. His face bore a ghastly pall and a trickle of blood ran down his right cheek from a cut above his eye. In terror, she felt his chest and wept with relief when she found his heart still beat. She gently lifted his head and clasped it to her breast, kissing the high forehead where the sandy hair began just slightly to recede. Tears ran down her cheeks as she stroked back the tumbled locks.

"Don't die, please don't die," she begged, kissing his unconscious face. "You can't die," she whispered. "I love you." With her handkerchief, she tried to stanch the flow of blood and discovered a large swelling on his forehead surrounded the cut. He groaned slightly at her touch, but did not waken.

She pulled herself together with an effort. He needed care. They had to get him off the street and away from the fierce heat of the afternoon sun. "Barney," she ordered, "get a blanket and some men to help us. We have to take him back to the hospital and put some compresses on his head."

"Yes, Miss Susan." Barney's eyes revealed his fright, but he obeyed her without question.

Johnny Lee appeared and Susan sent him for Dr. Morse.

"Tell him to meet us at the clinic. I want Dr. Morse to examine him."

Several men volunteered to help carry when Barney returned with the blanket. Under Susan's direction, they carefully placed Dr. Alexander's still form on the makeshift stretcher. With Susan walking beside them holding his hand, the little entourage carried him back to the hospital and put him to bed in his small, utilitarian room.

Susan had never been in the doctor's quarters before. Books covered most of the wall space. A miniature painting of a lovely young woman with striking blue eyes and sandy golden hair smiled at her from within a small gold frame standing on the desk. She immediately caught the resemblance. His mother, she thought. That has to be his mother.

I'll make him well for you, she silently promised the woman in the painting. Tears welled in her eyes. I will make him well.

Dr. Morse appeared, his usually cheerful smile fading as he looked at the still form on the bed. Susan watched anxiously as he gently probed Dr. Alexander's skull with skillful fingers. When he finished, he smiled at Susan.

"His skull does not seem to be fractured. He probably just has a severe concussion. If there is no bleeding inside of his head, he should recover fully."

"And if there is?"

Dr. Morse shrugged expressively. "We will pray there is not. Call me if his breathing becomes erratic." The doctor picked up his bag and departed. At the doorway, he turned and looked back at Susan with a gentle smile. "He is a fine young man, Miss McGuire. Sacramento needs men like him. We will hope for the best."

Not too reassured, Susan turned back to her patient with a sigh.

For three days she never left his side, sleeping on a pile of blankets beside his bed. Barney came in one afternoon to tell her Mr. Andrew wished to see her. She told him to tell the man she was busy. All thought of marrying Mr. Andrew and returning to Boston left her mind. This man lying here so still and pale was the only man she had ever or would ever love.

And if he does not love you? The imp in her mind persisted.

Be still, she responded. If he doesn't love me, at least he doesn't love anyone else. I can be near him. She knew then she would rather be by his side than be anywhere else without him even if he did not love her.

And if he dies? Her mind rejected the possibility. He can't die, she cried mutely, a frantic cry in spite of its silence. He can't. I won't let him.

But when three days had passed and he remained still and unmoving, the possibility that he might not recover loomed ever larger in her mind, even though Dr. Morse, on his daily visits, assured her all was progressing well. She continued to spurn the thought that she might lose him, faithfully moistening his lips, putting the compresses on his head, and bathing his face.

As the sun came through the window on the morning of the fourth day after the accident, Susan awoke with a start and rose quickly from the pile of blankets that served as her makeshift bed. Exhausted from providing for his physical care for so long without a rest, plus the constant strain of the fear he might never awaken, she had slept much longer than she planned. The compress on his forehead had dried out. She replaced it with a moist one and, taking the spoon, again dribbled some water on his cracked lips.

This time, his tongue came out and sampled the water. With a little cry of joy, she dripped more water onto his lips.

Again he licked it off.

"You are better, my love," she whispered, not daring to allow herself to hope. "You are better."

Barney joined her to help with Dr. Alexander's care as he did every morning. Together they bathed the lean body and changed the bedding.

"He's starting to drink, Barney. Look." She dripped more water from the spoon. Again the tongue flicked out to savor the moisture. "He needs sustenance now. Get me some milk for him. And watch Mr. Hobbs doesn't try to water it down."

Barney grinned. "I alluz watch him, Miss Susan. He'd have to get up right early to git ahead o' me."

She smiled. "Barney, I don't think anyone could get up early enough to get ahead of you. I don't know what I would do without you." She gave him a quick hug, affection for him rushing over her. How could she have ever even thought of returning to Boston and leaving him? She shook her head at her foolishness.

By the time Barney returned with the milk, their patient had progressed. Susan held up his head and fed him spoonfuls of water which, to her immense relief, he continued to swallow without choking.

"He's a lot better, ain't he?" Barney asked anxiously. "He looks to be a whole lot better."

"Now that he is taking some nourishment, we can be much encouraged, Barney."

"And now you and him is gonna finally admit you love each other?"

Startled, Susan stared at Barney.

He chuckled. "Easy to see as the nose on yer face, Miss Susan. Him too. Whenever he thinks you ain't a-lookin', he stares at you like there ain't no other woman in the world."

Susan blushed. "He's never given me the slightest hint that he loves me."

"No? You should'a seen 'im when he thought you were trapped in that fire. Like a madman, he were. Dragged me out to help him find you. I told him how you said for me to stay with Donny, an' that's what I was a-doin', but he hauled me off anyway. Told ol' Charlie to watch after Donny, 'cause them flibbertigibbet Dolan females was worse nor useless."

Susan laughed for the first time since Barney had dragged her to the side of Dr. Alexander's bleeding body. The laughter relieved some of her tension. She felt like a tight band around her neck had been released. "Thank you, Barney. I needed a good laugh. Now be a help to me and ask Mrs. Dolan to prepare some beef broth. I believe we are ready to go to the next step."

That evening, her patient feebly pushed away the spoon and opened his eyes for the first time. Susan stroked his cheek and smiled at him.

He looked dazed, then recognized her, whispering, "Susan." His eyes closed again.

Her heart leaped. Susan. Not Miss McGuire. Susan. He had never called her Susan before. She laid her head on his chest and wept.

The following morning, as she propped him up on a stack of pillows to feed him, he opened his eyes again. This time he looked truly awake, and, with a sigh of relief, she smiled at him.

"What happened?" he asked in a hoarse voice.

"Your horse threw you," she said. "We were so worried."

"Have I been . . . unconscious long?" he whispered.

"Four days."

"And you've been here the whole time. I . . . I've felt you near me. Oh, Susan, Susan." He reached for her and clasped her closely, his face buried in her hair. "I love you. I love you. Please, please don't ever leave me."

She raised her head, met his eyes and said, with a self-conscious little laugh, "I think I've loved you since the first time I looked into your eyes, back on the *Even Tide*. Although I was so sure I was in love with Donald that I refused to admit it."

A faint smile hovered on his lips. "I must confess I have also loved you from that moment. But I, too, refused to acknowledge it. I so feared you would reject me, a penniless doctor with no family, no social ties."

"Reject you? Me? The same Susan McGuire that Boston society ignored as the daughter of Irish immigrants? Don't be ridiculous, James Alexander."

He smiled. "Call me Jamie. My mother used to call me Jamie." His eyes softened as he glanced at the small portrait on the desk. "She died when I was ten." He met her eyes again and she saw the bitterness there. "Believe me, it has happened." In jerking sentences, he told her of the girl he had loved in Scotland. Of how she had rejected him because, after his father died, there had been no money, how she had left him for another man with wealth and title.

He had kept the feelings bottled up inside for so long that the story came out in bits and pieces, but Susan heard, in between the halting words, the aching cry of a young man who could not understand why he had never been accepted and loved for himself. Her arms around his waist, she held him, her head on his chest, savoring the strong, regular beat of his heart while he talked.

She met his eyes and smiled when he finished. "I love you. And I will never, ever leave you. Not for money, not for title, not even for Donny. Now rest. You need to rebuild your strength. I want you standing on your feet when we get married."

He chuckled softly. "I haven't . . . asked you to marry me yet."

"Then hurry up. I've waited for almost three years to hear you say it."

"Susan, will you marry me?" He pulled her to him with a surprising show of strength. His lips muffled her reply.

A month later, Susan stood on the pier at daybreak. The morning had dawned clear and chilly, and the oak trees showed touches of yellow. Autumn was in the air. She and Dr. Alexander came to bid farewell to Mr. Andrew and Donny. Mr. Andrew, although disappointed, had graciously accepted the return of the emerald ring when Susan confessed her love for Dr. Alexander.

Susan also persuaded Donny to accompany his grandfather to Boston with the promise that he could return and visit any time Mr. Andrew could bring him. Barney, Johnny Lee and the Dolans, even Old Charlie, all joined them on the pier to wish Donny a good journey.

"And Donny, dearest," Susan told him, kissing him again and again, holding him closely until he wriggled in protest in her arms, "they are going to build railroad tracks from here to Boston. Then you can come by train to visit. You've never ridden on a train. Won't that be fun? And you'll be learning your letters soon. You'll have to write to me."

So, accompanied by Pony and Horsie, the lead soldiers from his grandfather, and the set of blocks Barney had carved for him, Donny and Mr. Andrew boarded the steamer *Belle* bound for San Francisco where they would take a ship to Boston. Tears still stained the boy's cheeks, but he smiled brightly.

As the *Belle* swung away from the pier, the current caught her and pulled her into mid-river. Donny stood on the fantail beside his grandfather, waving and crying out, "Good-bye, Aunt Susan and Unca Jamie. Good-bye, Unca Barney, an' Unca Charlie, an' Johnny Lee, an' Miz Dolan, and . . . "

The blast from the *Belle's* horn drowned his farewells, but Susan called out, "I will always love you, Donny my dearest," and stood waving until the boat vanished from sight around a bend in the river.

She turned and smiled up at the man beside her. "And now we had better be getting back. You are still weak, and if we are to get married tomorrow, you had best keep up your strength."

His eyes gleamed as he smiled down on her. "And so all of our ghosts are laid to rest?"

"All of them. From now on, Jamie my dear, our lives will be very dull and ordinary."

Susan turned. Her eyes followed the wake of the *Belle* with a sense of closure. She had paid her debt to Donald, provided for Donny's care, and made her peace with Mr. Andrew. She finally felt she had arrived where she belonged. She had found what she sought, what had led her from Boston, around the Horn, to this wild and turbulent land. She had reached the end of her quest.

She rested her head against the arm of the man she loved so dearly and smiled. "Let's go home."

Susan's Quest

BIBLIOGRAPHY

Dana, Richard Henry; *Two Years Before the Mast* (P. F. Collier, New York, 1909)

Reed, G. Walter; *History of Sacramento County* (Historic Record Company, 1923)

Stevens, Errol Wayne; *Incidents of a Voyage to California 1849* (The Western History Association, 1987)

Thompson & West; *History of Sacramento County* (Thompson & West, 1880)

Upton, Charles Elmer; *Pioneers of El Dorado County* (Charles Elmer Upton, Placerville, 1906)

Winther, Oscar Osburn; *Via Western Express and Stagecoach* (Stanford University Press, 1945)

Susan's Quest

About the Author

The author, a graduate of Stanford University School of Nursing, lives in Southern California where she is in business with her oldest son. She has been published in professional journals, and several of her short stories have been published or won awards. *Susan's Quest* is her second novel. Her first, *Matilda's Story,* a biographical novel, has received critical acclaim.

The author is also active in community affairs. She is President of Liga International, Flying Doctors of Mercy, and flies with this group once a month to Mexico to provide medical care to the rural poor. As a nurse, she is a member of Orange County CA1 Disaster Medical Assistance Team, and has responded to disasters in Hawaii and North Dakota.

As a member of the Board of Directors of the Orange County Natural History Association, she is actively involved with the Orange County Natural History Museum, and is also on the Board of Directors of the Laguna Chamber Music Society.

Her third novel, *Katlin's Fury*, will be published in the spring of 1999, and work has begun on a sequel to *Matilda's Story,* entitled *Matilda's Story: The Later Years,*" which will cover Matilda's life from 1867 to 1906.